Of Gods and Genomes

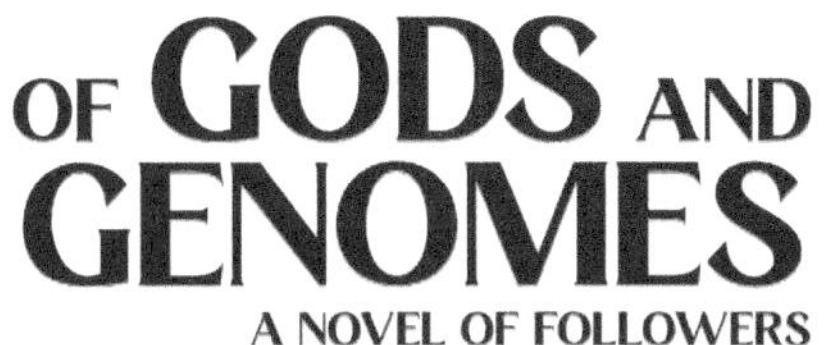

OF GODS AND GENOMES

A NOVEL OF FOLLOWERS

Nicholas Hellyer

HY Storyworks

For the followers.

FOREWORD

Social media is the worst.

I'm certainly not a fan, at least. The social market is a creature of cynicism that forces manufactured positivity down the throats of our eyes and thumbs. Creativity is far more removed than the forces behind these apps would have us believe. Rather than face that truth, in January of 2023, I set out to redeem the entirety of social media and save us from the pandemic of scrolling addiction.

Thus, I fell headfirst into the very trap the algorithm sets for us all.

I became a content creator.

My goal was simple.

*Use the .-*power*-, of social media to build a community and write a novel together.*

No ideas. No outline. No character, nor story, nor setting. I had recently seen a trend where Instagram accounts would do X things for every new follower. I adapted it to my needs. I would write 1 word for each follower of the account until we had written an entire novel.

This is how *Of Gods and Genome: A Novel of Followers* was born.

People were quick to hit the follow button and suggest ideas for the novel. While I dislike social media, I absolutely adore community. That was where the hope for this project lied: in the overlap between the two. When my little novel's

Instagram account found such a lovely abundance of support, I was thrilled. Soon enough, we had a long list of things to write, but due to the restriction I put on our word count, I didn't have enough words to write them.

It quickly descended into self-inflicted torture. I'd have nightmares about the follower count, or I'd simply find myself lying in bed late into the night, too anxious to sleep. When it did come, I would wake before my alarm clock to check the follower count. My spare moments were spent recording, editing, and seeking out ways to increase the number.

By day 100, I was spending far more time making reels than writing a book.

When time came for a necessary change, I found myself weighing my own mental health against the social repercussions of changing a project I had created. With the power of hindsight, I find the questions I asked myself in those days utterly hilarious.

Do I care more about a follower count, or writing a good book?

What does it mean to disappoint others?

Who is the decider of our potential?

What is the value of art?

The most obvious and true answer is *invaluable*. But, at my lowest points, I've fallen into the belief system of likes, comments and shares. The numbers will wrap your mind in their scaly fingers and cover your eyes from the truth of your worth.

Well, as Diedre Altair, Space Pirate Extraordinaire would say, that's a bunch of flerovium.

The truth is this: I achieved my original goal. I adapted the project and wrote an entire novel with 6000 people along for the journey. It's complete and messy and invaluable and lovely and it sometimes doesn't make sense but it never fails to make me smile.

Social media is the worst and I can't help but laugh at the fact that, without it, I never would have written this wonderful little novel.

Nicholas Hellyer

April

The evening drew a curtain of fog over the streets of Tombstone.

Cool air took root and bounced with the soft hum of music from Time's Tap. It wasn't often that the saloon stayed open so late, but the cold snap kept people from wandering home. Odd things would happen in Tombstone on nights such as that, where the chill sunk into the bones of the locals. Some blamed the drinking; a bar side stool filled bellies with warmth and chipped plenty of shoulders. Older townsfolk called it a curse; only on those sort of nights did the resting spirits of Tombstone come out to dance.

Many had their beliefs, few knew the truth behind the small tourist town. One who did was Gainsborough, the bartender at Time's Tap. A jovial old man with a round face, round nose, and rounder belly.

"Time's Tap, the hidden gem of Tombstone!" Gainsborough would chant as he served drinks. "The best place for a weary traveler to wet their whistle."

A musty place, even in the finest of weather, the saloon's interior gave the impression that it had gathered dust for a millennium, and that Gainsborough had served drinks all the while.

"We've been open for one hundred and thirty six years." Gainsborough said proudly. His audience was a group of college kids on a weekend road trip. "That buck above the door there? That's Igor. My great-great-grandaddy mounted him in eighteen eighty seven, just a year after he opened this place."

Igor the bodiless buck watched grimly over the saloon. Each time the saloon doors swung open, ancient dust trickled down from Igor's rack and landed on framed newspapers, photos of miners and cowboys, a taxidermy duck named McQuade that guarded the doorway, and eventually, the floor, where it would go unswept for many days.

Another who knew the truth of Tombstone was the present owner and manager of the saloon, April Minnary.

April sat at the end of the bar sipping a glass of whiskey. Thick hair fell in ringlets to her shoulders. The warm light in the saloon brought a golden-red tint out of her brown curls. She had a strong nose and a dangerous glare, which had gained infamy among the locals as being sharper than broken glass. As the owner of Time's Tap, she'd learned how to cut a bar fight before it happened, often with nothing more than a harsh word and her patented glare.

At that moment, April watched her uncle, Gainsborough. The older man had a habit of gabbing just before close. A bad habit. Given the nature of their saloon and the work they did after hours, April couldn't afford to have any squatters past last call. She needed to get ready for the *true* patrons of the saloon who would arrive after closing.

"Your great-great-great-grandaddy *in-law*, Uncle Gainsborough." April capped the correction off with a sip of whiskey.

Gainsborough combed back his thinning gray hair and sneered playfully. His thick, pale-pink jowls shook with the movement. "Need I point out your family ties, miss adoptee?"

April's eyes widened. "I was adopted?" She gasped emphatically and looked down at her dark hands. With faux shock, she traced a finger along her arm. Her reddish-brown skin was dark against the lacquered pine bar counter. "Why didn't grandpa ever tell me?"

April held the joke just long enough that the group of college kids shifted uncomfortably. Then, she and Gainsborough burst into laughter.

"We're just pulling your legs." Gainsborough poured them one final round of shots. "I *am* an in-law, and she *is* adopted. But we're the last of the Minnarys, so Sylas left this place to us."

"Grandpa Sylas left this place to *me*." April corrected again. Her glare turned sour. Gainsborough sneered again, though it was less playful that time.

"This is great!" One of the college kids said. His words

stretched as long as the night of drinking he'd had. "I told you guys Tombstone would be fun! The history alone—"

"We're a lot more than fun," Gainsborough cut in. "Tombstone's got magic, you see? A town don't get to be this old n' not have a bit of magic to it. What's your name, kid?"

"Magnus."

"Magnus, this town here is a mixing of times, you see? Come in close and I'll tell ya. Igor there, he watches over the passing of it. Watches over all of time, really. The comings and goings of people and things. All sorts of time passes in Tombstone, but it's still the present. Always, you understand?"

Magnus blinked blearily at the old man.

"I think you've had enough tonight, uncle." April butt in. "It ain't good to let tourists think our bartenders drink themselves rotten by close."

The kid named Magnus wandered down the bar haggardly. He was on the taller side, thin, lanky, and just around six foot by April's best guess. His long blond hair had been tied back in a bun upon arriving at the saloon a few hours prior, but now tendrils of it slipped from its hold and hung as loosely as he held to the bar. He had large brim rectangular glasses, though she couldn't tell if they were prescription or apparel. Perhaps both.

"I thought you were gonna stay quiet all night, miss." Magnus smiled. His breath smelled like cheap tequila. "Mind if I buy you a drink?"

April raised an eyebrow. "You miss the part when I said this was my saloon?"

"A free drink ain't the same as a drink someone else bought for you." Magnus stumbled through the words.

April considered the statement, then considered why she was considering a drunk man's philosophy.

"Look, kid, I appreciate it, but I'm good." April said.

The man nodded with his entire body. "*Kid*? I'm twenty two. Can't imagine you're much older. What, say twenty four? Five?"

She petrified him with her glare.

"Uh— right—" He pointed up to Igor. "Hear that Igor? She's good. Sorry to bother you, miss, uh?"

"April."

"April. That's a good name. People named after months are trustworthy." Magnus wavered a moment. "Enjoy your free drinks."

Clinging to the bar, he ventured back to his friends, who jeered at him.

April checked her wristwatch. Ten minutes to two.

"I'm going to have a smoke," April said. She tapped her watch. "Wrap it up, Uncle G."

Gainsborough waved her off and nodded.

The usual patch of dirt by the saloon door called to April. She braced against the cold night, tucking her neck into the black leather jacket she wore. It smelled of whiskey and cigarettes. Two of her favorite things. More than both, though, it still smelled like Grandpa Sylas. It had been two years since he passed, and far longer since he gave April the jacket, but his scent clung to it like he'd just worn it. It brought her peace, like her grandpa was still there, giving her a hug.

April leaned against the saloon's wall. Marigolds filled a row of planter boxes and drooped against the cold. She lifted one in her palm, then let it droop down as she pulled away.

The odd cold snap was a shame; marigolds were her favorite flower. Late August was summer's cradle, yet, a chill stirred. She patted a pack of cigarettes against her palm, shook one loose, and put it in her mouth. With a quick flick, she tucked a match under her belt, drew it out, and gave the dark lot a touch of light.

"Would you mind if I had one?" A voice asked.

April nearly spit the cigarette out. Her hand moved to the revolver hidden under her jacket. She only let go when the familiar face stepped out of the shadow. The silver glint of a long pole hammer stretched three feet over his head.

"Jesus, Gideon, what are you doing here?" April waved him away from the light of the doorway. "Get over here. We've still got locals in there. If they see you, they'll start asking questions."

"The Lord's name," Gideon chided. He lightly tapped April on the shoulder with his fist.

"Ah, yeah." April said, rubbing her shoulder. Even a light tap by the hale man made her arm numb. "My bad."

Gideon strode across the dark lot and leaned his hammer against the wall. The man was built like a bear. Short, staunch, and thick as an oak. Most of his bulk was concealed under a red gambeson he wore, but even it ran tight. His pale face had a flat nose that paired with a broad chin and cheeks. Atop his head, bright orange hair curled to just above his brows. With one hand, he took a cigarette April had offered and lifted it to his lips, right next to a scar she'd noticed the night before. A jagged thing that ran from his right cheek through to his upper lip.

"Well, for a newbie, your timing isn't terrible." April said. "Forty minutes off on your second night is better than most of you Middle-Agers. What were you again, eleven hundreds?"

"One thousand and two is my local year."

"Ireland, right?"

He nodded. While she had only known him for the day, April clocked him as the quiet type. In her experience teaching them, travelers from the Dark Ages usually had the hardest time adjusting. She blamed religious oppression.

"Let's start back up with your lesson." April said. "Remember what I said. Step one, awareness. What, when, where. Say it."

The grizzled man side-eyed her.

"I don't mean to kindergarten you, but it's important. First steps are the hardest. Saying things out loud helps your brain wrap itself around the concept."

"I do not know the word, *kindergarten.*"

"Doesn't matter." April wondered if the Irish had any quarrel with the Germans.

Gideon took a deep drag of the cigarette.

"I am a time traveler." He said meticulously. "My local time is the year 1002. I am currently standing in the year 2024."

April nodded. Gideon may not have felt it, but she his shoulders lose a hint of tension.

That was the nature of April's saloon. Time's Tap was a saloon for time travelers, and she often taught newbies. It had been that way long before she was the owner. Her Grandpa Sylas had taught her how to talk to people from all over the timeline and help guide them into understanding their ability. It didn't always end perfectly, but April tried her best.

Help the lost and you're helping yourself.

April felt a twinge of pain in her chest. Grandpa Sylas was still with her in every lesson.

"What did it feel like when you came here?"

She asked every new traveler the same question. For some, it was as simple as blinking. They'd open their eyes, and they were where they wanted to be. Many made rituals of it, though April steered her newbies away from that line of thinking. Far too many psychedelics involved.

"I was sitting outside my home. Then, the Lord above beckoned me—"

April winced. Religious travelers could be tricky.

"—He urged me to walk forward into the darkness of night. Your magic torches guided me—"

"—*Lights*. There's no such thing as magic, only electricity. Technology." April corrected.

"To name a thing after that which it produces is odd."

"Trust me," April said. "There's plenty of odd things in 2024, and light bulbs are *not* one of them."

She snubbed out the butt of her cigarette in the dirt. He was intelligent and inquisitive. It could have been much worse. Most Dark Agers denied the new reality and went mad. For Gideon, April figured she could have him traveling freely with two weeks of lessons, given that nothing got in their way.

"Stay here. You can't come in with locals here. Don't want them asking questions." She turned to the door, but the open sign caught her eye. It hung at a slight angle. She checked her watch. Two minutes to two. Biting her cheek, she tilted the sign so that it was level and walked in.

A newcomer had joined Magnus and his drunken crew.

A woman in a deep blue, nylon trench coat stood with their back toward the saloon's front door. Strange, April hadn't seen anyone walk in. The woman threw back a drink and filled the saloon with a bellowing laugh that April could recognize a mile away

"Diedre Altair—" April said sharply.

The woman turned. "—Space Pirate Extraordinaire, at your service."

They were shorter than April, with long, black hair hanging behind wispy bangs. As always, Diedre's skin was an unblemished, smooth beige with rosy undertones. They could have been a local to Arizona, a pretty Latina woman out for a drink, but April knew their true form. Behind their horrid, lime-green lipstick, she could count far too many teeth for a human mouth, an alien feature that drunken humans seemed to happily glance over for Diedre's traditional beauty. Just above a button nose, April picked out the feature that was Diedre's dead-giveaway: eyes with sparkling, amethyst irises.

"April! Just the human I've been looking for!" They spoke in a deep, lush voice with a hint of a foreign dialect, though it's origin wasn't within this star system.

"You know April?" Magnus asked.

"For practically all of time." Diedre said with a wink. "Hold my drink."

Diedre paraded along the bar as though they hovered over the floor. There was an unreproducible swagger channeled in each step. If the saloon had been full, all eyes would have been on Diedre.

April stood awkwardly as Diedre wrapped long arms around her and hugged tight.

"What's wrong, *partner?*" Diedre asked. "You seem a bit cold."

"It's a cold night." April said. "You're early."

"Can I be early if I'm coming from your future?" Diedre whispered. "Oh, ease up. So what? I'll keep my human skin on tight. No one will know."

"There are rules."

"Rules are for nebulous pigs." Diedre twirled toward Magnus. "Who wants another shot?"

April's right eye twitched as everyone cheered. There were rules for a reason. Mingling travelers and locals always stirred up trouble, especially in her bar. Diedre was often at the center of that trouble.

"Alright everybody, closing time. Get out." April announced. "Get back to your hotels, motels or whatever ditch yall are camping in."

"Come now, April. The party is just starting!" Magnus said.

"I like this one." Diedre added. "He'd like it in my time."

"What, the eighties?"

"Try again."

April's eye twitched again. "Get out of the bar or I'll grab that shotgun up there by Igor and so help me."

Magnus threw some cash on the bar. "Fine." He turned to Diedre. "You staying here with this party possum? Why don't you show us around town?"

"I could show you things you couldn't imagine." Diedre gave April a wry side eye. "But I've got business with this party possum. Maybe next time, kid."

On a bar napkin, he sloppily scribbled down a number. "Well, if you change your mind." He slid the napkin to them, took a step to gather his balance, then stumbled out the door.

Tap tap tap.

Gideon tapped on the window outside. April waved him in.

"I got him properly drunk, didn't I?" Diedre said. They took a flask from their trench coat and drank. "Shame. Your earth drinks taste good, but they don't pack any punch."

Diedre's beige skin shifted instantly to a soft blue hue. Their amethyst eyes grew to the size of orchids. Fleshy stalks sprouted from their eye sockets and lifted their large eye balls well above their head. Their torso elongated, as did their arms and legs, until they stood over seven feet tall. With a sharp *crunch*, Diedre's knees inverted backwards. That part of their transformation always made April's skin crawl.

"Dear lord," Gideon whispered. The poor man stood in the doorway, mouth gaping at the alien creature in front of him.

"Never seen a *myiad* before, beefcakes?" Diedre's alien face quickly folded into itself and morphed into a perfect reciprocation of Gideon's own features. In a perfect impression of Gideon's voice, Diedre spoke, "Myiads are shapeshifters."

All color drained from Gideon.

"Stop scaring my newbie, Diedre. I don't want you causing another heart attack."

"That was one time." The myiad shook their head, and with it, Gideon's face. "Look, April, I'll cut this quick. This visit ain't just star clusters and roses. I'm here on business."

April squinted warily. Business with Diedre was never

a good sign.

"What kind of business?"

The saloon door swung open and slammed against the wall. Every frame in the saloon rattled.

"Oops," Magnus wavered drunkenly in the doorway. "Sorry — Didn't mean to — think I dropped my wallet — "

His eyes landed on Gideon. They scanned up and down the soldier's attire.

"What's going on? There a circus in town?"

Then, Magnus noticed the blue skinned alien sitting at the bar, drinking from a flask.

Diedre nodded at him and smiled, their myiad lips reaching from ear to ear, revealing many more teeth than any smile warranted. As a cherry on top, Diedre shifted their eyelids to be vertical, and blinked sideways.

That seemed too much for Magnus. He blinked slowly, then fainted. His limp body rode the doorway all the way to the floor.

"Great." April said. "Thanks, Diedre."

"What, I can't have a little fun?"

II

Magnus

Magnus dreamed that he was in a cauldron. The kind in a children's fairy tale. He sat neck deep in boiling soup. Somewhere nearby in the kitchen, three witches decided how best to cook him.

"—you know what happens when locals find out about traveling. The council *disposes* of them—" one said.

"—ain't my fault you don't lock your doors, April."

"It's your fault he just walked in and saw an alien at my bar!"

Magnus groaned.

"—he's waking up—"

"—not quick enough. This'll help—"

Something touched Magnus' nose. A sharp scent struck him like he had just snorted a live bottle rocket. It jumped up his nose, exploded in his mind, and made him sit straight up and out of his dream.

He sat barside in the saloon. The woman named Diedre sat beside him capping a small vial of purple liquid and tucking it into their coat. April leaned behind the bar, arms crossed and staring.

"What was that, Diedre?" She asked.

"*Lorouxias* pheromones. Counteracts most toxins. A great cure for hangovers."

Magnus' head reeled. Thoughts came at him a thousand miles a minute. Where was he? His eyes darted hastily between April and Diedre, then he realized the big man in the gambeson sat on his other side. He was surrounded. He shoved himself off the counter and tipped his stool backward. For a single breath, he free fell. Two sturdy arms and a rock hard chest caught him.

"You okay, pal?" A deep, earthy voice asked.

"Yeah, sorry—" Magnus stood up with trembling knees. He turned to thank his catcher, but felt all air leave his lungs when he saw who it was.

A marble statue blinked at him, its hands out to make sure Magnus didn't fall again.

"You don't look so good—" The statue said, its onyx eyes examining Magnus up and down. Magnus shouldered past the stone man but only made it a single step.

The saloon was bustling with life, none of which was human.

Marble Man stood beside a table of equally stony humanoids, each with a different hue of rock-skin ranging from granite to slate, and each chipped in a variety of places. Just behind them sat a table of equally strange creatures that seemed to be made entirely of various liquids. Their shapes were less humanoid; one had many spindly masses of tentacles while another seemed completely round. Magnus whimpered as he watched one raise a mug and take a sip of beer, which he then watched sink into the creature's translucent body and disperse. Another table had a group of things that looked to be humans with dog heads. A Doberman, Scottish terrier, bulldog and shih tzu had paused their card game to stare at him.

"He's losing it." April said.

"Yep." Diedre replied.

Magnus didn't hear them. He rushed to the nearest corner of the bar, where a man in a police uniform stood by a rectangular prism with triangular eyes and a circular mouth.

"Officer, I need help—" Magnus placed a hand on the officer's shoulder. Suddenly, Magnus felt calmer. Relaxed, even. A soothing warmth emanated from his fingertips and circulated into his body. It seemed to him that the saloon itself had relaxed. The walls shimmered and waved. A black and white framed photo of a miner smiled and lifted a peace sign at him. Photos weren't supposed to move. At that moment, Magnus didn't care.

"Uh, hey, Psil. You got a freeloader." The rectangular prism said.

The officer turned around. Magnus' hand clung to his shoulder. He wasn't bothered by the speaking shapes, alien creatures, or even the officer, whose uniform was clearly labeled *PEA, Psilocybin Enveloped Astronomorph. Do not touch!*

Magnus was put off by the creature's face, which was a featureless cap of a massive mushroom, but even then, the tranquility he felt while holding on to its shoulder quelled all panic.

"Ugh," the fungus faced creature said. Magnus wondered at that— it didn't seem to have a mouth, but he clearly heard it speak. "Rude!"

The fungal creature pulled Magnus' hand off of its shoulder, and the rising tide of panic overtook him twofold.

"I have to get out." Magnus said to himself. He wasn't sure where *out* was anymore. The saloon wasn't particularly large, but it had become so filled with strange creatures that he couldn't find his bearing. One moment, he bounced against a leather-bound crew of pirates who looked mostly human, save for their unique allotments of eyes over their entire body; the next, he shouldered past two trench coat-clad figures who stood over nine feet tall. They walked at awkward angles, and Magnus could hear voices bickering under their coats.

Magnus needed a reprieve. His chest ached from how quickly his heart beat within it. He sat in an empty chair next to a table, and buried his face in his hands. Rest was fleeting, however, as he heard the muffle complaints of something below him. He jolted up to his feet.

"Excuse you". The chair said. It turned and waded into the crowd.

That was it. Magnus had lost it completely. He could feel his mind melting. Any minute, it would ooze from his ears in a thick, pasty goop.

Something grabbed his shirt from behind and tugged him backward. A long, stretched arm reached through the crowd like a sewing needle through thread and grabbed his coat. He was pulled to the bar and thrown entirely over it, landing on the rubber mat of the bar back.

Diedre's arm retracted to its normal length. April squatted in front of him.

"Having fun?" April asked. "Sit back here, keep your head down, stay where I can see you. You're going to be okay. Probably."

Every light in the saloon shut off.

"Shit." April mumbled. The saloon roared with the shocked noise of the patrons. "Change of plans. Follow me. You too, Gideon."

"Not me?" Diedre asked.

"I've had enough of you already."

Just as April took a step, the entire saloon began to shake. A heavy rumble rolled through the floorboards. Every breath in the saloon held tight. The shaking grew to a tremor. The walls rattled and threw framed photos and items from the walls, and more than one bottle fell behind the counter.

"Double shit." April said.

Magnus crouched down and covered his head and eyes. The building shook from its foundation to the ceiling. It grew into a crescendo of earthly groans and swelled to a final, cacophonous moment, an explosive sound, like an electrical transformer exploded directly underneath their feet. It rang throughout the building like dynamite in water.

"April?" Gainsborough called into the silence.

"There are candles in the back cupboard. By the sink." April answered. Using her hands, she traced the bar and let it guide her through the tenebrous room. One single corner of the room had light; a table which hosted three neon-green creatures. Light shone through their eyeballs like flashlights.

"Everyone, remain calm," April filled the room with her voice. She flicked on a flashlight and shot a beam over the bar counter.

"God is punishing our hubris. Time is not our domain" Gideon whispered. He touched his hands to his head in prayer.

"That wasn't god," Diedre said. "It was an earthquake. April, you haven't taught him about tectonic plates yet? And you call yourself a teacher."

"Must have escaped my mind." April said absently. "Uncle G, I'll check the fuse box. Newbies, with me."

Magnus watched as Gideon hopped to his feet. At least he seemed human. A *normal* human.

"You too, Magnus. Unless you want to stay here with Diedre."

Magnus looked across the bar at the Diedre. The myiad smiled a sweet, candid smile, until their canines suddenly grew four inches past their lips and tapered to a needle sharp point.

Magnus stood up and followed April. He did his best to ignore Diedre's laugh tailing them as they descended into the saloon's basement.

III

April

The basement had a dank odor. A mix of old whiskey and mildew. April led the men through hallways of thin-walled rooms, each filled with to the brim with whatever fit. Old stools and tables in one, Gainsborough's personal storage in another. April's office had a small desk and a mountain of tax documents and Time Council reports. Just a passing glance worsened her mood. A lot of paperwork went into managing an intra-dimensional independent business.

Behind her, Magnus followed closely. The poor kid's face was a torrent of expressions, mostly in the range of disbelief to fear. April had seen it before. Locals, those people who didn't have the ability to travel, had a harder time facing the truth.

Then, of course, there was the matter of his impending execution. April didn't know how to bring that up yet, so she decided to sit on it.

"How you feeling, kid?" She flashed the light back to his face. He was pale as a ghost.

"Fine." Magnus said. April could smell bullshit a mile off, but she didn't need a nose to pick out his lie.

"Mmhmm." She looked back to Gideon, who held the rear. "And how are you, Gideon? Ain't like you're used to extraterrestrials either."

Gideon only had a shade of color more than Magnus.

"Aye," He said. "It is still strange. The Lord's work reaches further than even the Holy Church knows."

"Sure." April shook her head and moved on.

They had only walked ten steps further into the labyrinthine basement before Magnus whispered in wonder.

"What is that?"

An aura of dim indigo light shone through an open doorway and bathed the man head to toe.

"That is our time dilation unit. TDU for short." April said.

At the center of the wide room, an apparatus of chrome and indigo lit the room. Eight poles sprouted from metal bases on the roof and ceiling. They formed acute angles, all meeting to suspend a glass orb four feet above the floor. A shifting fluid glowed in the orb, an indigo aura emanating from it.

Magnus leaned forward onto his toes. "What is a time dilation unit?"

April smiled. Asking questions was a good sign. A sense of curiosity meant that Magnus' hadn't lost his entire mind at first encounter.

"It's like a radio tower for travelers. That fluid in there is our signal." April said. "It isn't necessary for someone who knows how to control their traveling—" She glanced at Gideon. "—but the TDU helps newbies land at the saloon. Moths to a light bulb. It's better than a confused traveler popping up in the wrong time and causing a mess of things."

"Ah." Magnus nodded slowly. He wasn't getting it.

"Oh. Right. I haven't given you the preamble."

Magnus watched her with wide eyes.

"Time travel exists." She said, "Gideon and I can do it. We're travelers. You can't. You're a *local*— a person who can't travel by natural means a-k-a you're stuck in your local time."

"*Natural means?*" Magnus asked.

April walked on as she spoke.

"Travelers are born with a mutation in their genetic information. When an organism has that mutation, we call it the traveler genome. People who have the genome can time travel with a few limitations—"

"Time travel isn't possible. It's fantasy. Movie nonsense. Magic." Magnus said.

"Exactly!" Gideon added.

"No!" April said sternly. She unlatched the fuse box point. "It is *not* magic. Is electricity magic? Is running water magic? There's no such thing as magic. It's tough to wrap your head around, but here's a secret trick: don't worry about the details."

"Don't worry about the details." Magnus echoed. Unfortunately, he was a person who thoroughly enjoyed details.

Inside the fuse box, not a single fuse had been blown. April found that strange. She flipped them off and on one by one anyway. Hanging from the ceiling by a metal chain, the single light fixture of the room remained dark.

"Odd."

"A power outage is the least odd thing about tonight," Magnus said.

"The streetlights were still on. It's not an outage." April said. She tried flipping the electric room switch again.

"Maybe it's some routine power —"

Shattering glass echoed through the basement. April turned on her toes and immediately drew the .42 magnum from the holster under her jacket.

"Jesus!" Magnus said as he ducked away.

"Aye." Gideon tapped Magnus on the shoulder with his gloved hand. The muscular soldier didn't seem to put much into the hit, but Magnus yelped. "Don't speak His name in vain."

"Quiet!" April hissed. She combed the room with her flashlight, then aimed it down the hallway. Something about the pitch darkness of it unnerved her. Then she realized why.

A moment later, April was breathing heavily in the doorway of the TDU room. The room was dark. The ray from her flashlight bounced off of the chrome poles. They had been twisted and torn. Broken glass covered the floor. Not a single drop of time dilation fluid could be seen.

April shuddered to imagine what could break the TDU.

The chrome poles were titanium alloy. The fluid was suspended in a clear sphere of *lumenglass*; a material of solidified light molecules stabilized in the twenty fourth century. Nothing should have been able to break it, save for a moon-sized, ionized particle accelerator.

A shadow twitched at the edge of April's flashlight. She trained her sights on the cardboard boxes stacked against the wall opposite her. Silently, she followed the left wall of the room. She made sure to steer wide of the broken glass. As she came upon the boxes, she leaned over them, magnum first.

A rat chewed the cardboard on the floor. Beady red eyes peered up to April for an instant before it scurried out of sight.

"April!" Magnus shouted.

April turned sharply. The man clung to the doorway and pointed shakily to the opposite side of the room. She flashed the light to illuminate a shadowy mass of black, writhing limbs. She knew immediately what it was. An extra terrestrial monster whose name alone was a curse.

It was a velex.

Velexi were horror stories told over hard drinks and warm campfires. An extraterrestrial creature of pure carnage. One of the most vicious and mindless species in the known universe, they were hunted to near timeline-extinction centuries in the future. April had never seen one before, but the descriptions in stories made her sure beyond a shred of doubt. There was a velex in her saloon basement.

This specific velex was a large, ovular mass of space-black flesh, at least four feet wide by three tall. Dozens of thin, spindly arms sprouted from the thing's black body, each with a humanoid hand. Hundreds of talons skittered on the floor like a parade of scuttling cockroaches.

Then, the velexi song began.

Small slits opened all over the creature's body. Teeth chattered in each one of them. Velexi were said to have a hundred mouths over their bodies. A hundred tiny sets of razor sharp teeth tapped together in a discordant melody, excitedly awaiting their meal. The velexi song was an omen of certain death.

April shot twice. The velex was unnaturally quick. It rolled toward the doorway as a tumbleweed would roll in the wind, its dozens of arms catching and propelling it forward. The two shots grazed it, sundering two thin arms from the body. They writhed on the floor like decapitated snakes.

"Away from us, Satan!" Gideon lifted his hammer, but he too underestimated the velex' speed. Eight arms slammed him into the wall. The velex was focused on Magnus.

"Magnus, run!" April shouted. She shot twice more before Magnus stumbled into the dark hallway and disappeared. The bullets struck the velex, but only slowed its stride as it clawed through the doorway after the man.

April sprinted after. While the guy wasn't such a smooth talker, Magnus could run. He just made it to the staircase before a long velex arm caught his foot and tripped him. He fought to crawl up the steps, but the velex held him in place.

It crawled over him, savoring the final moment before its meal. April shot it twice more. Violet velexi blood sprayed over the floor and wall, but it simply ignored her.

Gritting her teeth, she threw down her empty magnum.

Luckily for Magnus, a wood chopping axe had been left out and was just within April's reach.

"Get out of my saloon!" Just as the thing's claws started to tear at Magnus' jeans, April dropped the axe into the creature's back. The swing alone severed three more of its arms. She buried the axe head so deep into its body, she couldn't see the metal glint from her flashlight.

The velex screamed out of its hundred mouths. Seven hands took hold of the axe and tore it out in a shower of dark violet. It threw down the axe and turned on April.

She didn't have time to react. The velex crawled over her like a steamroller. All breath left her as she landed on her back with the weight of the monster. Slick wet limbs dripped viscous slime on her. A hundred frothy mouths drenched her with spittle.

Through the folds of limbs, she saw Magnus stand up behind it, the axe held high above his head.

"Kill it!" April shouted.

Magnus hovered motionless. He was stone still; his face paralyzed with fear.

Then, a second shadow sprung across the light of the fallen flashlight. It passed so close to Magnus the loose strands of hair from his bun whipped in its tailwind. A human shape, nearly as dark as the velex, descended. April's screaming was drowned by the shrill hiss of a hundred mouths and the gurgling of alien blood.

The velex slumped over onto her, lifeless and still. April unwound herself from its arms. She shivered, wiping sweat and spit from her face. It wasn't much help, considering every inch of her was covered in velex mucous. A hand reached down to offer her a lift.

"Thanks," She began to say before looking up. "Oh. It's you."

"A rude thing to say to your savior."

The woman stood proudly over her kill. Her brown skin was nearly one with the dark room. Leather panels and straps covered her torso and legs as a tight fitting light armor. Malachite green eyeshadow framed pale, yellow-green eyes. Gold dust twinkled where it had been layered into the makeup.

"Sorry. Thank you, Kiora." April said begrudgingly. The woman's carmine red lips grew to a proud smirk. "Shit, we need to check on Gideon—"

"—I'm here." Gideon walked slowly through the hallway, leaning on his lucerne hammer as he walked. "Have we won, then?

"We're alive." April said.

"That may be enough for now." Gideon said simply.

Magnus closed his mouth, which had fallen ajar, only to open it again to speak directly to the stranger. "Who are you?"

The woman flicked blood off her left dagger and sheathed it at her hip. With her right dagger and her open left hand, she went to carve the velex.

"I am Princess Kekheretnebti of Kemet." She said, elbow deep in the velex carcass. "My traveler name is Kiora. You may call me either."

"Kekheretnebti?" Magnus asked. "As in the Egyptian princess from the twenty fifth century BC?"

April watched the man with a partly open mouth.

"Yes." Kiora paused and stood to look at Magnus. "You are well versed in history, local man. April has told me my homeland is called Egypt in the future."

"I have a minor in ancient civilizations." Magnus said.

Kiora grunted, nodded, then resumed carving the velex.

"Check its stomach for time dilation fluid." April said. "The bastard broke our TDU."

"The beast's stomach is empty." Kiora said. "This velex has been starved."

April knelt down and immediately gagged. The only smell worse than velex mucous was velex innards. Worse yet, Kiora was right. There was no sign of the fluid. Someone had snuck in, destroyed her time dilation unit, and left a hungry velex in her saloon's basement.

"Everyone upstairs." April commanded. "I need a drink."

IV

April

April left a trail of velex sludge from the basement to the bar counter.

Gainsborough had done a fine job of easing the tension in the saloon. In fact, he had done so well, the only people left in the bar were he and Diedre. Together they sat in low candle light. The amethyst eyed myiad hadn't moved an inch. They leaned their back against the bar counter and whistled.

"What happened to you?" Diedre asked. Their gaze landed on Kiora with a frown. "Who invited her?"

Without speaking, April crossed the empty room, leaned over the bar, and gripped the first bottle she could find. Like a sword from a stone, she pulled a bottle of cheap tequila from the counter.

"Where's everyone gone?" April said after a quick swig from the bottle. She held it to Magnus, who softly shook his head. Gideon sniffed at it, then refused.

"Once they heard gunshots, everyone packed up and left."

"That's good. Don't want anyone else knowing I had a velex in my basement."

The candles seemed to flicker at the mention of a velex.

"What?" Gainsborough asked. Even Diedre raised a brow.

"Not only that," April continued. "Somebody busted our TDU and stole our fluid."

She took another swig. The smell of velex scum was fading from her nostrils, or, her sense of smell was fading from the agave. Either way, the tequila seemed to be doing the trick.

Unfortunately, it wasn't doing the trick for Magnus.

"What is going on?" Magnus exploded.

April could almost see steam shoot from the man's ears. She'd expected a blowup— it was a reasonable response when a person's sense of reality was rug pulled from under them— but did he have to be so loud about it?

"That was a monster down there. And all the weird monsters up here, what the hell is this? It's a joke, right? There was a— an *ooze* person, and pirates with all sorts of eyeballs. A chair spoke to me! Ha ha, you got me. Good prank everyone, where's the camera."

"I told you the truth." April said. "Time travel is real. The monsters you're talking about are extraterrestrials from around the timeline. The '*ooze*' person was Looauamu.

They're a Gomo from the year 2321. The pirates were the space privateers. Rowdy bunch. Who else, the chair? That was Reginald. I don't know what era he's from."

Magnus's watched her with a wide, blank stare.

"Time travel. Time. Travel. We've got Renaissaunters from the Italian Renaissance, American Pioneers, Greasers, Olympians, Romans. People from the Ice Age are called Chillers, and people like Gideon here are Middle-Agers, from the Middle Ages. There's too many to count, past and future. There's the Roarers from the 2220s. Grays— you've seen those in movies, I'm sure. Zoombaatis are biomechs from the twenty fourth century— mind their exhaust ports if you ever meet one. Who else? Lovinians, Wicntibfos, Uul. Diedre here is a myiad."

"But you look human." Magnus pointed out.

Diedre answered by stretching their forehead upward until their face was three feet long. Seven sets of eyelids morphed from the new skin and blinked open to reveal seven additional sets of amethyst colored eyes.

"Myiads are shapeshifters."

Magnus was sheet white.

"Drink." April pushed the bottle toward him. "It will help."

"I'm feeling a bit... discombobulated." The poor guy struggled to spit out each word. "Can I have some water?"

"Get used to it, cowboy." April said. "Still drink wine, Kiora? Saving the bartender's life earns you a free glass."

"Yes." Kiora answered flatly.

For a single moment, much to April's appreciation, everyone drank in silence. She was lucky to be alive. Not many went toe to toe with a velex and still had their internal organs remain internal.

April eyed Kiora. It had been two months since the Egyptian princess came to the saloon. Coincidentally, it had been two months since April ended things between them. Still, her heart had skipped a beat when she looked up to find Kiora had saved her from the velex. April shook off the thought. That ship had already come to port and sailed off again. She was lucky Kiora had stopped at killing the velex and not her, too.

April shook off the thought again. It wasn't the time to be thinking about romance. But she did wonder why Kiora had shown up on this night in particular.

"Velexi can't travel by themselves. Someone brought it here."

"Who would drop a velex off in our saloon?" Gainsborough asked. "Who could *catch* a velex and hold it long enough to travel?"

"No clue." April said. She had met plenty of resentful travelers through her years. She had kicked her fair share of them out of the saloon. A velex, though? Dropping that off on a busy night meant whoever did it wanted people dead. It was too extreme for a petty fight. This felt personal.

April watched Kiora. The woman sat perfectly upright with a posture that could have been cast in bronze. When it came to petty grudges, exes were the first to come to April's mind. Kiora had also been the first to arrive at the scene. Was it sheer coincidence?

The entire timeline new of Kiora by her title. *Blades of Sekhmet.* She was infamous as the Time Council's go-to alien hunter. A feared one, at that. April liked that about her, or did, at least, before they tried to date. Cross-timeline dating was difficult, to say the least.

Even still, April was sure Kiora wouldn't want her *dead* for how things ended.

"I think I might have a guess." Diedre said. "Princess probably has one, too."

April eyed Kiora.

"I do." She said, "It is a private affair of the Time Council."

"Bullshit." April slammed her glass down. A globule of velex mucous slipped from her coat and splattered on the floor. "At this point, it's an affair of my dry-cleaner. Who is it?"

Kiora sipped her wine placidly.

April grit her teeth. Slowly, she turned to Diedre, who was always eager to defy the Time Council.

"There's word of someone causing time breaches." Diedre smiled wryly, like they were unwrapping an exquisite gift. "Time Council outposts are getting attacked, velexi popping up in strange places and eating the locals, yada yada. Didn't think they'd pop up here, or I would have warned you sooner, April."

"It's fine." April was a bit too sticky with velex guts to be truly fine. "So, who is it?"

"That's all I've got. Came here to see if you have heard anything through the wires or over a drink. Tell you this, though; the council is worried. They've got everyone trying to find whoever's doing it." Diedre whistled. "Capital B-Big bounty."

"Ah," Kiora pointed a sharp side eye at Diedre. "I feared you had begun to care about something more than money."

"I do." Diedre raised their flask. "A good drink."

April couldn't help but smile, herself. She hadn't always gotten along well with the myiad, but they could always agree on two things: the bureaucratic pricks in the Time Council could shove it, and a good drink was worth its weight in uranium.

"A council bounty big enough for you to take it, Diedre?" April asked.

"Yep." Diedre said. "Like I said. They're scared of whoever is dropping velexi where they don't belong."

"The only place a velex belongs is hilt deep upon my blades." Kiora said. The room seemed to grow cold.

"That, I can agree with." Diedre tilted her flask to Kiora.

April felt there was more left unsaid, not from Diedre, but Kiora. She eyed the princess carefully. Kiora had been trained in performance— the seat of a princess necessitated a certain stoicism. It had taken many months for April to crack it, and even longer to notice Kiora's tics and tells. April had a knack for it, though, something she attributed to serving drinks to the entire timeline.

"What do you know?" April asked flatly.

Kiora remained motionless. "Nothing more than what has been said by the exiled myiad."

There it was. Kiora's tell. The woman's face was too pure, too regal to show a shred of doubt. Her fingers, however, were the fingers of a fighter. Kiora had once told April she felt more comfortable fighting with blades than words. That is when April discovered her tell. When asked the question, her fingers moved subtly to the blade of one dagger at her hip. Drawing a blade was easier for her than lying.

"Right." April squinted. The problem April had found

was that even when she knew Kiora was lying, the princess remained a steel box. There was no cracking it open. "Fine then."

April stood up and wiped her hands down her body, sliding two more globules of velex mucous and guts to the floor.

"I don't care about the Time Council, or bounties, or even velexi. No one is going to tear down this saloon while I live and breathe. We're going on a field trip." April said. "But first, I need to take a shower."

"Actually," Magnus said. "I think I'll be going home now."

The man stood up, nodded goodbye to each person in the room, then slowly hobbled to the door.

"You can't go." April said.

Magnus froze in the doorway of the saloon.

"Why not?" He asked sheepishly.

"Cause you're an anomaly." She answered. "The Time Council doesn't like anomalies."

The man slouched as though he'd just been gut punched.

"What does that mean?" His voice was utterly pitiful.

"Means we gotta wipe your brain!" Diedre barked. They stretched an arm across the room and slapped him on the back. "Else the Time Council will send one of their hounds to eradicate you."

"Eradicate me?" Magnus echoed miserably. "You said you work for the council?"

Kiora pursed her lips. "My duties lie beyond paltry anomalies."

"As long as we tow you around, you'll be fine." April said. "We'll get you in a mnemosyne machine, wipe your memory, and get you back home. I'll keep you safe. Promise."

He hobbled to the bar counter and settled back into his seat.

Twenty minutes later, April returned to the main room of the bar with a moisturized face, fresh black jeans and a new shirt. Her black leather jacket still had a hint of velex-guts mixed with lemon scented leather cleaner.

Kiora sat alone at a table near the bar, perusing through a Vogue magazine. Gainsborough had brought out a mop and bucket and kindly taken to cleaning the trail of velex that April had left. Gideon and Magnus sat on either side of Diedre, who seemed to be enjoying the role of time-tutor. Magnus in particular had lightened up enough to ask questions again.

"So, what happens if I meet my future self? Or past self? Will we implode?" Magnus asked.

"Implosions? Not likely." Diedre huffed. "Explosions on the other hand—"

"No explosions." April cut in. "And no, you won't be able to meet yourself. There are limitations to time travel."

"Time traveling has limitations?"

April clapped her hands. "We'll have plenty of time to answer all of the questions you'll inevitably have wiped from your mind when we get going."

"I like these two, April." Diedre put a hand on their shoulders. "I didn't know teaching could be so fun."

"Don't listen to Diedre. They lost their mind in the Tang Dynasty." April said. "You have a spare pocket watch?"

"Nope, left mine with my co-captain on the ship." Diedre said.

Magnus checked his watch. "It's three thirty six."

"No not—" April began. "A *pocket watch* is what we call a hand held time machine. Locals like you can travel using a TDU, even if you don't have the genome. We call it *forced traveling*."

Gainsborough opened a drawer behind the bar. The clang of old phone chargers, various hand held tools and change shook with it. He reached in and pulled out a small black, metal box.

"Here," he said, and tossed it to April.

"Since when did you get a pocket watch, uncle G?" April asked as she caught it.

"Always had it." Gainsborough's eyes wandered to the bar counter, where he picked up a rag and wiped meticulously. "I'll watch the saloon, just make sure you keep me updated."

The pocket watch was cold in her hand. Its black frame of rigid metal fit nicely into her palm. The time dial sat atop it, a simple dial mechanism that changed the set date on a small analog screen beside it. On one side of the box, a tiny light bulb lit up in pale green. Next to it, a small activator switch, rigged with an intention-sensor, of course, as to not allow someone to accidentally send themselves through time.

"I've got my timewire." April said. "I'll keep you posted on our time stamps and coordinates."

April took a deep breath. It had been a long time since she left her local time. Operating a saloon for time travelers left little time for much else. That, and she didn't trust anyone to run her grandfather's saloon. Gainsborough would do in a pinch, but it was better if she stayed to take care of things. Besides, she liked the amenities of her year, though Earth politics had been getting under her skin lately.

When she was younger, she had explored all sorts of periods. For a class project about the Gettysburg address, she actually *went* to see Lincoln give the speech. She'd met Aristotle in person, then gone further back to watch Homer perform epics. And the future; she had spent plenty of nights space-clubbing with Diedre in her early twenties.

She was only twenty seven now, and the only place she ever visited anymore was the saloon. It was the only place she ever wanted to be. Her home. All that was left of Grandpa Sylas. All he had given to her.

Someone wanted to destroy her home.

April exhaled. She was ready.

Magnus, on the other hand, quivered on the verge of a nervous breakdown.

April was sympathetic. She'd met a few anomalies before. It was never their fault that they stumbled into the wrong place at the wrong time. Just a case of cosmic coincidence. A person's understanding of reality should be checked regularly to a healthy degree, not utterly dismantled in one fell swoop. Magnus was putting up a good fight against his own breaking mind, it was only fair that he shed a few tears and screamed once or twice. Everyone deserved a little mania at times.

"Chin up," Diedre said. The myiad's chin stretched out and tilted harshly up until it pointed at their nose. "Better to have lived and have your memory erased than be executed in a horrid, agonizing torture chamber. That's a human saying, right?"

"Look, kid." April glared at Diedre. The myiad shrugged. "It ain't fair. I get that. But it's still your choice, alright? I won't force you, I'll just tell you the truth. If you walk through that door, you won't have long. If you come with us, I'll make sure you get home and back to your life, alright?"

"Hardly a choice." He said shakily.

"Good. It's settled, then."

April held up the pocket watch in her hand. The tiny bulb shone pale green. "Everybody, lean in and grab my arm. Listen, newbies, forced traveling can be dangerous. You can keep your eyes open, but do not speak, unless you want your vocal cords shredded six ways to Sunday. We'd have to travel forward to Diedre's black market Neptonian doctor to fix em, and that's as bad as losing them in the first place."

Diedre's hummed in agreement.

"Don't move too much either. Relax your body, and you won't have any issues. Now, repeat after me. No speaking. No Moving. Relax."

"No speaking. No moving. Relax." Gideon and Magnus in unison.

"Good." April said.

With a twist, April set the dial on the pocket watch. It clicked into place, the tiny analog screen showing green, blocky letters. It began ticking quietly as a mechanical whisper in the silent room. The gears tapped against each other in a slow rhythm. It grew in speed, each tick growing louder.

"Where exactly are we going?" Magnus asked.

"England." April said. "Seventeen ninety nine. Shush up, now."

Magnus' eyes widened. His voice shook as he spoke.

"But— what is it going to feel like? Is it going to hurt? I don't know if I can—"

A hand clapped over his mouth. Kiora eyed him cautiously. Her face began to stretch like gum being pulled from a shoe, or a rubber band stretching as far as it could before snapping.

Rings of golden light formed out of thin air in the space just above each of their heads. Identical rings formed in the wooden floor under their feet. Their centers were opaque with a sheen like a pool of liquid gold. Each of them were being drawn in from above and below, wrought so thing that their physical bodies could pass through the fabric of time and space.

There was a soft feeling of being pulled, as though a toddler tugged at your sleeve. April felt her head and toes stretch into the fuzzy light, and knew the rest of her would come next. Her eyes crossed the boundary leaving her with lasting sight of the others, especially Magnus, whose eyes bulged with panic.

Just before April's ears broke through the horizon of light, she heard Magnus let out a sob through Kiora's clasped hand.

V

Magnus

Magnus' mouth opened before his eyes did. His dinner, along with far too much liquor, escaped his stomach the moment he felt ground beneath him. On all fours, he purged to the tune of Diedre's cackling laugh.

"Flerovium, kid, that was a dumb thing to do." Deidre gasped out the words between bellowing laughter. "But I'll never forget in all my forms the sound of your scream dragged along with us. That's richer than credits can buy."

Magnus heaved. His entire body felt like it had been set aflame and doused out a moment before he burned to a crisp. His stomach felt like it had been cut into thirds and braided.

"Say something," April said as she knelt by him,

carefully avoiding the puddle he had made. "What's your name?"

His face contorted as his mouth tried to shape words.

"I—I—I," he stuttered in a deeper version of his own voice as though his vocal cords had been stretched along a tanning rack. "I'm M—M—Magnus Du—d-du-Duvall. Why d-d-do I sound li-li-like this?"

"What part of 'do not speak while we're traveling' do you not understand?" April asked.

"Am I-I g-g-going to stay l-like this?"

"No." April said. "You're lucky. If you had opened your mouth a moment earlier, the vibration of your vocal cords would have torn your throat open while you traveled. Looks like they just got tugged a little bit. Give it time, your voice will return to normal. Probably."

"P-p-probably?"

"P-p-probably?!" Deidre mimicked him between heaving chuckles.

April stood and looked at Gideon. "You alright? Forced traveling is different from what you're used to."

"Uneasy." Gideon said, hovering a hand over his stomach. "It will hold."

"Better out than in!" Deidre said, slapping his back. Gideon took the myiad's wrist in his hand. He held a sour look. "Easy there, soldier. Don't spew your fuel on me. Just having a laugh."

Before Gideon could let go, Deidre shapeshifted their arm thin as a pencil and slipped from his grip. They smiled at the bewilderment in his eyes.

"Pitiful." Kiora spit at Deidre's feet. "Waste of the myiad gift."

The myiad's face changed swiftly. Skin sunk shallow and pulled taut against the bone structure of their cheeks and brow. Their nose sharpened to a point, as did their chin. An inky black overtook the whites of their eyes.

"Watch your mouth, *princess*." Diedre growled. April realized they had not only shifted their face, but something internal as well, bringing out a vicious rasp in their voice. "I may not be like the 'gods' whose boots you lick, but I still know wrath."

Kiora sneered. Her hands hovered to the dual daggers on her hips.

"Listen up!" April commanded. "We've been here for two minutes and three of you are trying to kill each other. Well, one tried to kill himself, but that's beside the point. If you all want to fight, I'll send you back to the paleos and you can hash it out there. Otherwise, shut up and play nice."

Gideon nodded. Kiora sniffed and turned away. A lingering growl hummed in Diedre's chest. April cleared her throat.

"Fine." Diedre's skin loosened from bone, their nose flattened from its jagged point, and their chin receded slightly from the pointed crest it had become. In a softer voice, still brimming with their patented air of sarcasm, they spoke. "Better?"

April nodded triumphantly.

"Where are we?" Magnus asked. He was able to speak without stuttering, but his voice was still far from normal.

Mid morning sunlight painted long strokes on verdant fields around the five travelers. To one direction, a road carried on through the country. Small spirals of smoke marked the otherwise dull blue sky. Along the other direction of the dirt road, even thicker plumes sprouted from an assortment of gray buildings. Some sort of factories, Magnus presumed. Not a soul could be seen in either direction.

Aside from the road and the two opposing landmarks, bare fields stretched beyond sight. Lush and green, they held few trees, save for a far off thicket to the west. Magnus assumed it was west; the sun was near the opposite horizon's edge, but the glow felt to be the renewing warmth of dawn, rather than a cascading dusk.

Blue cornflowers and pink dog-rose speckled the field beside the road. The air was humid and cold. Brisk. Morning dew topped the flowers and clung to mossy stones. The trees drooped with the weight of the chill. They seemed to be huddling together in copses for warmth.

"Where are we?" He asked.

"Dudley, England." April said.

With all his might, Magnus forced out a question that he felt rather silly asking.

"When are we?"

April nodded as though he had just correctly answered a question that hadn't been asked.

"Seventeen ninety nine. This was our nearest access to Portum." April said.

"What is Portum?" Magnus asked.

"A city outside the fabric of time. It's where the council operates."

"The seat of Portum runs all of time travel society. The Time Council currently holds it." Diedre added.

"It's in Dudley, England?"

"This is just an access point." She turned down the road

and left him kneeling beside his puddle of purged liquor.

Stepping in tune with her, Diedre walked along, though they took the time to glance back at Kiora and wipe dust off of their cheek with their middle finger. Gideon followed closely, his lucerne hammer cradled into his shoulder.

"Luck is with you, Magnus. None would go to such lengths to save an anomaly as April." Kiora said placidly as they looked down at him. The golden medallions of her necklace mirrored the sun's stare over him. Leisurely, she drew one dagger and squatted. "If you make her regret this decision to aid you, even for a fleeting moment, you will pray that a time hound found you before I did."

The Egyptian princess stood up, looked eastward to feel the warming sun, then followed the rest. He watched for a moment as the four strangers carried ahead. A foreboding feeling pricked at his neck, as though he had fallen onto a hornets nest, but the swarm hadn't gathered around him yet. He scrambled to his feet and ran after them.

His mind raced with questions. In no more than an hour, he had sobered up, met aliens, and traveled through time to the eighteenth century. How was any of it possible?

With burning lungs— Magnus was not a runner— he caught up to the crew and assumed a march directly beside April.

"How are we in England?" The first of his many questions, Magnus figured it was a good starting point. "Are you saying we time traveled *and* teleported?"

"Time and Space are tightly knit." April said with a finality that gave the impression she thought it was a sufficient answer.

Magnus had many more questions.

"If we wanted to go to this space-time city, Portum, why didn't we travel there directly?'

"Portum is a no-travel zone. You have to use access points, like this one."

"How does that work?"

"The council has deemed it necessary for the safety of Portum's residents." Kiora answered.

"And to protect their own asses." Diedre chimed in.

A low growl came from Kiora. Diedre grinned.

"But how can they prevent time travel in a specific location?" Magnus asked.

"Near-Future tech." April's voice was sounding more agitated with each question.

"How does technology stop—"

"I don't know all the science-y stuff." She said sternly.

Magnus looked at the others for an answer. Diedre shrugged, Kiora ignored him, and Gideon picked his nose as he marched forward.

How could something like time travel be prevented by technology? Then again, how could it be activated with a hand-held device resembling a pocket watch? Then again, again, why did Magnus think any of these limitations were strange when they were built on the already-estranged foundation of belief that time travel existed?

The thought brought another question to his mind.

"What are the limitations?" He asked.

Diedre clicked their tongue. "Now there's a question I can answer! Don't worry April, Professor Diedre has this one."

April waved a hand in the air without looking back. A silent, *take it away* gesture.

Magnus desperately wished he had brought a notebook. He'd have to commit what he could to memory and hope that most of it stuck. That half-hearted strategy had resulted in more than a few failed exams in his classes.

Diedre took a dramatic breath before beginning.

"It all begins with a little mutation. We can travel utilizing what we call the traveler genome. A microscopic mutation that has been seen to manifest in any species that reach a certain level of evolutionary intelligence. That means automatons, fullmechs, robots and homunculi can't travel naturally. Even then, the genome only ever develops in point zero-zero-zero-zero-zero-one percent of any given population. Don't be sad it missed you; the genome lottery has tough odds."

"Thanks, that makes me feel better." Magnus said. It did not.

Diedre took another large breath.

"Now, you may be thinking, 'Oh, time travel? That's magic, that's science, I want to travel back and see my ancestors, or Jesus, or the dawn of time!' Well, too bad! There are limitations. Three to be exact. Sort of like universal laws, similar to how you humans *thought* you figured out the laws of physics before the year 2102."

Magnus blinked.

"We don't have the right laws of physics?"

"No where close." Diedre said. "The first limitation is that each instance of the genome is dependent to the specific being it manifests in. Despite many attempts, it has nevyer been extracted, exchanged, or manufactured. Whenever a genome has been removed, it, and the host, have died in horribly grotesque, explosions of mutation. That's why almost all testing on the genome has been universally outlawed."

Magnus considered it. A selective evolutionary trait that allowed something to travel through time. He only ever half-listed in his biology classes, but he would bet Mr. Green would reel at Diedre's claims.

"The second limitation is what we call the *Far-Future*. If you travel beyond the year 2467 per the celestial calendar, you can't come back."

Magnus cocked his head. "What's so special about 2467?"

"That's the question everyone wants to know. There are lots of theories, but only one thing is for sure: no traveler has ever gone to the Far-Future and returned to tell about it. So we call it the Far-Future, and anything between 2200 and then is called the Near-Future."

"Isn't the word 'future' relative?"

"Knowledge of the genome goes widespread in the twenty-second century, so all the terminology is relative to then. We're currently in the Near-Past."

"Oh. That makes sense." Magnus said. He wasn't entirely sure it did. "What about the third limitation?"

"The trickiest of the bunch." Diedre sighed, as if preparing for a long winded, boring explanation of a universal mechanism.

Magnus started to get excited— he loved lectures. All excitement fizzled out when the long build up culminated into one word.

"Paradoxes."

The word fell from Diedre's mouth like it tasted sour. Magnus waited for more. No more came.

"What about paradoxes?"

Diedre shrugged.

"Can't happen."

"What do you mean, paradoxes can't happen?"

"The universe hates self-contradiction, so it doesn't happen. Time, space, even our personal senses of perception will warp to account for it."

He felt his face pinch at the explanation. Diedre must have recognized it, too, as they continued on.

"For example, let's say I travel back to the moment when I met you, in Time's Tap. The saloon would be there, but I wouldn't find my past self, or April, or even you. For obvious reasons, talking to my past self would spiral into countless threads of self-fulling circles that have no origin. The universe *hates* that. April and I are too close, as well. Even if we tried, we'd create a infinite loop of information simply by interacting. Now that you and I have become closer than strangers, it's likely it would be the same."

"The past versions of us wouldn't exist?"

"They *do* exist, we just wouldn't be able to perceive them. That's where it's tricky. The flow of time keeps us from interacting by changing our perception of what is happening. That's also why we can't change major historical events that have already happened in our personally perceived past. It's best to avoid paradoxes altogether — I've seen quite a few sad fools lose their minds trying to change the past."

They spoke in such a matter-of-fact way that Magnus' skull nearly cracked. His mind couldn't keep up.

"So," he attempted. "When a traveler is faced with the potential onset of a paradoxical scenario, some magical force of the universe alters their perceptions of space and time—but not the reality of the situation—in order to avoid it?"

"No such thing ha magic." April called out from the front of the group. "Other than that, you're correct."

"Of course," Magnus shook his head. "Magic. How could I have been so silly."

Magnus felt nearly as lost as when he first woke in the saloon. It was strange to imagine that something so conceptual as time-travel had so many boundaries. He felt like he was reading an old science fiction book he read as a kid. This conversation was the portion of the book when the author explained the inner-workings of the fantastical universe in an easily digestible fashion. Diedre's explanation, however, was obtuse and difficult to follow.

"Don't think too hard about it," Diedre said, noticing his face once again. "If you do, it all stops making sense."

April hummed in agreement.

A town rose from the approaching horizon. Distant dark shapes became red brick and mortar. Long lines of connected houses four stories high. Straightaways led buildings down lines of road that organized the town in a neat grid. A laborer town, Magnus presumed with what he could recall of the time period. Workers lived in lattice housing of small apartments, pieced together quickly with brick on any workable ground near a factory or mine. Towns like this could be built up in weeks, and once the factories stopped outputting, they'd be abandoned in half the time.

"We have to go through town." April pointed at Gideon and Magnus. "If we see any locals, you two keep quiet."

Gideon nodded vigorously while Magnus mimed a

zipper over his lips.

"Alright," April said. "Stick close."

VI

Magnus

The streets of the old town were empty, save for a few newspapers hovering on the wind. Once, they saw an older man sweeping dust from the street just in front of a less-than-appealing fruit stall. Over ripe apples rested in brown wicker baskets. He didn't say a word about April's modern leather jacket, nor Diedre's long trench coat. In fact, it didn't seem to Magnus that the man had seen them at all.

"Are we invisible?" Magnus asked at one point.

April cast a side glance backwards. "Invisible?"

"Yeah. You know… to the… *locals?*"

"You mean old man Lucian? He's blind as a bat. Everyone else is at the factory, that's why it's quiet." April answered.

They followed her into a thin alley. Magnus's shoulder's nearly touched the brick walls on either side; Gideon had to turn at a slight angle to keep his wide shoulders from scraping. After a while of squeezing through, the alley opened to a concrete courtyard, nestled in a tall valley of brick.

A metal door, smooth and scarlet in color, marked the end of the alley. They stood before it a moment before April raised a hand, and with the back of her knuckles, tapped the door. The door creaked and swung open from the soft weight of April's knock.

Magnus nearly jumped out of his boots at the metallic rasp of Kiora's daggers sliding from their holsters. Diedre and April drew their pistols only a half second later. They pressed their backs to the alley's edge, away from the door's entrance. Gideon also ducked away, leaving Magnus standing alone in the open doorway before the dark corridor.

April reached out, took his shoulder, and yanked him out to the wall.

"What's going on?" Magnus whispered.

"No doorman." Diedre eyed the corridor

"So?"

Diedre's right eye watched the door. Her left eye extended on a fleshy stalk from its socket and looked back at him. "Portum isn't the kind of place that's left unguarded."

"Something's wrong." April said. She squatted at the door's edge, peering into the dark hallway beyond the door. "New plan. Diedre with me. Kiora and Gideon, take the rear." April produced another handgun from under her jacket. How many did she have under that jacket?

She pressed the dark gray pistol into Magnus' hands.

"Know how to use this?"

"I— no I can't—" Magnus mumbled.

"Point the barrel. Squeeze the trigger. Don't shoot us."

With that, April stood and cautiously proceeded into the building, the shadowy corridor and her black leather jacket becoming one.

Magnus stood there miserably. His feet felt like iron. Kiora hissed behind him, and he suddenly found the motivation to walk again.

The hallway carried on for what seemed, at a glance, endlessly. Marble floor bounced the soft taps of their shoes like stones on a frozen lake. Fluorescent lights were embedded into the ceiling in regular intervals illuminating the hall with a sterile sheen. The corridor rose and fell in sharp inclines, then wound upon itself in turns that should have returned them to the entrance.

Magnus gave up trying to hold his sense of direction. The hallway obviously unnatural. Illogical, even. What little logic he had to spare would be better kept inside. What unnerved him more was the lack of outlets in the hallway. The gray walls were unbroken. Not a single door ventured out.

Gideon shared a look of mutual discontent. What they had stumbled into was unnatural.

Magnus bumped into Diedre, who let out an alien curse he didn't recognize. April had frozen in her tracks. Each watched as she knelt down and dragged her fingers across the floor. A thick, clear slime glimmered on the tip of her finger.

"*Velex*" Kiora growled in a low tone.

"Think this is your mystery bounty, Diedre?" April asked.

The myiad shrugged. "Plenty of people dislike the council. They're a bunch of autocratic, megalomaniac, fat-cat —"

"Speak more and your blood will mix with velex mucus." Kiora warned.

"Enough." April whispered harshly. "There hasn't been any news through the timewires. Either Portum has just been attacked and we're the first to arrive—"

"—Or no one escaped." Magnus finished. He didn't mean to speak, the words simply fell from his lips.

"Impossible." Kiora said. "The gods would not allow such an invasion on their home."

"There is only one God and His plan is unknowable," Gideon whispered. Kiora scowled at him.

April held up her fist. Everyone grew silent. Magnus shifted uncomfortably. A sinister feeling pricked at his neck again, like he was running towards danger. He'd already been tackled by one of those *velex* aliens, and it nearly ripped him to shreds. Was he cut out for what was to come? He was just a history major. Fighting wasn't his thing, *especially* the violent kind. In fact, with the handgun in his hand, he felt like he might puke again.

For nearly as long as he could remember, violence had made Magnus physically ill. Doctors had called it an acute psychological aversion. Even the thought of hurting a living thing made him tremble. His first hunting trip was cut short when he fainted at the sight of his father's hunting rifle. Sports had never gone well for him as all the little boys were raised to be vicious, and he rather enjoyed looking at the flowers in right field.

Now, Magnus stood in a dark hallway somewhere between the fabric of time, a gun in his hands, on a path toward deadly alien monsters. His head felt foggy, like he may drop at any given moment. To his surprise, he felt a little excited, too. Not about facing down a human-eating alien— that scared him speechless— but the fact that time travel existed. The possibility of exploring history. The secrets that hadn't yet been shared with him. The feeling of dread in his stomach had inextricably bonded to a sense of wonder at what lay ahead.

"The situation has changed." April looked at him as she spoke. "You're in over your head. Hell, I think I am too. But someone attacked my saloon and I can't let that go. You, though? You can go home. The council has bigger fish to fry right now. I'll cover for you and make sure you don't get eradicated, alright?"

Magnus nodded slowly, but his mouth spoke a different tune.

"No." He said. "I can't go back now. I want to— no, I need to see what's out there. Even if I won't remember any of it tomorrow."

Kiora placed a fist on Magnus' chest.

"A heart alone is a blade short of a warrior." Kiora said. "Do you possess the will to face what may come?"

Magnus' hands shook. He felt microscopic under Kiora's yellow-green eyes. She looked like the Cheshire cat; both wicked and wise.

"He will come." Kiora said with a nod. "I believe his fate is tied to ours. Seer Shai will wish to meet him."

April and Diedre shared in a joint eye-roll.

"It's your life." April said. "Just make sure you don't freeze up again."

The hallway returned to something of the natural world, flattening into a straight forward path. Gray walls had turned pale blue. White bulbs with wide cone caps replaced the fluorescent lights they had been walking under. Perfect circles of light warmed the floor, then receded into a short stretch of darkness before the next. It drew from him vague memories of hospital wings at night, long and empty stretches of a world where comfort was made sterile by anonymity.

A set of double metallic doors of an elevator marked the end of the strange hallway. April placed her hand on the wall beside the door. A square of electric blue light glowed in the wall and framed her hand.

Ding.

The doors lurched and made a heavy, grinding sound, then slid open slowly.

The first thing that struck Magnus was the smell.

Once, long ago, when Magnus was a kid, his grandfather had taken him to a slaughterhouse, with the hope to break his aversion. It did nothing more than leave Magnus with nightmares for months. He couldn't recall anything but the smell of it— he had blacked out soon after arriving.

When the elevator door opened in that strange hallway, Magnus' nose was brought back to that day in the slaughterhouse. A wafting scent of rotten meat and iron overtook him.

The sterile metallic sheen of the elevator walls dripped with maroon blood and shapeless chunks of flesh. Two mounds of what could be called corpses, were they not so mangled, oozed on the elevator floor. Hundreds of tiny bite marks and razor cuts left holes on the few places that had intact limbs.

"By the holy Lord above—" Gideon's words trailed off into a quiet, mumbling prayer.

Magnus' stomach overtook his mind once again. He turned and heaved. The taste of bile rose up to his mouth. Nothing else was left in him.

"Velexi." Kiora said. Tracing the tip of her dagger across a reservoir of clear slime among the pools of blood. She grunted. "Two. Velex mucus does not mix with other mucus of its species. See here. The separation of them."

"One velex is a party, but two's a crowd." Diedre joked. Four pairs of deadpan stares landed on them. "I joke when I'm nervous. The least you could do is courtesy chuckle."

The sound of April's boot squelching in the elevator made Magnus gag again. Even avoiding the mangled corpses, there was nowhere to stand completely free of blood or mucus.

One by one, each of them filed in, stepping cautiously around the bodies. Diedre hovered at the doorway, then shapeshifted their legs and splintered them until they stood on eight, each foot with its own shapeshifted shoes.

Magnus made a mental note to ask about that— how could Diedre control the shape of the clothes they wore as well?

The myiad's upper half remained human, but their lower half resembled a spider. Magnus didn't like spiders much. He was so bothered by the shapeshifting that it was hardly a surprise to discover Diedre had also taken on the capabilities of a spider; their eight legs stuck to the walls in the rare places that were free of muck, all in an attempt to keep their shoes clean. He had met a few sneaker heads in his time, but Magnus hadn't seen any one commit to their shoes as much as Diedre.

"If I get any velex guts on my shoes, you owe me a gloag of credits, April." Diedre said. They gave Magnus a side eye glance. "This is brand new marsdvark leather. They're like aardvarks, but from Mars. You humans discover them in the next decade of your time. It's the new 1600's beaver pelt. Or yeezys."

Magnus stared.

"Diedre, stop freaking him out." April said.

Ding.

The elevator's inner panel lit up with blue light. The doors slid closed, sloshing liquids out of the track. They closed with a thud. Gideon jumped at the shudder of the elevator. April placed a hand on his shoulder.

"We're fine. Look."

As April spoke, the gray wall opposite the elevator's door became translucent. Blue light emanated up from an immense cavern. Rows of crystals the size of building sat stacked upon each other in a web of glossy metal support beams and azure light. Clusters of platforms and smaller crystalline structures clung to the cavern's walls in the far distance. Above, countless crystals pierced the cavern's ceiling and aimed their glowing blue light down unto the city. Thick lines of wire wrapped their bases and carried the light down the cavern's walls to the buildings below. On the far end of the underground city, a structure rose higher than the rest. A citadel where azure light and metallic walls culminated into a grand staircase. It led up to a courthouse, with a face of clean stone and tall columns.

Gideon placed his hands against the glass and looked directly down. It was a long drop to the cavern's floor. A half mile at least. His knees wavered, and April steadied him. The thick mess of the elevator would not be a welcome floor for fainting, if any floor could be called such.

Magnus glanced down into the city and felt his chest tighten. An underground city that existed between the fabric of time. Sure. Why not?

Above, the large glowing crystals hummed with electricity and sent a constant buzz throughout the city. The cavern seemed to vibrate, but below, the streets of Portum were devoid of life. What kind of city didn't have people?

The elevator slowed and made a loud thud as it landed. April and Diedre readied their pistols, Kiora had held her daggers at the ready for the entire ride, and Gideon had maneuvered his lucerne best he could to get it into the elevator.

Ding.

Light flickered in the wide room beyond. Ceiling lamps hung low with broken bulbs. Most were dark, others glowed maroon under wet coats of bloody paint. Velvet ropes had once organized the room into lined pathways to the tune of hanging signs with phrases like *Traveler Security Administration Checkpoint* or *Baggage Claim.*

"Time travelers have TSA?" Magnus asked.

"What is TSA?" Gideon asked.

"Sort of a security measure, sort of socially accepted racial profiling," April said.

"Who's nervously joking now?" Diedre said.

"Wasn't a joke."

Kiora pushed through and stepped into the room. Her eyes darted each way, scanning for danger. She made a *tut* with her mouth, then waved.

The room was a battlefield. Tilted desks and tables had been thrown to each corner of the room. Multi colored splatters of alien innards scored the walls. Three mangled bodies lay among countless tracks of shoes and alien feet leading to the exit.

A soft slosh and gurgle came from Magnus's right. A furry creature lay on the floor, its brown hair matted and darkened by the crimson pool it lay in. At first glance, he thought it was a human. As he approached, Magnus realized the creature was covered head to toe with fur, and it had a vaguely dog-like head, similar to a pit bull. The creature lay on its back, cradling its stomach with large furry paws.

"Please—"

Magnus jumped.

"End it—" Its voice was a heavy groan.

"Step away from it." Kiora said in a haunted tone. She appeared beside Magnus. "Move your hands, *cantanea*."

"Please—" The cantanea whispered. It moved his paws to reveal a fist sized hole in its stomach. A hairless, black membrane bulged from the hole and sealed it, like something had been placed in the wound to stop the bleeding.

"These are not normal wounds." Kiora said. "They are markings of a velex brood. We must kill it before the hatchlings feast."

"End— the— pain—" The cantanea pleaded. "I— feel— them—"

"God save this creature's soul—" Gideon began praying.

"How do we kill the brood?" April asked.

"Kill the host." Kiora placed her dagger to the cantanea's neck.

"Wait!" April said sharply. She knelt by the cantanea and took its paw in her hands. With a free hand, she combed back the long fur atop the creature's head. "We're going to stop the pain, alright?"

Kiora raised her daggers, but April shot her a halting glance.

"But first," April said. "We need to know what happened here. Anything.—"

"Jesus—" Magnus whispered under his breath. Gideon punched him in the shoulder.

"—Who did this? Who brought the velexi?" April asked.

The cantanea let out a gurgled breath. Its eyes widened as it spoke. "Velexi—""

"Tell us who brought the velexi." April's commanded

"Deceiver—" The bulging stomach of the cantanea began to writhe. It spit froth and blood as it yelled. "They— are— biting—"

Kiora slid her dagger into the cantanea's neck. With a final, relieved gasp, its eyes grew dull. The wriggling black mass in its stomach stopped moving.

"Deceiver." April echoed. "What does that mean?"

Gideon knelt and placed a hand over the cantanea's face while continuing his prayer.

"Requiem Aeternam grant unto them, O Lord,

And let perpetual light shine upon them.

May the rest in peace.

Amen."

The moment of shared silence came to its end as April spoke.

"What does 'deceiver' mean to you two?"

Kiora kept her eyes on the corpse, wary of any movement from the velex spawn within.

"Jaakobah the Deceiver." Diedre said in a cold voice. Their skin shifted hues from rich beige to a dull blue.

"Who is *Jaakobah?*" April's patience was thin.

"Deceiver. Betrayer. Defiler. The Stricken. The Exiled. Choose a vile word and it can be attached to Jaakobah." Kiora spat each name out like a bite of rotten fruit. She stood abruptly and went for the door. "We must reach the Acropolis. The council will be there."

"Agreed." Diedre said, following in a close step behind her.

For the first time, April looked as confused as Magnus felt.

"Come on." April said. "We need to catch up."

Magnus's eyes drifted sullenly to the creature below. A hand took his shoulder. Gideon offered a grim look of his own.

"My old captain had a saying before we went into battle. Do not fight for this moment, but for the next. Then, you will see what must be done to reach it."

Together, they left the cantanea alone in the terminal and followed the others.

VII

April

Main Street of Portum looked like blood had rained down over a parade.

One silver lining was that people had escaped. April breathed a small sigh of relief. She figured their arrival was less than an hour after the attack on the terminal, judging by the freshness of the scene. Even predators the likes of velexi could not cover Portum in that short of a time.

"Their target is the Acropolis." Kiora set off two steps into a run. April followed quickly behind.

"What are we walking into?" April demanded. "Who is this guy?"

"His name was Jaakobah." Diedre said the name like it was sour. "He was a myiad of the council. That is, before he was exiled."

April wasn't sure why an exiled member of the council would have any issue with her. Before today, she'd never heard of him.

"Why was he exiled?" She probed.

"That is confidential—" Kiora began.

"—he was found experimenting on live test subjects." Diedre answered, happy to spite the princess. "When I was a myiadling, the older myiads spoke of him like a horror story. Never went into specifics about what he was doing."

"What does he want to do with my saloon?" April asked.

Kiora peered back. "Hasten your pace and you may ask him yourself."

April groaned. An extraterrestrial, shapeshifting murderer wanting to shut down her saloon definitely wasn't on her new-years bingo card.

No one messed with her saloon. They could mess with the entire timeline of the universe as long as they left that place untouched. Jaakobah was about to find out he picked a fight with the wrong bartender.

The streets of Portum were barren, which April was glad for. The scene at the landing terminal had turned her stomach, though she tried to keep her face as sturdy as she could. A few knocked out teeth and a broken nose were all part and parcel for a saloon, but what they stumbled upon was grotesque.

Kiora darted down streets, turns and alleys like she had memorized the city. A hundred paces from the elevator terminal, blood-stomped tracks tapered out and gave way to clean streets, save for the velex slime that led in the direction of the Acropolis. If they weren't already, doors clicked locked as the rag tag crew ran past. Curtains were drawn by hidden hands. A few brave, or stupid, depending on how one looked at it, Portumites peeked through second story windows as April and the crew passed by.

Though the concept of Portum had been explained to her many times— a city outside of space and time— April could never understand the technical workings of it. She'd eventually given up trying to. With the technology of the timeline, time could be shifted for an individual, so why shouldn't space be shifted for a building? Or a city? Not everyone needed to understand how a modem worked to use the saloon's wifi. When one walked across Portum, time and space never aligned. What should have taken more than an hour to cross by foot, with Kiora as their guide, they crossed in minutes.

Kiora slowed to a complete stop just before the Acropolis' entry staircase. April had read history texts of battles with velexi. It could not prepare her for the scene.

"Heavenly lord," Gideon exclaimed.

Velexi were fueled by one thing, that much was widely known. Blood lust. On a battlefield, velexi had been recorded to be more vicious than in their natural hunting practices. They were granted the title of the *"Universe's Greatest APEX Predator"* in 2188, which is when humanity first made contact with the velexi home world of Velerex. It was soon after that a united front was formed among all sentient life in the universe to exterminate the velexi threat. The Time Council took the procedure a step further and set forth a campaign to remove velexi from the entire timeline, past, present, and future.

Another thing known of velexi: they were damn hard to eradicate.

Maroon cascaded down the entirety of the staircase like a waterfall. Blood pooled into the street and touched the corners of the nearest buildings. Dozens of extraterrestrials lay in crumpled mounds, haggard and draped upon the Acropolis' entrance. A single velex corpse lay among them, its onyx black skin crisped and smoking from charred wounds of photon lasers.

Kiora bounded up the stairs four at a time. April shared a wary glance with Diedre before running after her.

Inside the Acropolis, they followed a trail of death through lobbies, hallways and offices.

"If there were two velexi, then one must have made it inside." April pointed out. "Stay alert."

In sharp contrast to the rest of the building, the antechamber to the council's meeting room was relatively clean. It seemed no guard had survived long enough to make it.

Large marble doors hung double-wide against the wall of the antechamber, set in a frame of pure gold. A glass mosaic stretched the length of the doors. At the top, humanoid creatures with animal heads stood in a line, their hands open and dropping gifts of food, fabrics and technology down unto a crowd of tiny figures at the bottom. Humans stood among the figures, naked with hands raised to catch the droppings. Other species in the crowd raised their own hands, paws, tentacles and hooves. Without slowing her step, Kiora crossed the antechamber and pushed open the doors.

"Wait—" April yelled. It was too late. The marble doors

echoed a stony, ear wrenching rumble into the chamber as they swung open.

Twelve thrones rested at perfect intervals along the ovular wall of the Time Council's meeting chamber. Behind each, fifty foot tall statues of the council members stood over their respective thrones. Each a humanoid body with an inhuman head. They cast powerful glances down at the central dais in the chamber. Light refracted down from the glass mosaic ceiling of the room in shades of glossy blue and twinkling green.

On the central dais, an inhumanly tall figure stood wreathed in dark robes. It turned a hooded head slowly to April, but the face underneath remained hidden. An eerie shadow clung to the hood, as though light itself could not pass the shelter of the fabric. The figure's robes cascaded down its hulking form and bunched up on the ground, obscuring every inch of the wearer from view.

"*Jaakobah.*" Kiora hissed.

Another shape writhed underneath Jaakobah. April squinted to make out what she could of its features. A humanoid figure, with an hourglass frame draped in a cerulean silk dress, torn and bloodied. Her head was that of a jade green serpent. Shai, April recalled. A myiad of the Time Council. One of the few April had met in person, though she had been a young girl at the time. Breath lifted Shai's chest in small, fragile rises. Jaakobah's robed foot pinned her to the floor. Beside him, a velex waited deathly still, as though in a trance.

"Kekheretnebti," A deep voice said in a slow, broken rhythm. It came as a rigid gargle, as though each word pained the speaker. A chill traveled down April's spine.

"April Minnary. An unexpected turn. I believed one velexi would suffice in the destruction of your saloon—"

"Silence!" Kiora shouted. "Release her."

"Ah, Kekheretnebti the *Blades of Sekhmet*." Jaakobah announced. "Your patron god, Sekhmet, was here but a moment ago. He has fled, but I will find him."

"Lies."

"This is a chamber of lies." He leaned his weight onto Shai. "Do you not agree?"

Bronze daggers glinted under the stained light of the windows above. Reflected light glimmered around Kiora's quick feet. She crossed the chamber in an instant and leaped at the figure, her blades pointed down like a serpent's fangs. Just before she found her mark, Kiora froze in the air. She hovered just in front of Jaakobah, motionless.

"What is this?" Kiora demanded.

Jaakobah let out a single, rickety laugh. Then, he clicked his tongue.

The velex beside him broke from its trance. It barreled into Kiora, throwing itself, her, and her daggers skidding across the stone floor. As she was pulled away from Jaakobah, she began to move freely again. She reached for her blades, but the creature wrapped her in its countless arms. Together they rolled in a tight grapple off of the dais.

"Kiora!" April shouted as she charged in.

"Eat stardust, you 10 foot freak!" Diedre fired their laser pistol at Jaakobah. As the photon laser approached, it slowed down to a static halt just before reaching its target. There, frozen in the air a foot from Jaakobah, the photon laser flickered, then shot back toward them. It nearly took off Diedre's left eye stalk.

From underneath his robes, Jaakobah brought out a laser rifle and aimed it at them.

"Scatter!" Diedre shouted.

VIII

Diedre

Diedre and Magnus found cover behind one of the statues of the council members. There was just enough space between the statue and wall for both of them to stand, backs against stone, shoulder to shoulder.

"My pistol won't work against him." Diedre said, tucking the laser pistol into its holster under their trench coat.

"Why not?" Magnus asked.

"You didn't see it? You blind or something?" Diedre figured anyone with a brain could have seen the trick. Then again, Magnus was human, and he was from the twenty first century, no less. They weren't quite sure he did have a brain.

"See what?" The man asked innocently.

Diedre grinned wildly. It wasn't often that they got to teach newbies. April hogged all the fun— and avoided a lot of the important bits, like explosions.

"That's it. You're gonna be my protégé." Diedre laughed maniacally as photon lasers blasted the stone beside them.

"Is this a time to be kidding around?" Magnus.

Oh, he had much to learn. A fight was the perfect place to kid around. Who ever wanted to die with a frown?

"Time for a lesson on Expressive Singularity Defense Force Fields."

Magnus' eyes seemed to spin with the words.

"ESD for short. You see how nothing we throw at Jaakobah can touch him? Like there's an invisible wall around him? That's an ESD force field. Near-Future tech. I've only ever seen it used on ships, never as personal armor. Wish I'd thought of it—"

"He's untouchable?" Concern spread like wildfire across Magnus' face.

That wouldn't do. If Diedre knew one thing about teaching, it was that a teacher needed to inspire their pupils.

"Not untouchable." Diedre corrected. "You know how black holes absorb everything, even light?" He nodded. "ESD's use quantum white holes to push everything away."

"Even light?" Magnus asked, daring a peek at the unnaturally dark shadows of Jaakobah's black robes.

"Bingo." Diedre chimed. They rifled around in the inner coat pocket of their trench. Putting on an armor of white holes was insane. Diedre could respect that about Jaakobah. Luckily, Diedre knew the best way to fight insanity: with a dose of itself. "A-ha!"

They pulled a pack of astro gum from their pocket.

"What's that?"

"Gum. Want a piece?"

Magnus shook his head. Another photon laser blasted the wall beside him.

Diedre threw the pack of gum aside and shoved their hand back into their trench coat.

"A-ha!" They said again, more enthusiastically.

In their hand, they held up a small glass vial, no larger than a thumb. It had no cap, no seal, and looked to be empty. Diedre peered through the clear glass at Magnus.

"It's empty." Magnus said.

"Seems that way, doesn't it?" Diedre's brain tickled. The vial brought a pinched smile to their face. The moment before a big explosion was always so exhilarating, Diedre could barely contain their excitement.

Slingshot, Diedre thought. They envisioned a slingshot. The handle, the prongs, a stretchy material. As they envisioned, the five fingers of their left hand receded into the palm. It then split into two, thick prongs. Between the tips of the prongs, folds of stretched skin sprouted out and bridged the space, resulting in a fleshy appendage that resembled a slingshot.

"Pop quiz, protégé. What happens when you throw antimatter into a forcefield that repels matter?" Diedre asked.

Magnus' eyes widened in confused terror. Diedre loved that look. It was a sign of a plan coming together.

"Times up, kid. The answer?" Like a sweet treat, Diedre's mouth watered at the word. "*Annihilation!*"

Drawing back on the stretched skin, Diedre pinched the

vial into their fleshy slingshot.

"Are you a good shot?" She asked. "April said you hesitated back at the saloon."

Magnus winced, then sighed. "I can't hurt things."

"What do you mean by that?" Diedre stared at him.

"It's a psychological block. I can't hurt anything on purpose." He looked down miserably at the gun in his shaking hands.

Diedre grunted wonderingly. How was this kid alive if he didn't fight for life?

"That's one lucky life you've been living. I sometimes wonder if I'd be a straight edge like you if I didn't have the genome." Diedre had never actually wondered that. They loved their life. "Hand me that gun as soon as I slingshot this antimatter at him."

He nodded. "Will it hurt him?"

"With any luck." Diedre grinned. "We'll be alright though. When you hit a starship with antimatter, the entire sector lights up, but the ESD and antimatter sort of cancel each other out. I'd recommend covering your eyes."

"This is insane." He whispered.

"Yeah it is. Got any better ideas?"

Magnus shook his head. Diedre loved that look. The best time to enact an insane plan was when no one else had anything to counter it. Desperation loved insanity.

"Let's do this, cowboy."

IX

Gideon

Behind a statue to the left of the entry doorway, Gideon held his lucerne hammer tightly to his chest. Between his fingers, he rubbed the cross at his neck.

"I can do all things through Christ who strengthens me."

He tilted his head out of cover to get a side glance at the Jaakobah. He seemed focused on the alien woman and the man from April's time. Lightning bolts of crimson spat from his magic wand and hit the stone wall beside the two. Gideon heard Diedre's cackle clash against the crackle of the lightning. *Photon lasers.* That's what the alien had called them. The words meant nothing to Gideon. What was a photon? Was it like lightning? What he had called witchcraft at first sight, April and the others had named *technology*. Jaakobah had *technology*. The dark robed figure wielded metal wands and lightning. Even light itself seemed to avoid Jaakobah, as though the touch of God had abandoned him.

Gideon shook his head. The holy light of the Lord could pierce the hearts of the most egregious sinners. This was an opportunity for Gideon to achieve two things he had hoped for on this crusade through time: seek out the powers that claim to be gods of time, and cleanse their sins of self idolatry with the righteousness of his hammer. He had not told April this plan; he feared she would not have understood his holy mission. In that moment, however, he knew she would see the light of the Lord as He showed it through Gideon's hammer unto the unfaithful.

Twisting out of the cover, Gideon locked his glorious gaze upon the demon that had tackled Kiora. April struggled against its wicked arms, squirming to avoid its talons. The chatter of its teeth sounded of a roaring sea of bones.

"Come off of the woman, unclean spirit!" Gideon planted his feet hard onto the marble floor and swung his lucerne hammer with all the strength God had gifted him. The demon dubbed velex reached out a tainted hand toward him, but the reach of the lucerne was further. Its wide sweep carried dust and grit in its tailwind and slammed heavily into the velex, breaking into its skin and shattering teeth in a handful of its mouths. The crumpled creature slid across the stone leaving a thick trail of velex mucous and violet blood.

Triumphantly, Gideon smiled, though a feeling of shame bloomed in his stomach and ruined the moment. The victory was not his, but the Lord's. Gideon's nemesis had reared its head once again. Pride.

His captain had warned him of pride. It was a thick drink in the harshest winter; a lifeline easy to drown oneself in. Pride in one's faith was never misplaced, but Gideon struggled with his personal pride. He found great satisfaction in a victory, not only for the Lord, but for his own strength.

It felt *good* to crush his enemies under his hammer.

Gideon immediately knelt and bowed his head in prayer.

"Move your ass!" April tackled him as she shouted.

A lightning bolt — *photon laser*— struck the wall behind him. He rolled for a moment, then found his feet and took cover behind a statue. April hunkered by him, their shoulders touching.

"What the hell, man?" April said. "I appreciate the save, but you can't just close your eyes and pray in the middle of a fight."

Gideon nodded. "The Lord sheds the light of salvation upon the devout. If penance is due, then I must pay."

April's mouth was agape. She was unfaithful. He knew that. Still, he had taken a liking to her. She reminded him of his own captain. Strong willed and wise. Maybe one day, he could show her the warmth of God.

"Shit, Gideon, this ain't the time to be a bible thumper."

"That's not a term I'm familiar with, but if you'd like to hear the good word of the gospel, I can—"

"April!" Kiora's voice called through the *cracks* of laser against stone.

Gideon peeked out once again and found that the

Jaakobah had three robed arms extended from his cloak. Magic wands— *laser rifles*— extended from the dark sleeves of each so that no part of his flesh could be seen. One fired lightning at Diedre and Magnus, another at himself and April, and the third at Kiora, who had taken cover behind the next statue over.

"What?" April yelled.

Gideon wasn't sure Kiora heard. He could hardly hear over the squealing sound of three laser rifles firing. It sounded like a flock of birds. Cawing crows diving toward a carcass. Each bolt screeched through the air and blackened the stone wall beside them.

"Draw his attention!" Kiora's voice barely pierced the cacophony of lightning cracks.

"What does she expect me to do?" April complained. She drew her revolver and looked at Gideon. "Have you shot a gun yet?"

Gideon shook his head. He hadn't, nor had he wanted to. In the short time since his genome had awoken, he had seen plenty. Self pulling chariots, magic wands with lightning, and metal crossbows called *guns*. It was a powerful tool, that was a point he could not contest. But just as crossbows in his time were not to his taste, so too was the thought of the future ranged weapons. Gideon preferred spreading the grace of God with his own two hands and a hammer.

"Just keep your head down. If Jaakobah gets within spitting distance of us, then you hop out and swing your hammer, alright?"

"Aye." Gideon answered. Another reason why he was becoming more fond of April; she drummed up perfect plans.

"Good." April stood just high enough that she could reach her revolver over the statue's base. Her gun didn't sound of birds, but of shields bashing together in a battle field; explosive and violent.

As she stood, photon lasers came more rapidly toward their cover. Gideon tucked in his arm after one singed his arm hair.

Then, a flicker of movement caught his eye. Not that of a photon laser, nor of April, but the bronze glint of Kiora's daggers.

X

Kiora

Kiora sprang forth like a serpent. This was her element. The haze of battle, not only by way of smoking photon lasers, but the haze upon the minds of those ill-prepared to defend their lives. When it came to the hunt, Kiora was always prepared. Knives sharpened by whetstone. Muscles poised to move and strike in a moment's notice. Rage had blinded her a moment before. She recalled her patron, Sekhmet, the warrior god of the Time Council, encouraging her to quell the rage. Disallow it from controlling her. Despite the many great lessons her teacher had given in the way of the hunt, that single idea had always escaped her.

At that moment, she felt great rage. A blinding thirst to sink her knives into the Deceiver. He stood over Shai, a goddess of the Time Council, and mocked her. He mocked Kiora. Rage rose within her. She had garnered attention for that very rage. Kiora, *Blades of Sekhmet.* Rogue criminals, vagabonds and enemies of the council had all come to know her as such.

Her legs pulsed furiously as her feet pounded the floor in sprint. In her left hand, she artfully twirled her dagger, Patience, between her fingers. Another poor habit, but one she indulged in. Her other dagger, Time, held its angle in her right hand, thirsting for Jaakobah's jugular.

The two most powerful warriors are patience and time.

April had read that quote to her once. A man named Tolstoy had written it. Kiora had become so fond of the idea that she named her bronze daggers Time and Patience.

Kiora, Blades of Sekhmet, had hunted many of the council's enemies. She had faced unimaginable weapons and circumvented all possible defense systems. Jaakobah appeared to have an ESD force field, though it could have been a different type of Near-Future tech Kiora hadn't seen before. Now that she was aware of it, she could see the faintest distortion of light in a bubble around him. Its edge was three feet from his body. Considering how her dagger interacted with it, anything that approached would slow down to a complete stop before ever reaching him. There, an approaching object would be frozen, trapped in the force field, a fly caught in a spider's web.

Even still, Kiora was always prepared.

Along the hilt of Time, she slid her thumb and depressed a hidden lever under the linen handle. The famed daggers, Time and Patience, held many secrets for many applications. This particular secret opened microscopic slits at Time's base, and released a film of refined antimatter over the blade. It was, however, a balancing act; just the right amount would need to be released. Antimatter was extremely volatile. Kiora had heard plenty of stories of some poor soul getting their hands on a vial of raw antimatter and annihilating an entire city by accident.

It was a fine needle to thread. A step away from the edge of the forcefield, she thrust Time forward. Jaakobah had reacted poorly to her speed. He fumbled to redirect all three laser rifles at her. It was too late. Time touched the edge of the force field.

Unfortunately for Kiora, she was also too late. Rage fell to the wayside of confusion in the final moment of her strike. Something glinted near her blade, frozen in time at the edge of Jaakobah's force field. A clear vial? How had it gotten there? A metallic glint approached it. A bullet. It hit the outer edge of the ESD bubble and carried its declining speed directly into the vial.

The vial shattered. Glass shards on the side nearest Jaakobah remained motionless. On the side facing away from the forcefield, shards tapered down through the air, floating to the ground and landing like crystalline snowflakes.

Kiora had only a moment to cover her eyes and curse Diedre's name before an expansive, white light overtook the room.

XI

April

April's throat burned. Dust filled the air in a thick, hazy cloud. A sharp ring bounced around in her skull. Her head felt like a rattle snake's tail. She had vague memories of waking up hungover after long nights of drinking at the Prescott Rodeo.

All colors seemed pale and whitewashed in her vision. The bright white marble floor stung her eyes. Slowly, she sat up. When had she been knocked over? How long had she been out? Gideon lay next to her, lost in a coughing fit of his own. Above, the statue of a council member leaned against the wall. Both arms and the head had broken off and fallen around them like miniature meteors. An index finger had fallen near and almost pinched her head to the floor

What happened? One moment, Kiora charged. The next?

It came in a slow series of images. A blinding white light, like an explosion, but she couldn't remember a sound. A silent combustion. It had sent a shock wave that cracked the thick walls of the room and tore down half the statues lining it, but there wasn't a scratch on her. None that she could see or feel, at least. During the flash, it almost felt like the air around her thickened and squeezed her.

"Kiora?" April called out. Her heart pounded. "Gideon, get up."

"The Lord shall smite thee with an inflammation, and with an extreme burning." Gideon spit dust.

"Focus! It's no time for verse."

Scanning the edge of the room, April caught a flicker of movement. Diedre and Magnus picked themselves up from the floor. Rays of light from above shone down from the open ceiling. What remained of the mosaics lay on the floor, the colored glass deflecting beams into dust. It reminded April of a music festival.

Her heart raced further. Each hasty beat encouraged her to take a step forward. Kiora had just charged head first into an explosion. April obliged her heart, and approached the center of the room.

"Kiora?" April said aloud. She kept her revolver ready. "Are you in there? Say something. Kekheretnebti?"

A haggard voice boomed.

"Fools. All of you. Allowing these wretched myiads to rule the timeline. They distill it into your hearts and feed it to your children. Despair is manufactured in this room."

The words landed in April's ears, slithered down her spine and chilled her to her core.

"Why do you want to destroy my saloon?" April called out. She slowly skirted the edge of the dais, keeping her revolver aimed at the center of the dust cloud. All else in the room settled and became clear, but the cloud remained still over the dais. "What beef have we got, huh?"

"Do you not see the hypocrisy in it all? A council overseeing eternity. Infinite resources at their fingertips. Time itself can grant this to them. What do they do with it? Build statues in their own likeness. Strike down those who stand against their order. Your saloon is a piece of a deranged system. A small piece, but one that must fall with the rest."

What April found deranged is that a universally feared murderer was speaking of what he found deranged.

"So destroy the Time Council, my saloon, and then? What next?" April asked.

"I will bring an end to despair."

Since entering Portum, despair was all April had seen. A pathway of despair had been painted with blood and stamped by Jaakobah's footprint. She had felt quite a bit of despair when a velex threatened to kill her in Time's Tap. Jaakobah's preaching about hypocrisy struck April so violently, she couldn't help but take a hint from Diedre and be a little snarky in response.

"Were you going to do that before or after the indiscriminate killing?"

"The council is hardly innocent." Jaakobah growled. "Food to feed the poor, shelter to house the unfortunate, medicine to heal the ill. I have killed the council today, yes, but how many have they allowed to die when an answer is within their reach? They have harbored despair, made it the work of their millennial terms. The genome can cure it all. Erase despair in its entirety. My universe will never know of hunger, disease, or unnecessary pain."

Despite the concerning interest in total control over the universe, April didn't think it sounded too bad. That sent another chill down her spine. His words preyed on empathy. She had seen despair. She had *felt* despair. Maybe not at the behest of famine or disease, but she was no stranger to pain. April knew what it was to be lost. Feel helpless. Grief woke with her alarm clock and laid in bed with her each night.

"I know of your grief." Jaakobah spoke as if reading her mind.

April wondered if he *could* read her mind. With extraterrestrials, she could never be sure. Diedre could shapeshift into an exact replica of, well, anything they wanted. The odds of Jaakobah reading minds wasn't exactly zero.

"Never knowing your parents. Your dear grandfather, Sylas, abandoned you."

A sharp pain twisted April's chest. She grit her teeth.

"He didn't abandon me, asshole."

"To we who travel through time, is death not abandonment?" Jaakobah's voice slithered through the dust. "What would you give to breathe life into his memory? Or, perhaps, stop his life from ending altogether?"

April froze. She fought her imagination like a siren's song, but it lulled her to dream of the possibility. She had wondered before, what life would be like if Sylas hadn't passed on. They would share a whiskey at the saloon, Fleetwood Mac humming through the jukebox, Sylas laughing through a story of his recent venture to Alpha Centauri, or a trip to the grocery store earlier that evening. Grandpa Sylas could make any story worth listening to.

Imagination. Nothing more. April didn't know much about Jaakobah, but he wasn't called *the deceiver* for nothing. He was selling tonics and snake oils. Lies and manipulation. He wanted power, and he'd twist his words in any way he could to get it. Living in the United States, she'd heard every kind of rhetoric from every kind of politician. The tyrant before was always to blame for the next one.

Aside from his reputation, April knew one thing without a shred of doubt: there were limitations to time travel. Her grandfather was gone. The genome couldn't bring him back, nor bring her to him. There was no rule bending, no defying the limitations, no magic.

"Bullshit." April said. "It's impossible."

"I have discovered a way to surpass the limitations of the genome." Jaakobah said. "Your grandfather could live again, April. Join me, and let us erase despair together."

Softly squeezing her grip, April shot three times at the shadow within the dust.

"Consider my offer, April. Once I bring an end to the council's rule, I will return to your little saloon. I expect an answer, then."

A wicked laugh trailed his words. The shadow twisted and stirred up the thick cloud of dust into a vortex. In a blink, the shadow dissipated, the vortex stilled and rolled off the dais, leaving only Kiora and Shai alone in the center of the chamber.

XII

April

"Are you alright?" April asked as she approached Kiora.

Her eyes darted around the chamber, looking for any sign of Jaakobah. Travel dampening technology was always active in Portum. A directive of the council. Had Jaakobah somehow turned off the dampeners? He *was* once a member of the council, maybe he had some secret back door access. Either way didn't seem too far-fetched to April.

Jaakobah's claim of breaking the limitations of the genome, however, reeled in April's mind. A lie to lull her in, surely. That drew a different question to mind; why did Jaakobah want April to join his inter-temporal crusade?

There wasn't a single mark on Kiora, let alone the expected aftermath of a point-blank Diedre-explosive. For that, April was thankful.

"Children—" Hissed Shai. Green fluid glazed the blue scales around the myiad's serpentine mouth. "One named by spring, come near and hear me."

Kiora shot a demanding look at April. Her eyes were red and puffy.

For April, the sight of the dying myiad was insubstantial beside Kiora's tears. As if a second explosion had been set off within her, April felt her own eyes swell. In years of knowing Kiora, and months where they had tried dating, April had never seen the woman shed a tear. Even when April had shown her *Marley and Me*.

She knelt by Shai, and listened.

"Dark flower of spring, your bloom brings omen and succor. The rainstorm has yet to come. Jaakobah will not rest until the council fertilizes his thorny flower bed."

"What is up with people and speaking in verse?" April mumbled.

Kiora hissed sharply.

"I mean—" April added quickly. "What did Jaakobah mean about surpassing the limitations? That isn't possible, right?"

"The Deceiver can not bend the fabric of time. He has tried before and failed. Deceit to slither near. His teeth drip with venom. Jaakobah has become a distillation of his own malice. He will find the remaining council members and—"

Shai fell into a coughing fit, spitting dark blue blood onto the dusty marble.

"What must we do, Lord Shai?" Kiora asked.

"The universe has blessed me with a vision. April, you will be Jaakobah's unraveler. You must lead the fight against Jaakobah. Kiora, I place you in service of April Minnary. Vow to be her guardian, her blades, her knife's edge, until death do you part, or Jaakobah is slain."

A hot, jagged frown struck April's face. "No, that isn't —"

"By each moment left within me, I vow." Kiora said with a steel voice.

"Uh," April stared into snake-headed woman's eyes. Pupils like sapphires watched her from a scaled face. With each word, the color in them grew duller. Pale sky blue, with gray clouds forming overhead. "I'm not interested in leading anyone in some grand time-war. Or whatever. I'm just here to save my saloon."

Kiora sneered viciously at April.

"—your Lordship." April added. The addition didn't seem to dissuade Kiora's sneer.

"Place trust in those near, and be wary of trust; this storm precipitates duty and betrayal. Seek out Osiris, High Lord of the Council. He holds the key to defeating Jaakobah."

"Lord Osiris has been hiding for centuries. How are we to find him?" Kiora asked.

"Osiris may be found when Queens place crowns upon their own heads."

Shai's mouth stilled. The silence of the room was broken only by the heavy thuds of Deidre's marsdvark leather shoes. They crossed to the dais and peered at the dead myiad. Kiora sniffled.

April was struck by an uneasy feeling. How could she comfort Kiora? They had been friends, even lovers, once. But their relationship had been reduced to steely words and short glances. Now, the woman held one of her own gods in her arms and wept. April didn't think she could find a hallmark card that said, "*Sorry one of your gods died,*" though she was sure it would sell in a 2024 etsy shop.

Hesitantly, April reached out a hand to Kiora's shoulder. It hovered for a moment, but never landed.

"Bow your heads. A god finds rest." Kiora said.

Each did, save for Gideon, who eyed the half-serpent half-human body skeptically. The dust cloud settled around them.

"What do we do now?" Magnus broke the silence.

"*We* do nothing." April said. "I'm going home."

"What?" Magnus asked.

April walked toward the entrance of the room while she spoke. "I'm not interested in cosmic power grabs or political takeovers. Jaakobah wants something, otherwise he wouldn't have left us alive. I figure out what it is, I convince him not to destroy my saloon, and the council deals with the mess they created—"

A hand wrapped her wrist like a steel cuff. Kiora held her in place, malachite eyeshadow smeared around bloodshot eyes.

"We must seek out Osiris." Her voice was hoarse. "Shai was Seer of the Council. Her visions are foretellings You will be Jaakobah's unraveler."

"I'm not going to trust the dying vision of some extraterrestrial. I don't owe the council anything, dead or alive." April retorted. Kiora's expression became steel. That was a face April was familiar with.

Diedre clicked their tongue and whistled. "You may want nothing to do with Jaakobah, but from my seat, it sounds like he wants you on his side of temporal-xenocide.

Now, I didn't think that was your brand of whiskey, but, who knows, I've been surprised before."

The myiad drew their eyes up from the corpse and gazed at April. Their amethyst stare could freeze fire if Diedre felt too hot.

"Shit." April said under her breath.

"'Shit' is right." Diedre said.

The words hung in the air and settled with the broken glass on the floor.

"Shit." April said again. She dug her hands into her jacket pockets as she trudged toward the door. Kiora matched each step she took, only a foot behind. "Mind giving me some space?"

"Shai has named me your blades." By Kiora's tone, it seemed a great struggle to say the words. April noticed her eye twitch as she repeated them more sternly. "Shai has named me your blades. I must follow you in this fight."

"Wow," April said. "That's all it takes for you to commit, huh? A divine edict?"

She expected a pointed retort, but Kiora silently scowled.

"Fine." April sighed. "We will find Osiris or whatever. But listen, I'm only in this to save my saloon, got it?"

"I'm in." Diedre said. "If Jaakobah's hunting down all of the myiads, my name is on the chopping block."

"This isn't going to be some space-time-adventure-party. I'm going to handle this the way I do things: alone."

"Total flerovium" Diedre waved a hand. "He's got force fields, pet velexi, and who knows what else. Better if we stick together."

"No one is alone if they accept Christ into their heart."

Gideon added.

Magnus shuffled a step away from him.

"You did not see as I did." Kiora's voice softened. "His skin repelled the annihilation of matter. I was protected by proximity alone. It is not only an ESD forcefield, but his body has become something else. *Distillation of his own malice.* It is unlike anything I have seen."

That damned ounce of softness in Kiora's voice trickled into April's ear and unsteadied her heart. She had always called it Kiora's third blade. The Egyptian princess could disarm any combatant with her daggers, Patience and Time, but all she needed for April was a word.

"Jesus." April sighed. Gideon punched her shoulder. "I admit, I'm in over my head. I don't hunt down extraterrestrials, or fly space ships, or whatever you do, Gideon. I manage a saloon where people can have a drink in peace. If the universe's number one most wanted is trying to destroy my home, I'm going to do everything I can to stop him. If you want to 'team up,' or be 'crime fighting buddies,' or whatever, leave that shit at the door. We're gonna stop Jaakobah, and we're not gonna like it, alright?"

The four others shared a confused look.

"No—I mean—I'm gonna save my saloon. No comic-book super-team stuff, alright?"

"What is *comic book?*" Gideon asked.

April shook her head. "Don't worry about it. Let's get out of here."

XIII

Magnus

As they approached the entrance terminal to Portum, it dawned on Magnus that his neck had been pulled from the chopping block. Then, a second dawn broke; his neck had been placed on a much larger, sharper, chopping block.

"Wait," Magnus slowed to a stop as he constructed the thought. The blue light of Portum's crystalline cavern poured down over the street corner they were crossing. "If Jaakobah isn't hindered by the three limitations, how are we alive? Couldn't he remove your genomes, or get some tech from the Far-Future, or maybe right now, he's going into the past to kill us before we ever meet him!"

"His title is warranted." Kiora answered. "The Deceiver speaks lies to threaten put fear in our hearts. None have broken the limitations before, and he is no different. He speaks of erasing despair, yet he sows it in his flight toward power. Do not listen to his empty promises."

It seemed to Magnus that she spoke more to April than to answer his question. What did she mean by his empty promises? His curiosity got the better of his mouth.

"He promised you'd see your grandpa again." He pieced it together. "That's what he meant. Without the third limitation, you could travel anywhere and see anyone, even if you witnessed their death. Paradoxes wouldn't matter."

Magnus regretted his curiosity immediately.

April's demeanor changed. She grew rigid, her shoulders tense, her fists balled and pressed into her leather jacket. She shared Kiora's eerie presence. Together, they radiated silent rage. Magnus could see why they had a history — they were quite alike.

The heavy sound of her boots led April's cold voice.

"It's impossible."

Magnus waited for more, but April had said all she desired to.

A way to bring back the dead. That was Jaakobah's promise. If it was possible, April would be able to go back to a time where her grandfather was alive and be with him again.

Though he didn't know April well, Magnus could surmise that her grandfather's death was a gaping wound on her heart. Jaakobah had prodded that wound with a fiery stick and promised to heal it.

Even if he could break the limitations of traveling, April would never join his side. She wasn't that type of person. She'd brought Magnus along in order to save his life. A total stranger. Then again, it was her saloon that put his life in jeopardy. He didn't know her well enough to be sure, but even at their first meeting, he knew she was a kind person.

Despite it all, Magnus could only recognize the others as a short step above strangers. How long had he known them? They had traveled back two hundred years, but how long had they actually *spent* together. With all the time shenanigans, he wasn't sure.

What he did know was that Jaakobah gave him the heebie jeebies. Just thinking about his gravelly voice made Magnus squirm like cockroaches were crawling over his entire body.

A silent solemness spread over the group as they crossed the city. A strange, sheltered fear. These special few who traveled through time suffered from the same debilitating fears as everyone else. Unknown. Loss. Loneliness.

An odd feeling came over Magnus. He was certainly afraid; that much had been true since he woke up in a saloon full of aliens. At that moment, however, realizing the time travelers shared many of his fears, he felt more grounded. Comforted, even. As though his internal voice has stopped shrieking and taken a deep breath. They may have the traveler genome, but they were still human. Most of them. Despite knowledge of the future and access to the infinite history of the past, they still laugh, cry, and bicker. They were afraid. Alive. They seek out ambition and preserve what they can against the inevitable end. Every living thing across time, even those who could travel through it, faced the inescapable truth of mortality and its associated conundrums. That was worthy of a thesis.

As April led the group through the elevator terminal and out of Portum, Magnus wondered if she would consider a quick stop in 2024 so he could grab his notebook and a pen. There had already been so much worth writing down. He had an itching feeling there would be much more to document before it was all over.

The return journey to the surface streets of 1799 was much quicker than the entry into Portum. Once out of the elevator, they had returned to the surface street in less than a minute. The once non-euclidian hallway had become a straight stretch of twenty feet. Magnus wasn't sure how long they had been underground, or if they had really been underground at all. Space, along with most of his understanding of the physical world, had become an abstract concept.

In the sky above the town of Dudley, the sun hadn't moved an inch.

"Every access point to Portum is an intra-temporal hallway. It's a static connection between two points in time." April said off of his look. "We spent a relative thirty six minutes in Portum, but less than a second has passed since we entered."

"How can you tell?" Magnus asked.

"I have a really good internal clock." April grinned and brushed her thumb against her nose, flashing a wristwatch. It wasn't a fancy, time-travel gadget as far as he could tell, just an analog wristwatch with a two mechanical dials. "Get in close, everyone. We've got all the time in the universe and it's probably not enough. Now, it seemed to me that we don't stand a chance in hell against Jaakobah in a gun fight. Anyone have another idea?"

None had a word to say on that point, though Kiora seemed to boil under her skin.

"Shai has given us an answer." Kiora said. "Osiris. The High Lord of the Council—"

"Osiris, Shai, Sekhemet, are all the Time Council members named after Egyptian gods?" Magnus blurted out. Kiora gave him a scornful look at being interrupted. Again, he cursed his unfiltered curiosity. "Sorry."

"They *are* the Egyptian gods." Diedre answered. "Myiads visited earth in the early years of human civilization. You ever watch that show *Ancient Aliens?*"

Of all the things Magnus had witnessed and held his sanity through, he felt like his mind might shatter at the mention of *Ancient Aliens*. "The TV show that said the pyramids were docking stations for alien starships? Are you telling me that *Ancient Aliens* was correct?"

"Of course not," Diedre said.

Magnus let out a huge sigh of relief.

"They only had about eighty percent of it right."

"'*When Queens place crowns upon their own head.*'" April cut in. "That's where we can find Osiris' hiding place."

"From what does he hide?" Gideon asked.

April looked expectantly at Kiora.

"Council secrets." She said coldly.

"We'll ask when we find him." April patted Gideon on the shoulder. "Any ideas where we can find a queen crowning herself?"

Kiora shrugged. Diedre shook their head. Gideon stared at the ground.

"Cleopatra." Magnus mumbled. "In one of my ancient civ classes, someone brought up an old story about

Cleopatra's rise to power. In antiquity, some historians believed she crowned herself at her coronation, though there's no evidence of it."

"Who is this *Cleopatra*?" Kiora asked.

Diedre laughed. "Your great grand kid about seventy times removed."

"Well actually, Cleopatra was Macedonian—" Magnus began.

"When was her coronation?" April asked.

Kiora shrugged. Diedre shook their head. Gideon stared at the ground. All eyes darted to Magnus.

Magnus had the answer to a history question that time travelers did not. Time travelers! The moment tickled his ego. A smug satisfaction swept over him. Even the skill of time traveling could not compete with the well studied.

"March 22, 51 BCE." Magnus smirked.

"Give me the pocket watch." April said.

Magnus had forgotten he had it in the first place. He took it from his coat pocket. The little box felt cold in his hand. Heavy. The light on its side glowed red. When he handed it to April, the light flicked to soft green. She clicked a button, turned a dial, and handed it back. The light turned red in his hand.

"It works better if the holder knows exactly when and where we're traveling. Just press that dial down, think really hard about Cleopatra's palace or whatever, and it'll start." April said "Remember what I told you about forced traveling?"

"No speaking. No moving. Relax."

"That's right." She nodded to him. The dial clicked as he pressed it, and a loud ticking followed. The light remained red.

"Red light," Magnus said quickly. "Red light, is that good or bad?"

"It's fine. Now shush." April said.

A churning of excitement, disbelief and fear boiled within him. He remained silent as the circles of light appeared above his head and below his feet. Not a sound came from his throat as his body stretched like taffy and traveled through time.

April

Humid air struck April. It filled her nostrils and unfurled over her like a thick, wet blanket. Her eyes opened and adjusted to the shift of light. High overhead, a blazing sun boiled a cloudless sky. Sea salt trailed a light breeze and tickled her nose.

"Where are we?" April looked at Magnus. He stood, mouth agape, staring past her. "What?"

April turned and couldn't help but gasp.

Across a murky green bay, a stone tower rose from an island. A wall at least ten feet high encircled the tower, but was dwarfed entirely by the structure. From the ground to half its height, the tower was a square pillar of beige stone. Above that, the middle section of the tower was an octagonal shape that stretched further up. Atop the middle section, a cylinder shaped tube pointed skyward and rounded off its tip with a dark weathered stone roof.

Beyond the island that held the tower, April took in the mainland. Immense wooden ships rocked in the water and dotted the long harbor of the city. Wide buildings lay on the earth and covered the horizon, earthy yellow and brown homes of stone, with dark wooden lace ceilings.

Below her feet, April stood on exquisitely cut stone tile. They had landed on a separate island in the harbor. No more than fifty yards from her, the stone tile cut off and gave way to a short drop into the water. Another fifty yards in the opposite direction, a palace of yellow, beige and white stone rose from the earth. Hanging banners of gold and red adorned countless open windows, none of which had glass.

April recalled reading in a history book about when glass was first put into windows. It was in Roman Egypt, but she couldn't recall exactly when. She glanced at Magnus, the ancient history wiz kid. He'd probably have the answer, but she didn't think it was that important either way.

Many of the palace walls were engraved with various symbols and shapes that one could find in history textbooks with little context paragraphs that were, more often than not, far from correct translations. April recognized some hieroglyphics that Kiora had taught her, but even they seemed old and dusty compared to the newer art and tapestries adorning the place. The ground was clean cut and mostly tiled over, save for a few palms that had remained while stone was set around their bases.

A blaring horn turned April on her heels. A ship coming into port.

Her nerves were on edge. They had just walked away from a gun fight, and before that, she'd nearly been torn apart by a velex. She pinched her brow. A near-death experience wasn't an excuse to fry your nerves. Fried nerves lead to an *actual* death experience.

Across the bay, a glisten at the tip of the strange tower caught the corner of April's eye. She squinted against the harsh light and peered at it. Another glisten. A flash of light. A momentary thing. A quick burst and then, a plain old tower.

"What is that?" April looked to Magnus once again, but the man still stood agape.

"The Lighthouse of Alexandria." Magnus whispered. He turned to the palace. "And this is Antirhodos, Cleopatra's palace. They both fell to earthquakes centuries ago, I can't believe it."

"It ain't centuries ago any more." Diedre said amusedly. "It's local time, and we're tourists."

Magnus closed his mouth and gulped audibly.

"You're positive this is the right—" A thundercloud of cheering voices cut April's sentence. Pounding of feet rattled the laid stone below and shook the palm leaves atop the trees. The entire island seemed to shake. Gideon clung tightly to his hammer, as did Diedre to their laser pistol. Further along the esplanade, April spotted three locals walking together. Women with smooth purple silk wrapping their bodies, and so much gold jewelry they shined as bright as the lighthouse. They scuttled past two guardsmen standing by a portcullis in the palace's wall.

"Sounds like the coronation has begun." Diedre said as they hid their laser pistol under their trench coat.

Kiora marched forward. "If Osiris has hidden a clue to his hideaway in this time, I will find it."

"Wait a second," April said.

To her surprise, Kiora listened. She turned slowly to reveal a submissive scowl on her face. Somehow, the tortured look was more ominous than her standard glare. April certainly appreciated when Kiora listened to her, but the somewhat gray area of indentured servitude unsettled her. She didn't want Kiora to be her *blades*, as Shai had bid her to do so.

"We don't even know what to search for." April glanced at Magnus. "Any ideas from the history buff?"

"An ankh, Atef crown, the lotus, plenty of symbols were associated with Osiris." Magnus posed. "He was seen as the lord of the afterlife, so anything to do with death."

What a stroke of luck that the one local April gets stuck with in this mess would be a historian.

"Alright, we're looking for ankhs, crowns, death in general. Spot something, say something." April said. "Diedre, can you get us through those guards?"

"Sure." Diedre brought their laser pistol out from their trench coat with a sinister grin. After a cue from April's stern glare, they acquiesced. "Fine, if you want to do it the boring way."

The myiad's face began to ripple. Skin became like the surface of a pond; tiny waves bounded out from the nose to the back of their head. Diedre's skin became darker, shifting from blue to a fleshy bronze. Their nose grew longer and rounded off into a soft button, their eyes sharpened to strong points, enhanced by a deep shade of eye shadow just below their brows. The black hair on Diedre's head shrunk to a cleanly-chopped, neck length cut. Only their eye color remained the same; pale amethyst irises that sheened in the broad sunlight.

Watching the process made April squirm. Staring into the eyes of an amorphous shapeshifter made April's own skin want to crawl away. She had to give Diedre one thing; they understood traditional beauty standards. The face and body they had adopted was that of an early classical era supermodel.

"Am I pretty enough?" Diedre batted their long eyelashes. "Follow me and don't say a word. Let me work some myiad magic."

The two guards stood on either side of a portcullis in the palace wall. Padded armor of red linen and gold lace covered each of their shoulders and swept down their bodies to short cut skirts. Over the fabric, identical iron chest pieces covered each, adorned with red and green jewels in lines down the sides of the torso. Underneath the padded skirts, iron greaves covered their legs from the shin down, meeting leather sandals on their feet. Feather plumes sprouted and draped over kettle helmets they wore on their heads.

As Diedre approached, they regained their postures and stood up straight. Their eyes latched onto Diedre's swaying curves, their pronounced swagger, and their large, butterfly-lashed eyes.

For a moment, it seemed to work. The guards simply watched, stunned by confidence, or presence. Diedre nearly walked right between them, until sense snapped back onto the guard's faces like a drawn rubber band.

"Halt!" A husky voice came from one guard.

"No entrance without a pass." A squeaky voice came from the second. April noticed his hand shift toward the sword on his belt.

"Peace, friends." Diedre's rich voice dripped effortlessly into the air like rose petals on the wind. April wasn't sure how they managed it, but their voice adopted a sultry tone more deviant than their appearance. "I'm here for the coronation of our queen. I'm a dear friend, though it seems I've lost my pass. Don't you think you could let me in? A personal favor."

A fish to chum, Husky took the bait.

"All deserve to see her majesty claim the crown," Husky grinned lasciviously.

"What's this?" Squeaky prodded Gideon's hammer with a finger. "Never seen nothing like this."

"Do not touch it." Gideon growled. "It is a holy device."

"Don't mind them," Diedre put a hand on Squeaky's chest. "They've traveled over far seas to see the Queen, and her esteemed guardsmen."

"Is that so?" Squeaky said. He couldn't decide where to cast his gaze. "Strange clothes they wear overseas."

"Drop it, Tentahkt." Husky commanded. "I can let you slip by, but the foreigners aren't to be let in without explicit —"

Clunk!

Kiora hammered the back of Husky's head with the hilt of Time.

"What the—" Squeaky was cut off as Gideon pounded the back of his head with a heavy fist.

The two guards slumped to the ground, clattering as their metal bits hit tile.

"No fun. I almost had them." Diedre pouted. They didn't seem too bothered by the outcome either way. Their voice distorted along with their face as both returned to the usual humanoid form Diedre appeared in. The shorter, Latina woman with amethyst eyes that April knew. "Hammerhead, what part of 'don't say anything' do you not understand?"

Gideon shrugged. "Don't touch my hammer."

"He has a point," Kiora agreed as she spun Time into its sheath.

April felt like a chaperon on a school field trip of murderous toddlers. Working alone would have been much smoother. Too late for that. She wondered if Gainsborough was having better luck at the saloon. He'd probably be drinking by himself in peace. Now that April thought of it, he may be in danger, too. At the very least, he needed to close down the saloon until she got back. April pulled out her time wire.

"Is that a cell phone?" Magnus asked.

"Time wire. For sending messages across the timeline." April said.

"Who could you possibly be texting right now?" He asked.

"My uncle." She tapped. She sent the message with a sharp click. "Alright, we can't just stand over these two arguing til someone finds us. Shush up and start moving."

The portcullis opened to a short passageway through the palace wall. A tunnel, ten feet long, with light pouring into each end. Cheers and chatter from beyond the tunnel were amplified against the stone. April could hardly think as she approached the roiling sound. Thousands of feet stomping, hands clapping, and voices chanting all sorts of competing cheers.

Pausing only to take a deep breath at the end of the tunnel, April stepped forward into the courtyard of Cleopatra's palace.

XV

Kiora

Time and Patience sat in their holsters on Kiora's hips. Her fingers itched to draw them. She wasn't partial to dense crowds, and the majority of the courtyard was packed shoulder to shoulder.

Kiora rebuked her own weakness. A sappy sweat formed on her palms. An unnerving tension fell into her gut like a stone cast into a pond. *Kekheretenebti, Princess of Kemet,* had grown accustomed to masses of this size, but *Kiora, Blade of Sekhmet,* much preferred the vast emptiness of space, or April's saloon on a weeknight.

Of course, she recognized that the two identities made one person. The difference was a matter of presentation.

Kekheretnebti the *princess* had never felt peace in her

own body, yet she could don the mask of a politician. Golden robes and ostentatious jewelry fit nicely upon her. It was a requisite. Striking the mass heart of Kemet with but a command was a pass time leisure. Born as Kekheretnebti, the lifestyle was more than simple conditioning. It was a wrathful spirit of politics, subterfuge and wit. It swelled within, flexing sore muscles against rich fabric and golden chains. When Kekheretnebti's traveler genome awoke, she discovered her true nature: Kiora, the free, daring spirit who longed to rip through the chains of silk and gold.

In that courtyard of her homeland, despite three thousand years separating herself and the people calling for their Queen, a piece of her, Kekheretnebti, felt naked in the crowd. She was without her fine linens, jewelry and regal makeup. Her true nature was laid bare for her people.

These were not her people. The name Kekheretnebti was buried deep in the sands of time. Kiora had seen enough of the timeline to understand. Conquerors came and passed, as did Queens, Pharaohs, and the like. The council persisted. A guide for civilization. Advancement. What worth was the legacy of a pyramid? A pile of stones on a tiny planet. Upon the scales of divine determination, time outweighed gold. Kekheretnebti was a stranger to the people of Cleopatra's Kemet.

Kiora felt no sorrow in being forgotten. Kekheretnebti struggled with the inner thought. Even still, the crowd made Kiora nervous.

Sekhmet, her patron myiad within the council, had taught her many things of fighting, the history of the future, Near-Future technology, and self regulation. It was the premiere quality of myiads, and, though Kiora was only human, the teachings of Sekhmet, along with some highly classified mutagenic alterations, allowed her a decisive control over the functions of her body.

Kiora had never told anyone of this. Even April. Mutagenic experimentation was outlawed by the council. She and Sekhmet had made a pact of secrecy. In return for undying loyalty to the myiads and the council, Kiora would be given supernatural abilities beyond a human body's natural limits. She could live free of the chains of her home time and planet, without worry of struggle or fear, so long as she bade her blade to the council's rule.

For the particular technique she wanted to employ, momentary focus was all that was needed. A breath inward, timed with a beat of her heart, and a breath outward in similar rhythm. Conscious activation of her mutagenic qualities. A numbing shiver dripped down her spine, through her nervous system, echoed to her fingertips and wavered her knees. After a moment, the sweat in her palms dried. She tapped together the fingers of her left hand. They were completely numb. A sinister trade off, if only temporary. She quelled anxiety at the cost of dexterity. A dangerous solution in a dagger fight; an apt one for deceit.

Thousands filled the wide courtyard. They wore clothes not dissimilar to the apparel of Kekheretnebti's time; richly woven linens ranging in various degrees of white, blue, and purple, with some draped and others tightly knit to a person's torso. Often they wrapped high on the men's legs and formed breathable skirts, whereas the women wore long gowns cut to the ankle. Many in the courtyard wore gold bangles and bracelets, which, between cheers, clattered like a windstorm in a treasury. The footwear Kiora observed was the same as her own leather sandals. It seemed that hadn't evolved much since her time.

A stage clung to one edge of the courtyard, its back wall the palace itself. Walls stretched outward, wrapping the crowd and courtyard in stone arms. Guardsmen lined the walls every twenty paces, and plenty more wandered the courtyard. Upon the stage rested a simple throne of black stone, carved and painted with hieroglyphs.

Kiora's first instinct was to search for a sculpted message. What is written in stone persists long after the writer.

Between two vomitoriums upstage left and right, lines of hieroglyphics painted stories across the palace's wall. Kiora recognized none. Many had been freshly cut and painted, telling of Cleopatra's ascension to the throne. Black and red painted symbols depicted strange wars with sea travelers, old men in purple robes, and Cleopatra claiming the land. None pointed to Osiris.

"See anything?" April asked.

"Nada." Diedre answered. Gideon shook his head.

"All sorts of things!" Magnus said excitedly. "Oh, you mean clues? No. None of those."

She sighed and looked at Kiora.

"Anything in the hieroglyphics?"

Kiora shook her head. "None direct us further on our task."

"You sure you brought us to the right—" Diedre began.

Inward with a beat of her heart, outward in rhythm. Activation. Another wave of numbness swelled and rose through Kiora's throat like steam, then tickled her ears until the courtyard's chorus of chatter became the dull sound of a distant waterfall. Focus was needed, not mindless bickering.

Inward for four beats of her heart.

Her entire body grew numb. The natural state of her mouth, tasteless; the distant waterfall of sound, silent; the light peeking through closed eyelids, blackened. Scents of sweat, dust and salt subsided from her nose.

Outward in rhythm. Second activation.

Her senses became strings on a harp; idly silent, awaiting a single pluck to release a pure note.

She plucked sight, and opened her eyes. Light swelled and blinded her. Shadows harshened into black shapes. She could only pass a glance over the courtyard before she closed her eyes. In that glance, she took in more visual information than she could have in an hour studying the place. The walls of hieroglyphics bore no answer nor insinuation, nor did any in the crowd seem a living carrier of a clue. Another sense was needed.

Kiora plucked her sense of hearing. A thousand conversations within the courtyard entered her mind.

"—then the little one said—"

"—patra will be—"

"—vying for illegit—"

"—ing one anoth—'

"—freedom from their—"

Tick. Tick. Tick.

There. A thousand conversations bore no oddity, but among them, Kiora heard ticking. It was not from her companions, though each drum of the second hand on April's wristwatch sounded like roaring thunder. This ticking was different. Near, but covered.

Tick. Tick. Tick.

The chambered ticking was soft. A mechanism of sorts. Unnatural to the local time. Kiora had found a traveler in the crowd. But where?

Tick. Tick. Tick.

Kiora's nervous system shivered. It fought the unnatural mutagenic process. If she continued to push her human body to the extremes of sensory intake, it would shut down entirely.

Urging her nerves a single moment further, she plucked at her hearing again. The ticking struck like a hammer on a bell. It could have shook the earth where she stood. In fact, it *was* shaking the earth. The ticking came from below her feet. A hollow echo of the ticking trailed each strike.

Deactivation.

A starship could have fallen on her Kiora fell so quickly. Her body felt like it had been set on fire, then doused with dark matter fuel. Each of her muscles quivered with exhaustion.

"Are you alright?" April asked. It took a moment for Kiora to realize she had been caught. Warm arms cradled her cold, numb body. April looked down at her with eyes like brown tourmalines. "What happened?"

Kiora rolled from April's arms and caught herself in a squat. Desperately, she tried to hide the spasms in her weakened legs.

"Osiris has left us a sign buried in the sand." Kiora's lungs burned with each breath. "Below us there is a sound. That of a clock ticking. An indicator of the Time Council."

April cocked her head. "Really?" She listened for a moment, but only furrowed her brow at Kiora. "How the hell could you hear a clock ticking below ground?"

"My senses are guided by the council." Kiora said stiffly. With strained effort, she managed to get back to her feet. She would not allow herself to rest while Jaakobah lived. "We still must find the entrance."

"I could ask someone to show me around." Diedre's voice shifted to the damsel intonation they had put on before. "It won't be hard to convince a big, burly man to sneak away." They cast a wry glance at Gideon, who shifted uncomfortably. "The voice works for beefcakes, here."

"I am a married man of God." Gideon said sternly. A bright blush in his face brought out a barking laugh from Diedre.

"That will not work," Kiora rubbed her temple. The myiad's laugh pounded against her skull, each rise a hammer driving a stake further into her splitting headache. "The council is not so daft as to allow an accidental discovery of their secrets. The path forward will only be found by a traveler."

"Here," April took Kiora's palm and placed two orange pills in it. "I keep Advil on me at all times. Take these."

"I do not need your medicine."

April stared at her until she swallowed the pills. While she hated to admit it, Kiora was fond of the little orange pills. They helped with the subtle pains. It was a small but appreciated pleasure that they tasted sweet, as well.

"A clock hidden underground." April said. "That's something, but if we don't know where it is, we're still at square one."

An eruption of noise swelled from the crowd and took over the courtyard. Kiora fell to her knees and cradled her head. The ache of overusing her body was made worse by the feverish screams. Wavering on the edge of consciousness, she breathed deeply. Like a ship in a stormy bay, her cloudy mind fought against the lapping waves of aches. She did not know how long she knelt there, nor could she open her eyes. April placed a hand on her shoulder. It felt far away. Only when the crowd ceased its bellowing and gave way to a single, enchanting voice, was Kiora able to regain herself.

"My people," The rich voice echoed against the walls of the courtyard. Sheer silence had overtaken the crowd. Nary a breath was let loose, nor a pin dropped "In the wake of my father's passing, I come to you in mourning, and in need—"

Kiora kept her eyes low as she opened them.

Upon the stage stood a short woman made taller by her presence. Midnight dark hair lay evenly cut at her shoulders. Pristine white fabric clung tightly to her figure. Gold belts and tassels lay over her chest and arms reflecting the sun's light unto the crowd. Kohl lined her eyes, sharpening even the barest of side glances to dagger points. Full, red lips were touched by carmine, and blue lapis lazuli shadowed her sharp gaze.

Regal pride swelled within the part of Kiora that was Kekheretnebti. She respected the woman named Cleopatra. Kiora was skilled at playing the role of princess. By a single glance alone, she knew Cleopatra had perfected it.

"That's her?" Diedre whispered. Magnus shushed her. The myiad delivered a swift elbow to his side.

"Focus," April whispered. "Any eyes on an entrance to the underground?"

"Nope." Diedre answered. Magnus and Gideon stared at the stage. "Stardust, kid. Pick up your jaw, I don't want my protégé drooling over every woman we meet in the timeline. Not a good look."

"Not just any woman. It's *Cleopatra*." Magnus said. Diedre wound up to elbow his stomach again. He braced his hands to block the blow, but Diedre shaped their elbow in a wide curve around the block and hit the man's other side.

The throb in her head slowed to a soft drum. Between the orange pills April had given her, and the silenced crowd, her nervous system had time to stabilize.

"'When Queens place crowns upon their own heads.'" Kiora said. "The myiads of the council do not place secrets in space, but in time itself. At the moment Cleopatra crowns herself, what we seek will be revealed."

"You've got a plan? Let's hear it." April said.

"Take the stage. Seek out a secret entrance to the underground." Kiora said simply.

"And when we have a hundred guards waving swords at us?"

"Kill any who stand in our way." Kiora couldn't understand what part of the plan April found confusing.

"Thou shalt not murder." Gideon said.

Diedre side eyed him. "What's the hammer for, big guy?"

"Divine retribution."

"I'd rather not kill anyone, either." Magnus said. "What if we change the future?"

"Don't worry about that. Major historical moments iron themselves out one way or another." April answered.

"How does that work?" Magnus asked.

"Paradoxes and the universes, blah blah." Diedre said.

"That doesn't explain—"

"We're not killing anybody." April put an end to the point.

Kiora didn't try to hide her scowl. It would be difficult to be April's blades if she were unable to stab freely, but such is the nature of a task given by the myiads of the council. Simplicity does not exhibit true devotion.

Again, Kiora scanned the courtyard. The walls stood high over, with guards marking the battlements every ten paces. She counted eight entrances to the courtyard, six on the level of the crowd, and two on stage that passed into the palace itself. A cover was needed. Panic would be best. Large crowds without easy escape routes tended to erupt with the slightest cause. A gunshot near a herd of animals.

"Myiad," Kiora said. "Do you have an explosive device?"

"I have a name." Diedre glared, then held open the side of their nylon trench coat. Strapped to the inside flap, a dozen devices of different shapes and sizes rattled. "I also have explosives. What are you looking for? World War 2 grenades? 2202 EMP hand detonators? M80s? Pick your explosion."

"Why are you carrying all of that?" Magnus asked in a mousy tone.

"Something of this time." Kiora said. "True panic makes the best cover. Justified fear builds the best panic."

Diedre's eyes lit up and shifted to a light shade of lavender. "Greek fire!"

"No setting people on fire, either!" April added.

"We'll only use a little."

"Do not act until Cleopatra places the crown upon her head." Kiora warned. Diedre simply grinned, took Magnus by the arm, and receded into the crowd. "We must take our position. When the panic begins, take the stage and seek out the entrance."

April wore a concerned look, but waved a hand for Kiora to lead.

Kiora slithered through the crowd, a cobra in the sand. The tension in her stomach had returned. This time, however, Kiora was in control. The hunt was her element. Albeit, she was hunting for clues, not a council-wanted extra-terrestrial.

Blending into the crowd was a simple thing. Thousands of faces and twice as many eyes were plastered to Cleopatra; none spared a glance at the strange three figures winding through. The queen's speech carried on in much of the same ways as Kekheretnebti had given in her time. A pity, that. Empty promises of strength and unity to come under the blossoming queendom. Kekheretnebti knew the ruse— she was taught to turn a crowd's opinion before she could walk. Rulers brought bright futures by dimming the present, and casting a shadow over the past.

"—today I claim the sole leadership of Aegyptos."

The crowd erupted. Every voice struck Kiora like a thousand needles in her ears. Still, she persisted, fighting her own weakened body with a steel mind.

Upstage of Cleopatra, a line of young men and women stepped in accordance with each other toward the soon-to-be queen. Each was dressed in sheer white robes, so fragile that light shone through and touched their naked bodies. They too wore makeup on perfectly sculpted features, though none matched that of their new queen. Marching in rhythm, they encircled the throne, then split open to reveal a young man holding a red pillow. Upon it rested a pschent, a tall double crown, with a concave cylindrical base of deep red, and an inner oblong white helmet that rounded up and pointed to the sky. Kiora thought it strange. In her time and opinion, the pschent was of an older fashion, and a weaker showcase of power than the vulture crown Kekheretnebti wore. Among her travels, however, she had learned not to judge the evolution, or devolution, of culture too harshly.

The man knelt before Cleopatra and offered the pschent to her. A thousand sets of lungs held their breath. Even Kiora caught herself staring— Kekheretnebti understood the significance of the moment. Not just the crown placed upon Cleopatra's head, but the hopes and dreams of an entire people. More than the thousand in the courtyard, but the millions whose lives would be liable to this single woman's actions. None knew of the future to come, only of the present.

Cleopatra took the pschent with both hands. She lifted it high above, holding it for the people of the earth and the gods of the skies to witness. With an inscrutable expression, she placed it upon her head. Louder than before, a rampant joy overtook the crowd. Cries of laughter bounced against the courtyard's walls. Stomping shook the palace stones, and hats were thrown high into the air in celebration. Somewhere behind, Kiora heard the blaring horn of unknown instruments singing out.

Panic sparked. Not in the crowd, as expected, but rather, in Kiora's chest. The moment they had sought was present and passing. Diedre's distraction was nowhere to be found.

XVI

Diedre

Diedre giggled to themselves as they strapped the brass container of Greek fire to the base of the tree. Rigging explosives made them feel like a myiadling again. Something about the smell of soot and sulfur really was nostalgic.

Of course, they had listened to April's wishes. The explosion would be in the back corner of the courtyard where the crowd tapered off to an empty patch of stone tile, and a lone tree cast a little shade overhead. It would have been fun to see a guard or two stop, drop and roll, but Diedre figured there would be plenty of time for fun when a psychopath wasn't hunting down their entire species. With their wide smile, they clicked the firing pin into place, and looked up to Magnus.

"All set. I told April we would only use a little but I lied."

His face dripped with horror. Diedre's smile only grew wider.

"Oh, don't give me that look, you're gonna make me blush. If there's a chance for a boom, you've gotta go big. You want to pull the trigger?"

"I think I'll pass this time." Magnus said.

Diedre grunted. "Oh yeah, that quirk of yours. You really don't like violence, huh?"

Magnus didn't answer, only drifted his gaze to the stage where Cleopatra spoke.

That would not do for a protégé of Diedre Altair, Space Pirate Extraordinaire. Explosions could wait; their pupil needed help.

"Trauma, huh?" Diedre asked in their best *2024-bro* tone. They grew their shins a few inches so they could speak to him eye-to-eye. "I get that. I've been drenched in a lot of guts in my time. Does things to your brain. You know, I could teach you how to torture someone. That doesn't have to involve killing at all—"

"No thank you, Diedre." He said in a thin voice.

Damn. What kind of protégé gives their teacher the cold shoulder like that? Diedre deflated back down to their natural height and watched him. He held himself tall and stiff, with arms crossed in a brooding manner. They had plucked a nerve, but they couldn't just keep quiet— there was a bomb armed behind them. They were too giddy to keep still. How was it that Magnus couldn't feel the same thrill?

"So what, you can't even kill a mosquito—?"

"I'm trying to listen." Magnus adjusted his glasses and

watched the stage.

An odd sense of pride swelled within Diedre. Yes, they would have to put a microgrenade in Magnus' pocket for the cold shoulder treatment, but, at least they had found a way to stir him up. That was a step in the right direction. If they were going to fight Jaakobah, Diedre needed to toughen him up. Get him ready for the fight. He was already defensive. In Diedre's eyes, that was only a short walk from prying fingernails off of a torturee.

"What's ol' Cleo saying?" They asked with feigned interest.

"Something about her brother. There are theories about Cleopatra's rise as a sole ruler, but we're sure her father instructed that she and her brother co-rule after his death."

"You sure like your history."

"Don't you?" He asked. "I can't imagine being able to time travel. The answers to history's greatest questions at the tips of your fingers."

Diedre yawned. "It ain't all that."

"How can you even say that?"

"Look, cowboy. Once you see some, you've seen it all. That whole 'history repeats itself' saying should be written into stone and set in the center of the universe."

Magnus shook his head. "History doesn't repeat itself. Any two actions, no matter how similar, are unique. Every single factor in the decisions that lead to those actions are unique."

"What's the point if the results are the same? The very palace we're standing in doesn't last. Hell, some of ol' Cleo's actions push it to that end. Same as the Pharaohs before and the Romans after. Different actions, same consequences; the fall of an empire. That's history, kid. Assholes control all of the money, food, power. It crumbles. Rinse. Repeat."

"Then why are you here?" Magnus' asked. He was irritated again. The outer corner of his left eye twitched, sweat beaded at his brow, and his voice had changed tune. One more point for Diedre. Pretty soon, they'd have him throwing punches.

"I'm here to have a good time and shit on the system." Diedre answered mechanically. The words fit in their mouth like an old friend. It was a sermon they had plenty of practice preaching. A creed, one could call it. Diedre often did.

"From my angle, it looks like you're risking your life to save the system."

"Only thing I'm saving is my own skin—" Diedre's voice trailed off as they spotted a guard marching directly toward them. "Keep quiet, I'll handle this."

Closer to the wall, a second guard approached with his sword already drawn. A third and fourth, Husky and Squeaky, approached from the opposite wall. They husked, squeaked and closed in, trapping Diedre and Magnus into the corner of the courtyard.

"Stardust!" Diedre said as they pulled out their laser pistol. "Double stardust, April! How are we supposed to save everybody if we can't kill everybody?"

"What do we do?" Magnus asked.

Diedre glanced around. The corner of the courtyard was clear of people, which made it great for explosions, but less so for escaping a crowd of angry guards. The closest entrance was at least forty yards away and blockaded by a thick sea of people. Yellow stone walls rose at least twice their height.

"Here." Diedre handed him the detonator. Panic lit in his eyes like a light switch had been turned on. "No one's going to get hurt with this one."

"You said the anti-matter wouldn't hurt anyone, and it nearly killed us all."

"Yeah, it did." Diedre let out a quick snort of a laugh. "But these are normal-matter *distraction* explosives. Don't be a gas giant— stay focused on your girl Cleo. When the time is right, hit this switch."

"Okay—"

Diedre darted toward the courtyard's corner where the two walls met. Twenty feet, give or take. That was their estimate. They visualized their arms elongating and shape shifting out from their chest. Each swing of their stride became heavier. As their arms grew and monopolized their body's mass, the rest of their body shrank. In only a few strides, Diedre was no taller than a toddler, but with arms that could reach twenty feet and take hold of the wall's ledge.

Like a slingshot, Diedre yanked their small body into the air, flew ten feet above the wall, then came down onto the battlements. It was a thin walkway with a far drop on either side. Plenty of space for the small framed myiad.

Peeking over the edge, Diedre caught a glimpse of Magnus' wide-eyed stare. His mouth was agape in awe. Just behind him, the assortment of guards stood frozen in similar amazement. Diedre was used to being looked at in that way— everywhere they traveled, they left people awestruck.

The moment didn't last long. One guard snapped from

the stupor and yelled at Magnus. Another moment, and Diedre's pupil would be in bronze shackles.

"Strap in, Cowboy!" Diedre yelled. They sucked their right arm back into their body. The spare mass exploded into their left arm, building muscle fiber in a ripple down the limb and extending it further. With a quick whip, Diedre planted their hand on Magnus, twisted up a handful of his jacket, and like a fish on a hook, tried to reel him in.

Instead, Diedre nearly threw themselves off of the wall. Their frame was too small, and with the majority of their mass shifted into their left arm, they didn't have the leverage to pull the man up entirely. He floated five feet above the ground like a piñata. Diedre had never seen a piñata kick at the people underneath it, but then again, they'd never seen someone attack a piñata with swords.

Diedre took what mass they could back from their left arm and shaped muscle into their legs. They took a slow, heavy step, then another, and another. Diedre began running along the battlements. Then, Diedre began laughing. Like a hyena's yip, Diedre's cackles echoed into the courtyard. Magnus swung haphazardly along the wall's rim, only inches over the heads of the crowd. Diedre tried their best to hold him away from the wall, but they couldn't stop every single brush up he had with outcropped stone.

"Eight seconds, cowboy, let's see how long you can go!"

Magnus yelled in a frail voice, but it quickly was cut off by a loud grunt and *thud* as he smacked against a stone outcrop.

"Sorry about that!" Diedre shouted. He looked a bit green at the gills, but Magnus gave a grunt in response. "This is fun, ain't in?"

They had lost the trailing guards on the ground; the crowd was too thick to chase a person hovering overhead. What they had gained, however, was the attention of a thousand panicked Egyptians.

Ahead on the wall's battlements, two bulky guardsmen climbed out from a trap door and pointed bronze tipped spears toward them.

Diedre shape shifted the arm holding Magnus into a thin rope, and slammed their feet into the ground. They condensed all of their spare mass into their legs. As sharply as slamming the brakes on a starship, Diedre skidded to a halt. Magnus, however, carried the momentum and swung over the battlements. Diedre's rope-thin arm swept the two guardsmen off the wall opposite the courtyard. Magnus squealed as he soared in their grip and hung over the opposite side.

"Pull me up!"

Diedre hadn't thought to look at what was on the other side of the wall.

Below, Magnus dangled on their arm above a sheer drop into the ocean. Jagged crags pierced the frothy water like fangs from a foamy mouth. Luck had it that Diedre had chosen the one wall that bordered the island's edge.

Rather than reeling him in like Diedre had tried before, they used her heavy frame as an anchor to swing him back and forth. On one particular high swing, Magnus' hands clasped the wall's ledge.

"What a ride!" Diedre shouted excitedly. "Oh boy, you'll fit right in with the crew! Once we wrap up this business, I'll have to show you Paul!"

Between dry heaves, Magnus managed to get out the

question. "Who's Paul?"

"My starship, of course!" Diedre grinned. Magnus rolled over and spewed out a milky mix of green and yellow liquid. "There it is, bet you feel right as meteor rain, now! Where's that detonator?"

"I dropped it." Magnus clutched his stomach.

"What?" They leaned over the ledge and looked below. "How could you drop it? What else were you holding on to?"

"My dinner." He whimpered. "My sanity."

"Quark your dinner." Diedre jeered. "How are we supposed to cause a distraction without an explosion?"

"I think we're alright." Magnus sat up against the wall's ledge and pointed a thumb toward the courtyard. Only then did Diedre see the riot they had caused. Half of the crowd screamed in terror, while the other looked up to them with reverent stares. Some knelt and offered open palms to the sky. "Your laugh was louder than any explosion."

"You don't say." Diedre put a foot up on the ledge and smiled.

Cleopatra was gone, ushered off by her guardsmen, surely. In her place, standing beside the throne, Diedre picked out three figures, dressed in clothes far removed from the time.

For the moment, all eyes were on Diedre, but it wouldn't stay that way forever. April and the others still needed cover. Wouldn't be easy to find whatever secret Osiris left if a legion of guards was trailing them.

"Time for your next lesson, my young protégé."

"What's that?" Magnus asked.

"Play the cards you're dealt." Diedre said. They covered

their face with their hands. "And bring a few in your sleeve."

Feathers formed and sprouted from Diedre's forehead. Combing their hands down their face, Diedre revealed a sharp beak where their nose had been. With a grand sweep, they cast their arms skyward. Skin erupted into white and brown feathered wings.

Those who had knelt in reverence now called out for Diedre, chanting the names of each of the Egyptian gods. A choir of *Horus, Shai, Osiris, Ra,* and many others poured from the crowd. The people pleaded for blessings of fortune, health, weather, and for Cleopatra's ascent to the throne. Even the guards laid down their weapons and rose palms to the sky.

Diedre bloomed feathers out from their torso. The blue nylon coat they wore absorbed into their skin as their body took on the shape of a falcon. Their shoes melted into their skin and grew out into arched leathery toes, each equipped with its own finger-long talon.

The shifting was internal as well. Each myiadling went through rigorous study to understand the physiology of living matter across the cosmos. Diedre shifted bone marrow from their human skeleton, both hollowing out their new bones and allowing the relocation of mass to their lungs. Hollow bones allowed easier flight, and strong lungs kept one in the sky longer.

"Ready for a second ride, cowboy?" Diedre screeched in a half-caw-half-speech. Careful to avoid stabbing him with a kitchen-knife-sized talon, Diedre once again took a hold of his jacket with their hand. Or was it their foot? The names of body parts never translated perfectly between creatures when they shapeshifted.

Tipping forward off of the wall, Diedre spread out their wings and flew above the courtyard with Magnus in tow.

XVII

April

"What do you see?" April asked. She scanned over the heads of the cheering crowd, seeking any sign among the havoc.

"Nothing." Kiora said with a growl. "The myiad was too late. They have doomed us all."

April didn't respond. If some secret passage were to be found, complaining wouldn't be the key.

A human sized shadow of a falcon screeched overhead and blotted out the sun. A moment later, it swooped down, deposited Magnus on the stage beside April, and rose again, drawing the attention of a thousand local onlookers.

"How's the search going?" Magnus asked. His eyes seemed to spin.

"About as well as your distraction went."

"I'm ready to leave Egypt."

"Not yet." April said.

By her limited knowledge of Ancient Egypt, nothing seemed out of order. Certainly nothing that indicated an alien had deposited something there to be found. Carvings on the courtyard walls hadn't shown any particular signature of a traveler's touch. Cleopatra had crowned herself; April witnessed it just before Diedre's laugh cut into the courtyard like a nuclear siren. The myiad's volume amazed April. Maybe it was some sort of internal shapeshifting they did to bolster their voice.

That wasn't important, now. April could wonder about Diedre's habits all day and still not understand a thing about them. She only had the moment to find a secret passage left by an Egyptian god.

Assess. That was the first step. April knew how to solve a problem. That's what running a bar was. Problems with drunks, paperwork, and money. Assess. The stage was bare, save for the throne and Cleopatra's golden shawl. It must have fallen off when Cleopatra's guards ushered her into the palace. A glint under the fabric caught April's eye. Underneath, its gold sheen hidden by the gold fabric, Cleopatra's crown lay on its side. A golden viper statuette jutted out from the front and reflected sharp sunlight in a glittering dance over the stage.

"The moment is gone." Kiora said tiredly. She'd had an uncharacteristic fatigue to her voice since they had entered the courtyard. "The crown lies on dirt and stone."

April drew back the shawl and inspected the crown. It wasn't a jewel encrusted, fluffy based bauble that a

European king would wear with a scepter in hand. Kiora had told her the name of it once. A pschent, she recalled; a combination of a hedjet crown and a deshret crown. On a red base, a white oval pointed proudly to the sky. Attached at the front, a golden viper seemed to watch April with taunting emerald eyes.

"What now?" Gideon asked. "Can we return to the past and attempt it all again?"

"No," Kiora said. "The third limitation will prevent us. Our presence has altered this moment too heavily. Returning threatens paradoxical repercussions, blinding our perceptions of the true reality."

Gideon answered with a blank stare and a shrug.

April sighed heavily. In a single day's time, she had been covered in enough blood, velex mucous, and Diedre quips for a lifetime. She was tired, and annoyed, and, most regrettably, stone cold sober.

"This is why I prefer to work alone." April muttered.

"As do I." Kiora nodded.

"Seriously?" April asked. A beast of anger rose within her and set its eyes on Kiora. "If I left right now, you'd be breathing down my neck all the way home."

"I do not wish to be bound to you." Kiora said.

"Yeah, I've heard that one before." April jabbed.

"What is happening?" Magnus whispered. Gideon shrugged again.

"You wish to stir the past? I have plenty to say." Kiora closed the distance between them with two strides.

"April, Kiora." Magnus said meekly.

"What?" The two women answered in unison. Magnus flinched as they turned their heads in perfect synchronization.

"Is now a good time to have this conversation?" He shifted as he spoke, raising his hand to fend off a glimmering reflection of light on his face.

April watched him carefully, then eyed the crown. "Magnus, move."

As he turned, the crown reflected sunlight past him. It beamed to the throne and highlighted the soft indents of carved hieroglyphics.

"Kiora, what do those mean?"

Kiora knelt down and felt them with her fingertips. "They depict the death of one's body. The journey of the Soul. Judgment in the Duat." Her finger came to an unmarked area just below the seat. "It ends before the final verdict."

Tilting the crown carefully, April moved the glare to mark the place where Kiora's finger touched. The black stone absorbed light, revealing an unnatural crimson glow. The illuminated hieroglyphic looked like a drawing of a beaker in a chemistry class, with four lines across the top of the tube.

"What is it?" She asked.

"A djed pillar." Kiora whispered. "A mark of Osiris."

Her fingers traced the center of the glowing shape. At her touch, it depressed into the throne. A mechanical grinding rumbled under the stage. The throne turned of its own accord and revealed a dark hole into the earth. Warm, heavy air seeped up from the depths.

In the crowd, a guard yelled, followed quickly by the responses of a dozen more. Diedre had held the attention of the people as long as they could, but a stranger taking the

Queen's stage wrenched their attention. A thrown stone landed by Magnus with a heavy thud, then another by Gideon. The stage became a drum under the steady beat of stones; a choir of guardsmen yelled in its rhythm.

"Go!" April yelled as she took a handful of Magnus' coat, dragged him to the edge of the hole, and dropped him in. His yell echoed into the depths. Kiora drew her daggers and jumped after him. "Gideon, get in!"

"No," He said, holding his lucerne hammer at the ready. "I will protect your escape—"

April hooked her foot behind his legs, took him by the shoulders, and swept him from his feet, dropping him directly into the hole. Elongated Irish curses trailed his descent.

"Diedre!" April yelled. Amidst the commotion of the crowd, it was impossible to know if the myiad heard her. Instead of yelling more, she rose a finger into the air, spun it in a circle, then tapped her wrist. A universal sign for *wrap it up, it's time to go.*

An ear-hollowing screech crashed into the courtyard and silenced the crowd once again. Diedre flew in a wide arc, rose above the courtyard and silhouetted themselves against the sun's light. Then, they stooped. Form and feathers receded into a human shape. Their skin returned to soft beige, the features of their face human, and the blue nylon trench coat emerged as a flapping cape behind them.

April had always wondered at that— how was it that the coat changed with Diedre? Some aspect of myiad shapeshifting, she figured. It wasn't the time to wonder.

In their human form, Diedre let out one more hawk-like screech before diving at top speed into the hole.

"Dramatic, much?" April mumbled to herself. She cast a glance at the ring of guards on the stage. Despite closing into a circle around her, they seemed too terrified to actually approach. "Alright. Well, uh— don't trust the Romans!"

April hopped into the hole.

If the djed pillar marking wasn't enough to convince her that they had found Osiris' secret, the ominous hole into the underground sealed the deal.

It was pitch black, deathly silent, and impossibly deep. After the initial sense of plummeting, a sense of weightlessness overtook her. Gravity ceased to exist. She had felt moments like this before— it was a signature side effect of traveling. The hole slipped between the fabric of space, therefore, it slipped beyond the gravitational forces of the visible universe. It didn't feel like she was falling because she wasn't.

Direction held no meaning in this place, if it could be called a *place*. Each of April's senses had been left at the entrance. Her body most likely didn't have a physical form at that instant.

Grandpa Sylas had explained it to her, once. When travelers slip between time and space, their physical bodies transcend the boundaries of those dimensions. A being's soul travels, not their physical matter. The body simply assimilates into the matter near where it departed, and the soul claims new matter from where it arrives. Some bar patrons told April of their bodies changing after traveling, freckles where they hadn't been before, a half inch change in height, and even discoloration in hair tones. April never had experienced anything such as that.

What she had experienced was the feeling of nonexistence. That's what she felt after jumping into the hole. Natural traveling often felt like a blink of an eye. Even forced traveling with a pocket watch was quick, though it left her feeling queasy afterwards. This was akin to the single hallway entrance into Portum. A static passageway from one space and time to another. Her mind remained conscious as she traveled, but her physical form had been left behind. All that she was simply drifted as pure energy on a dimension that what was left of her thoughts couldn't comprehend.

Then, the burden of weight filled her, and she felt the panic of falling in the dark once again. She only fell for a moment, before she landed on a warm cushion that let out a grunt.

"Constellations, April, when did you get so heavy?" Diedre mumbled.

"I— can't— breathe—" Magnus wheezed. The first to descend, he laid at the bottom of the dog pile. Gideon lay atop him, then Diedre, and finally, April sat at the pile's peak. Kiora had somehow managed to catch herself on two feet beside them. Crouching, she held her knives out and poised.

"Where are we?" Gideon asked as he pressed his weight off of Magnus.

"The past." Kiora said. "Further than we should be."

"How do you know?"

"A feeling." She glanced at April.

April felt it as well. The tunnel was an intra-temporal passageway, similar to Portum's entrance, that much she was certain of. It could have taken them to any time in existence.

"Give me the pocket watch." April said. Magnus produced the small watch from his pocket. Red light from the tiny bulb warmed the room. As it passed to April's hand, a green glow took hold.

"What do you mean, 'further than we should be'?" Asked Magnus. "I thought traveling too far forward was the issue."

"Cretaceous period." April said. "Shit. I'll wire my uncle in case we need a rescue."

"Flerovium," Diedre whistled. "We're pretty far back."

"Could someone tell me why that's a bad thing?!" Magnus asked. April wasn't sure if he was excited or terrified.

"Traveling this far back gets messy." April whispered. She tapped a message to Gainsborough on the time wire.

"Why?" Magnus whispered back.

Diedre made a grand moment of clearing their throat before answering.

"In layman's terms, the further a traveler gets from their local time period, the less control they have when traveling. Having a TDU act as a tether in your target time decreases the chances of making a wrong turn, so to speak."

"Ah," Magnus breathed heavily. "I see."

They stood in a dark, stone box of a room with one open cut doorway leading to a dark staircase upward. On each side of the doorway, a flickering wooden torch hovered at eye height. Firelight and shadow danced along the earthy walls and illuminated carved hieroglyphics, among countless other languages, only some of which April recognized as human. Various English words marked the walls, along with a few she could read in Spanish, German, and various alien scripts. She had learned a word or two in most languages around the universe. Glancing above, April confirmed a short suspicion she had; the ceiling was solid. The passage from Ancient Egypt was a one-way ticket with no return service.

"This room is secure." Kiora whispered. Two quick steps took her to the room's entrance, where she crouched underneath a torch. Her feet were deathly silent on the stone floor. "Nothing can be seen." Gingerly, she placed her foot upon the first step, felt it for a brief moment, then began to climb the stairs.

April stalked carefully behind. Magnus followed suit, while Diedre and Gideon casually strolled at the rear. After twenty steps, the dim light of the torches below became a small fleck in the dark distance. Each forward step put April on edge. It had become too dark to make out the floor below. The entirety of her trust was placed upon Kiora.

How had she gotten herself into this mess? Only a few hours prior, she had been pouring beers and worrying about rent. She tilted her own head at the thought. A few hours? Traveling distorted a person's perception of time, but April had built a knack for feeling it. Based on her energy level, the time they'd spent in Portum and Egypt, and how sober she felt, it had been three hours at most. Three hours had taken her from a normal night in Arizona to a dark cave in the cretaceous period.

Above, a tiny speck of light manifested. April would have called it her imagination, but the light grew a touch with each step. Like leaves on a dying wind, her nerves settled.

By the steadied breathing of her companions, it seemed

they, too, found comfort in the existence of light. Ragged breaths grew more tame, reinvigorated after the long journey upward. Only Kiora held the heaviness in her breath. It was a rare sighting for the Egyptian Princess to let her weariness show. Something had happened in the courtyard when Kiora fell to her knees. April doubted she'd ever get the truth of it.

As the light above grew nearer, darkness found definition. A newfound trust bounced in each step now that the shape of the floor could be seen. The sight of her own feet brought a smile to April's face.

Watching her own feet, April was deathly unaware that Kiora had stopped. She walked directly into the back of the woman, felt her foot slip from the step, and began to fall backward. The smooth stone walls offered no hold. Behind her, Magnus would catch her and surely fall along with her, and they would snowball into Diedre and Gideon and tumble their way into the hole from which they just climbed out.

In the time it took April to gasp, she felt a sharp tug at her shirt. Kiora's hand had taken the flap of her jacket in a steel grip and pulled. Together, they fell forward onto the stairs, April tucked tightly in Kiora's hold.

"Silence." Kiora spoke softer than silk. She held April with a similar touch.

Strange sounds hopped down the staircase. Music. A familiar melody whose name bounced at the tip of her tongue. It haunted the stairway and puttered against the walls in a soft whisper that faded with the light. Dry piano chords accompanied a heavy voice.

"Is that *Hallelujah?*" Magnus whispered.

He was right. It clicked in April's ears. The heavy voice was a rambling mutter of incorrect lyrics, but the chords were perfect.

Kiora cast a sharp glance back at Magnus and placed a finger over her mouth. Unfurling her hold on April, she rolled to her feet again and prowled up the stairs, the skilled silence of her stealth soiled by the clunking of the four behind. April did her best to keep quiet, but the black leather boots she wore weren't a perfect match for a stealth operation. The steel toes lent themselves to ass kicking rather than back stabbing. At this rate, she'd have to stop by the saloon and grab some old sneakers.

As they climbed the stairs, the light grew brighter, and so, too, did the music. Now close enough to make out the words, April heard the gruff voice singing the tune in a way that she had never heard, nor did she think anyone should. The voice was akin to nails on a chalkboard, but dragged down three octaves to become a deep, unsettling tremor that tainted the stairwell.

A wooden trap door was the finale of the drawn-out staircase. Bright light peeked through the trapdoor's frame. Kiora drew Time and Patience from their sheaths. Music dripped in a discordant tune from the edges of the door.

April shivered as though worms crawled on her neck. She couldn't pin what was more unnerving, the abyssal cave behind, or the wicked music ahead. She raised an ear to the door. Whoever sang the tune was no more than a few feet from the entrance. With one hand against the trap door, she hovered the other near the light peeking through, and raised three fingers. Two. One. With a heavy slam, she threw open the trap door and rushed into the light.

XVIII

April

Blinding light poured over April. It seeped into her eyes, her face, her skin. All she could make out was the shadowy silhouette of Kiora passing by her. Stumbling into the light herself, she held her revolver at the ready. A clang of piano keys. Kiora grunted heavily. A man's voice heaved with it.

As her eyes adjusted, April watched Kiora wrestle another person to the floor. Two women rolled in a tight grapple, both the same shape and color, with matching leather tunics and dagger holsters on their sides. The two daggers, Time and Patience, lay on the floor away from the tussling women. A stone pit formed and fell into April's stomach. There were two Kioras.

April was in a waking nightmare.

"Hey!" April yelled. She pointed the revolver at the ceiling and pulled the trigger. The two Kioras froze, their hands wrapped around various parts of the other. "Split up. Kiora, get away from her."

The two Kioras twisted to their feet in counter motions. Their bodies were dexterous and fluid. Crouching a few feet apart, each held a pointed stare at their counterpart.

"It is a Jaakobah!" Left Kiora said. "Shoot him!"

"Do not listen to him, April." Right Kiora hissed. "He is the Deceiver!"

"Vile speaker of lies!" Left Kiora spouted. "Shoot him!"

"Shut up!" April shouted. "I can't think with one of you yelling in my ear, let alone two. Look me in the eyes!"

Both Kioras twisted their heads in a serpentine jerk and watched April.

Eerie. She didn't like that. Kiora could loose daggers with two eyes. Four became a storm. Aside from the shiver down her spine, April had no sense of which was the true Kiora.

"They've got the same eyes." April said. "Diedre, I thought myiads had trouble shapeshifting eyes."

"*I* have trouble with eyes." Diedre answered. "Thanks for bringing it up."

"Diedre?" Left Kiora spoke. She squinted and blinked. Her pupils shifted from brown to emerald.

"Ha!" Right Kiora laughed. "I knew it!"

"Diedre, my little myiadling!" Left Kiora approached Diedre with open arms. As she walked, she shrank down two feet. Her skin turned pale and brittle, her head shed hair from its crown, and her face grew a large, bulbous nose. Shifting with the rest of her body, Left Kiora's voice dropped like a sinking ship. The leather harness she wore melded into her skin, only to be replaced by the shifting shape of a floral Tommy Bahama shirt, jean shorts, and flip flops. "You're alive! I was afraid I was the last myiad. Save for Jaakobah, of course. It warms my heart to see you."

"Osiris." Diedre said. April noticed a subtle shift in Diedre's tone. Fondness broke through their usual jaded, sardonic demeanor. It shorted out quickly as they raised a fist and punched the squat man across the chin. "You asteroid! You know Jaakobah is causing issues and you're still here?"

Osiris rubbed his jaw, whimpered and nodded.

For the leader of the Time Council, he certainly wasn't what April had expected. He had shifted to what she could only presume was his preferred state; a squat old man with skin nearly as white as the little hair he had on his head. His voice was the same that sang *Hallelujah* before; deep and rickety, with a habit of cracking into a high pitched squeal.

"It is already done." He said with a short frown. "There's no use. You and I are the last of the myiads. I warned them. They did not listen, and so, it is done."

"The last of the myiads?" Diedre asked. Their eyebrow twitched. It may have been her eyes adjusting, but April thought that Diedre's skin shifted towards a blue hue for a single moment. "Jaakobah has already found the others?"

The squat man whistled and tidied a stack of fallen books as though he did not hear the question.

"Lord Osiris." Kiora knelt as she spoke. "Is it true? The council is slain?"

"Careful, you're kneeling on my research." Osiris waved a hand and picked up a crumpled wad paper beside her.

"Hold on a moment. Yes, it's coming back to me. You are Sekhmet's human, correct? Ah, sorry for your loss."

Kiora kept her eyes plastered to the floor. In a soft voice, she asked, "What loss do you speak of?"

"He certainly put up a good fight. After that mess in Portum, Sekhmet gathered the entire council and faced Jaakobah on Mars." Osiris smiled placidly. "A lovely place for a final stand, isn't it? The fields of Cydonia. Truly operatic! But alas, even myiads can't fend off a velexi horde forever. Ah, what was your name, dear?"

"Kekheretnebti."

"Kekheretnebti" Osiris rolled the name over his tongue "Tea! Would you like some tea, Kekheretneb-*tea*? Sit, sit. We are safe. A place of safe-*tea*. I will prepare drinks." The squat man hurried out of the room.

Silence followed his exit.

It was only then that April took her surroundings. A long, dusty room filled from floor to ceiling with towers of books, papers, tomes, dvds, cassettes, vhs tapes, signal transponders, temporal message tubes and hologram illuminators. Some shorter stacks had tumbled over while Kiora and Osiris wrestled, spilling paper into the limited open floor space. LED lights lined the ceiling in a zig-zag pattern. Dust and cat litter tickled April's nose, though no cat was to be found. A grand, white piano sat in one corner, dusty and stained.

April took up a paper from a stack near her and glanced at the written scrabble. The single page had a dozen languages, different scratched diagrams and alien anatomies. Not a single sensible phrase she could parse. The place was a mad scientist's laboratory.

"Why exactly did Osiris go into hiding?" April asked.

Diedre shifted uneasily. "Dunno. I was young when he left. The older myiads said he needed to seclude himself for some 'grand research.' Never said much more."

The myiad flashed their amethyst eyes at April, then tilted their head at Kiora. Without words, April knew what Diedre intended to say. The Egyptian Princess knew more than she was letting on.

What kind of research would the council hide from other myiads? April found the question was as unsettling as the news of the council's demise. It was too riddled in politics for her liking. That's one reason why she never liked the council much; too big of a scope. Trying to rule over the entire timeline bound to have its own special sort of corruption. April kept her scope on the edges of her saloon's property line.

Much good that did her in the end. Jaakobah still wanted it destroyed for some god forsaken reason.

"How is it possible that the other myiads have already fought Jaakobah and lost?" Magnus asked. "Aren't we in the past?"

"Time isn't linear." Diedre said. "Now that we know they're gone, it would break the third limitation if we tried to interact with them when they were alive."

"Oh. The third limitation." Magnus said meekly. "Of course. Makes total sense."

April glanced at Kiora. Still kneeling, the woman clasped her daggers with white knuckles. Bristled rage speckled the princess's face. Sweat beaded on her brow.

"Kiora," April said softly, attempting to raise a white flag between them. Kindness had once been a thing they shared, but the concept had become foreign. Still, April tried to offer a hand to an old friend. "It isn't over yet. We can still stop Jaakobah before—"

"It is not for the Deceiver that my insides boil." Kiora said in a vicious tone. "It is for a god who has abandoned his people. Osiris hides away, praising safe harbor while the rest lay down their lives."

"The Lord works in mysterious ways." Gideon said amusedly. He scratched at the chin of an orange tabby that had found his leg. April glared at him. He shrugged and picked up the cat.

"Look," April said, ignoring the image of the hulking soldier cradling a tiny cat. "I agree. It ain't right. It's a coward's choice. But truth be told, I don't think Osiris has all his bolts and screws—"

Diedre gave an agreeing harrumph.

"—but if Shai was right, that coward in there might have a weapon to stop Jaakobah. That's what we need to find. Don't point your daggers at the one saving grace we may have in this fight."

With a deathly scowl imprinted on her face, Kiora nodded.

"I nearly forgot! I had cookies in the oven!" Osiris said, emerging from the door with a platter of cookies and tea. He set the tray down on a stack of books near the center of the room. Holding the orange cat in one hand, Gideon took up a cookie in the other and bit into it with a smile.

"Shai told us to find you." April said. "She said you could help us stop Jaakobah."

Osiris set tea bags into an array of mismatching cups and filled them with hot water from a chipped kettle.

"Diedre, dear, do you take sugar?"

"Two spoons." Diedre answered.

"And you, Kekheretneb-*tea*?" Osiris asked. Kiora glared at him in silence. "None for you, I take it. And you, the one without the genome? How do you take your tea?"

"How did you—" Magnus stammered. Before he could answer, April pressed the kettle back down to the tray with a loud metallic *thud*.

"We don't have time for tea."

"Time is all we have!" Osiris's emerald eyes glittered at her. "And yet, we never have enough, so it seems. Would you give all that you have for another moment of time? Or would you give all of your time for another moment with all that you have? That is what we must ask ourselves in every passing moment. It is invaluable. It is all that we are given in life. Only time is ours. Nothing more or less. Life does not exist once time is gone. What worry is there in using it while it is present? Sit and drink tea; time is abundant and fleeting."

The squat man continued to pour drinks. April passed a befuddled glance at Diedre, who shrugged, waved a finger by their head and silently mouthed the words, *he's nuts.*

Kiora stabbed Time into a book pile beside her. "Tell us how to defeat Jaakobah before your cowardice brings about the end of the universe." She took Osiris by the collar and lifted him to her eye level.

"Would you prefer Splenda, Kekheretneb-tea?"

Cautiously, April placed a hand on Kiora's shoulder. She let go of the man, took up Time and trudged to the corner.

A mad man held the key to stopping another mad man from leading a crusade across the timeline. April sighed. It was all above her pay grade. A manager of a saloon, that's what she was. A drink slinger. Yeah, that saloon was primarily for time travelers, but that was the family business. A haven for people with a strange gift.

Osiris shoved a steaming mug into her hand. Three loose bits of leaf had escaped the strainer and twirled in the amber tea. It smelled of turmeric and lemon.

A mad myiad. Maybe *she* was the mad one, trusting the dying words of a council member. How could she get the information she needed from Osiris when speaking to him was akin to speaking to a drunkard at closing time?

April felt a slight pinch in her brain. That was *exactly* the kind of work she specialized in. The only way to get through to a person in a state like that was to meet them on their level, and make them think they're the smartest gift to the universe.

After blowing on the tea for a moment, April took a sip and spoke the words Osiris had said in a tone of utter agreement. "Time *is* all we have. And it is *never* enough."

"You're getting it!" Osiris said as he offered a mug to Gideon. The old soldier was too preoccupied with the cat to accept.

"But what's there to do with the time we have?" April asked earnestly.

Osiris paused and glanced at the ceiling in thought. "That's a question. An answer? Drink plenty of delicious tea!"

"An answer. Surely there's more than tea. Research?"

"Research! Yes, that is another answer. Drink tea and research. Tea-search!" The squat man chortled at his own wordplay. April joined in enthusiastically. The two shared a bellowing laugh that rattled the book-filled room. The others watched silently, save for Gideon, who had petted the orange tabby into a roaring purr.

"What is it you research?" Asked April as she wiped a tear from her eye. With what little she knew of the man, he could have been searching for the optimal temperature to brew tea, but every moment she kept him talking was an opportunity to glean information. Maybe he wouldn't have a direct answer to stopping Jaakobah, but he was the oldest myiad of the council, and in turn, a contender for the oldest living creature in the universe. If the mad myiad didn't have any insight, none would.

"Research." Osiris spat out the word and slumped his shoulders. With a hop, he sat on a stack of books across from April. That was good. He was enjoying their conversation enough to settle into it. April could keep a counter-crawler gabbing all night if they sat at her bar. "Never enough time and too much time to think about never enough time and too much time to think about never enough time and too much time to think about—"

The man stopped, his sudden stillness violent against his jolly demeanor. A murmured scramble fell from his open mouth as his eyes flicked back and forth across the ceiling. A chill came over April, and she couldn't help but follow his gaze. The ceiling was bare wood, crossed with support beams. She jumped when Osiris spoke again.

"Apologies, thought I felt a breeze. Where was I?"

"You were telling us about your research." April urged.

"Oh," Osiris said. "Yes, I was, wasn't I? A great answer. The greatest. What you seek, or have sought. Desire and desired. All desire one thing before the curtain falls. The great sought for which I seek. A way *out*."

"A way out of where?"

"Of time. Haven't you been listening? It is all we have. It binds. It shapes. Yet there is so little. Even we who think we have the better hand. Time is the house. Time is the empire. Time bests even us."

"Travelers?" Diedre posed.

"That is it, little Diedre. The great curse." He glanced at Magnus. "Non-travelers are more blessed than we. You, human boy, can you imagine it? Smelling the feast and starving beside the table. Time ad infinitum to illuminate our inconsequential existence. We may journey through time, but may we affect it? No. Might we utilize it? It utilizes us. We are sand in an hourglass, not the eyes to watch or hands to turn. Glass boundaries surround us. We do not see them, but we can feel them. No permission, only compulsion. Speak out as we may. Shake your loved ones to sleep and cradle them awake. Time fills empty pockets and blind eyes. Dictation purposeless. Hollow propriety. Wastefulness. Acquired. Exhausted. Time. That is the research. I've gathered my own time's culmination in a little, red box. To protect it. Even Jaakobah couldn't achieve it. Ha!"

April held to the edge of the book stack she used as a seat. They were mad ramblings to the tune of a haunting melody. It cast an anarchic shadow over the room. All hope drained from her like a broken pail in a well. No amount of pulling at the rope brought water before it leaked through.

Shaking her head, she gulped, and blinked away water that had formed in her eyes. Had she blinked at all during his speech?

"What couldn't Jaakobah do? What is *'time's culmination?'"* April asked.

Osiris burst into scream. *"My* time's culmination. *Mine!* None other's. It is mine alone, and it shan't be taken from me! It won't be! Ever! Ha! I've already taken it from myself! Try as you might, none may, even Jaakobah! Burned are the records. Scarred is the path." As he spoke, his short body stretched taller. By the final word, he towered over April, bending over her to keep his head from scraping the ceiling.

Kiora's daggers glinted in the corner of April's eye. Aside from Osiris' heavy breathing, the room was silent. Kiora placed herself behind the mad myiad. With a warning glance, April bade her to step away.

Looking into the mad myiad's emerald eyes, April found a dullness reflected in the stare. If the soul could be seen through the windowpane of the eyes, Osiris was an empty house with the lights off. April had never met the mad myiad before, but she could recognize the absence. Behind the dull green glare, something was missing. Something more than just his mind.

A quiet bell chimed from the doorway. Osiris lifted one long, stretched arm and gasped an elongated breath at his wristwatch. He put a hand to his cheek as his body shrunk down to the squat man he had been.

"What is it?" April asked.

"I've forgotten to feed the little ones." Osiris said, rushing toward the door. "They get so antsy when I miss their dinner time, chewing holes in the roof and whatnot! If you'll please excuse me—"

A short moment of uncomfortable silence followed his exit.

"How long has he been like that?" April asked.

"He's had a tea-thing for as long as I can remember." Diedre answered.

April glared.

"Osiris has always had a marble loose," Diedre shrugged. "The marble bag held up in the past."

"That bag of marbles is torn to pieces." Gideon chimed. He laid on his back across a table of stacked books and chewed on a cookie. The orange tabby loafed on his chest.

Taking up another piece of paper from a nearby stack, April scanned it over. More nonsense strewn across multiple languages, sketches and tea stains.

"Alright. It's time you spill some council secrets. What do you know about this place? Why is Osiris hiding? Does it have to do with Jaakobah?"

All eyes fell upon Kiora.

"I know nothing." She answered.

"Bullshit." Diedre said. "You may be the council's watchdog, but you're too clever to not peek behind the curtain."

"Silence," Kiora hissed. "You bring shame to the myiad species—"

"*Tell us.*" April said. Kiora returned a stone glare. "You're my blade, or whatever. A vow on your honor and life and all that? I'm commanding you to tell me."

That struck Kiora like a hammer to the chest. She opened her mouth to rebuke the command, but no words came. It was checkmate.

Through gritted teeth, she forced the words out.

"Osiris' research necessitated secrecy."

"What is his research?" April asked.

"He sought a way to bypass the three limitations."

April hesitated. Her heart fluttered.

"That's impossible—" April stuttered. "Jaakobah lied. That's what you said! You told me it was all lies! Is that why he was exiled from the council?"

Kiora nodded silently.

"Jesus." April said. Gideon's pointed stare burned a hole in her shoulder.

Imagination ran rampant in April's mind. If the council believed it was possible, did that mean Jaakobah had pulled it off? Had he broken the few limitations the genome was bound to?

Unhindered time-travel. The possibilities of it were endless. She could bring back her grandfather. She could meet the parents she had never known. Paradox would not be a hindrance.

Osiris' words struck April with new meaning. Had Osiris overcome the limitations where Jaakobah had failed? If Jaakobah was lying, would he actually attempt to take over the timeline on the back of a bluff?

"Do not wonder, April." Kiora warned. "Jaakobah seeks control, nothing more—"

"—Why do you think Osiris is here?" Diedre spit the myiad's name. "That bastard—"

"—Osiris seeks to protect the timeline from threat." Kiora answered harshly.

Diedre's skin wavered into a scarlet hue. "Protect the *council's power* from threat."

The two drew their weapons in sync. Laser pistols aimed their barrels at bronze daggers.

"Please, we shouldn't turn on—" Magnus began

A shrill scream cut his words short. Before it ended, April had her revolver drawn. Gideon set down the cat in favor of his hammer.

All eyes landed on April. Pausing only a moment to check the chamber of her revolver, she marched toward the doorway.

XIX

Magnus

The rest of the house was no different than the room where they had arrived. Stacked piles of paperwork made ravines of hallways. A serpentine path carved through the house, into side rooms, up staircases, and, at points, blocked entire routes.

It enamored Magnus, in a way. The home was a library without bindings. What history could he derive from the scrabble of the mad myiad? A time traveler with thousands of years of life collecting thoughts on questions that modern historians hadn't even asked yet. Beyond history, the implications that could be drawn for the fields of physics, mathematics, philosophy, it all astounded him. History has born proof that mad men could be leaders of thought.

Pursuers of knowledge that lost pieces of themselves in pursuit.

Exceptions to the rule, Magnus reminded himself. Mad men were, more often than not, simply mad. Still, he desired nothing more than to stay and organize the grand mess of the home. More pressing matters were at hand.

He followed at the rear of the group through the winding home. April led, though the hallway urged them in one direction. They passed quickly through, glancing into off shooting rooms. Each was similar to the first; wooden framed ceilings high enough to shelter towers of books well above Magnus. At the end of the main hallway, light peeked through the glass window of a door. April charged and shouldered it open. A bit much, Magnus thought, but he was a stowaway on this ship across time, and it didn't seem a good moment to question the ship's captain. The open door poured daylight over the travelers.

Tall, thick kapok trees surrounded the house, which had an external appearance of a modern log cabin. It sat squarely in what seemed a dense jungle. An expansive yard of clean cut grass stretched to meet low set cycads at the jungle's edge. Leaves the size of Magnus hung from the low branches of the nearest tree, dripping moisture and offering a landing pad for fist-sized insects.

Magnus had abandoned the majority of his skepticism in Egypt, but what lay in the yard washed clean whatever remnants had remained. Three black feathered creatures crouched in the short grass, each one at least five feet long from head to tail. They stood on two haunch legs, with two short arms equipped with talons thick enough to match Kiora's daggers. Cocking large heads, they bore long fangs that glistened with saliva.

"Raptors." Magnus whispered in disbelief. "They *do* have feathers."

At the center of the three velociraptors, Jaakobah stood, his flowing black robe covering his frame head to toe. He towered over the velociraptors. In a charred black hand of long, scarred fingers, he held Osiris by the neck. Even against the harsh daylight, Jaakobah's hood cast an opaque shadow over his face.

Osiris wriggled in the grip. The old man's skin shifted to a purple hue. His eyes bulged. Short legs writhed and reached for the ground, shifting into long wiry strings. They dangled helplessly a foot above the grass, thin and weak. Raspy attempts at breath gargled in this throat. Tilting his head, Osiris pointed his gaze toward Magnus. A silent plea for help. For relief. Anything.

A flash of bronze cut the air in an arc towards Jaakobah's hood. Kiora's dagger, Time, held still in the air just before Jaakobah's head.

"Kekheretnebti," the maleficent voice oozed into the yard. As if on cue, the dagger fell to the earth. "Haven't you learned?"

"Unhand him!" Kiora shouted.

The hood of the cloak cocked. "Unhand him?" Jaakobah's black fingers squeezed Osiris' neck until a shattering *crack* echoed into the surrounding wilds. The old myiad went limp, his bulging eyes and twisted mouth forever frozen in pleading frown. Loosening the tight grip, Jaakobah let the corpse fall. Osiris landed beside Time. "Satisfied?"

Another flash of bronze, this time Patience, soared toward Jaakobah. So, too, did the velociraptors. Jaakobah caught the bronze dagger with the same hand that held Osiris. He sidestepped the first raptor and plunged the dagger into its neck. The other two circled him for a brief moment before pouncing. At the same moment, Diedre shot off their laser pistols at him. The lasers froze against Jaakobah's invisible force field but did not dissipate. Instead, in a lightning flash of bronze, Jaakobah used the flat of the dagger's blade to redirect the lasers. The flickering beams bent briefly before jetting out and striking the remaining raptors.

"You have my thanks for leading me here. Shai would have kept the secret to her grave, had you not arrived in time." Jaakobah's voice nearly sounded appreciative. "April, our moment is forthcoming, but this present will not do. Your time is running out."

"Why me?" April tossed out the words like heavy weights. "Why are you so damned stuck on me? You're like an obnoxious ex."

Jaakobah's voice slithered out from his hood. "A debt. Mercy is my payment."

"Mercy begins *after* xenocide." Diedre said. "That makes sense."

"Sense must be abandoned at times. It is a derivative of what has been, not what will be." He said. "My list is expended, April. It is your turn. August thirty first, 2024. Your saloon will burn. It is your choice whether or not you burn with it."

In a single blink, Jaakobah was gone. Magnus scanned surrounding jungle, but the black robed giant was simply gone. Vanished. Was that what natural traveling looked like?

Silence set into the yard. A thick silence made denser by the surrounding jungle.

Diedre staggered forward. They stood over Osiris' corpse, deathly still. Magnus thought he saw them whisper something, but he didn't hear. He stood by the cabin's doorway dumbfounded. Millions of years into the past to find Osiris. Just a few minutes to kill him.

Magnus couldn't help but feel guilty. The loss of a great mind was a tragedy the likes of the library burnings of Antioch or Alexandria. Jaakobah not only sought to take control, but he wanted to erase what had been. Each page of the mad Osiris' indecipherable rambling had become just that: indecipherable.

What was he thinking? Magnus shook his head. A person just died, and he could only think of preserving history. What of preventing further death? Jaakobah's destruction? Osiris had been their saving grace. Or, at least, that's what loose information they were operating on. If Osiris did have the key to stopping Jaakobah, could it still be found?

"What do we do now?" Magnus asked.

Kiora walked out just far enough to reclaim her daggers. Without a word, she turned and marched toward him. If he hadn't had the forethought to step out of her way, she would have marched *through* him. The cabin's door slammed as she threw it open, then slammed again as it closed behind her.

"Same thing as before." April pulled the door open and followed after Kiora.

No more than two seconds had passed before Magnus heard their muffled shouting trail down the hallway. He didn't need a minor in ancient history to see theirs was much more recent.

Carefully avoiding puddles of raptor blood and feathers, Magnus made his way across the battlefield to Diedre. The ESD forcefield they had told him about was no joke. In the broad daylight, Jaakobah's lethality had been put on clear display. The Deceiver was untouchable.

Magnus placed a hand on Diedre's shoulder. The myiad's skin was ice cold.

"Another rule for you kid," They said in an obsidian voice. Their skin adopted an indigo hue. "Don't die."

"Don't have any plans." Magnus answered.

The sound of a spade staking the ground turned him on his heels. Gideon stood behind him, leaning a single boot on a rusty shovel

"Let us bury him and drink to his memory." Gideon said.

"I can drink." Diedre answered. "Pick him up, beefcakes."

Gideon reached down to pick up the man, but quickly recoiled as though he'd been electrocuted. He winced and stuck his finger into his mouth.

"What's wrong?" Magnus asked.

Gideon eyed the corpse. "He is cold."

"Cold?" Diedre asked. Bending down, they put a hand on Osiris' arm. They immediately hissed and recoiled. Their skin rippled in a wave up their arm and shook their entire body. Flashes of electricity spat out from the ends of their hair. The myiad stumbled back, staring at their hand.

"Are you alright?" Magnus nervously shuffled away from the corpse.

"Beefcakes is right. It's cold. *Boomerang nebula* cold."

Magnus shook his head. "I don't know what that means."

"Colder than cold. Something else, too."

Magnus didn't like the uncertainty in their voice. Certainty was Diedre's entire personality. When they lost that, it seemed to him that everyone should be worried. "What do you mean by *something else?*"

"When I touched him, my nerves fired into defensive mode. Like a shock rifle. Touch him yourself and see."

"No, I think I'm okay—" Diedre grabbed Magnus' hand and pressed it onto Osiris' arm.

A sharp squeal erupted from Magnus' lungs. Slowly, he let go of the wince and opened his eyes. His hand touched the corpse. It was cold, but not surprisingly so. Nothing about it felt peculiar. At least, not any more than touching a dead person.

"Why can I touch him? Why can't you two?" Magnus asked.

"Don't know." Diedre said. They leaned in and squinted at something on his neck. "Unbutton his shirt."

Something about disrobing a newly deceased space-alien-god didn't settle well in Magnus' chest. That was, until he noticed what Diedre had seen.

A scar poked out from under the man's short sleeve. Why would an alien with the ability to shapeshift have scars? If his time with Diedre had taught him anything, it was that myiads were in total control of their physical form. There's no reason a shapeshifter should have lasting scars.

Each button revealed more lined scars across the

myiad's chest. Hundreds of thin cuts that had healed over into scar tissue. None had been fixed by myiad shapeshifting, and though he couldn't be sure, Magnus had an uncanny feeling that none were created by shapeshifting either.

"Jesus, Mary and Joseph." Gideon whispered.

"Stardust, Osiris." Diedre sighed.

The final button came undone, and Magnus laid the shirt open so that the entire torso could be seen. Every inch of flesh had the sheen of scar tissue. Over the man's heart, an inch wide X was still freshly scabbed and swollen. It resembled the mad sketches Magnus had seen inside. He shuddered. Self inflicted torment of a tormented mind. One could only guess at how long Osiris had been alone without his sanity.

A grave whisper came from Diedre.

"Cover him back up."

Before Magnus could fold the shirt flaps back over Osiris' torso, Gideon took him by the arm.

"Wait," The soldier said. He squinted at the corpse. "It is a map."

"A map?" Magnus's lips curled with disgust. "That's morbid."

"A map of what?" Diedre asked.

Gideon pointed at the house, but still held a squinted stare at the scarred torso. "I worked as a carpenter before the war. This is a sketch of the home. See there, that is the door on his belly. That hallway passes the kitchen, and these doors we passed as well. Here is where we emerged from the stairs."

Appalled and intrigued, Magnus followed Gideon's

finger until he began to recognize the scratches. It was indeed a bird's-eye map of Osiris' house.

"Why?" Diedre asked. "Neptune, we can change our shape at will, why carve it into your chest?"

"*Scarred is the path.*" Magnus pointed at the only fresh wound on Osiris. A red, scabbed X. "Something is in that house, something Osiris wanted found."

A strange giddiness bloomed in him. Despite the grotesque avenue of delivery, the prospect of a treasure hunt excited him. Of course, it was tragic and morbid, but what sort of ancient artifact could be so precious as to necessitate such morbidity?

Magnus stood and dusted off his khaki pants in an attempt to keep his hands from shaking. A treasure hunt released more adrenaline into his bloodstream than any gun fight could.

"We have to tell April and Kiora. This could be what we —" Magnus' words trailed off. Diedre's skin had sunk into a dark, midnight blue. He added quickly, "—we should bury him, first."

"Go find your treasure." Diedre said. "I'll bury him."

"You sure?" Magnus asked.

"Some species in the universe stay with their families their entire lives. Growing. sleeping. Dying. All together. Strange, isn't it? I suppose you may not find it strange. Humans often do."

Deidre paused. Magnus felt that he should say something, but no words came to mind.

"One big, dysfunctional family. That's what we are. Were. We myiads. The Time Council. I never wanted a part in it. Never needed the ego trip of reigning over the timeline.

It pissed me off. They killed a lot of people too, you know. You would have been executed. You didn't do anything wrong. Walked into the wrong place at the wrong time. But you broke a rule, and that gets you killed. You're lucky it was April's saloon you stumbled into."

Diedre snorted.

"Look at them now. All gone. I'm the last living myiad, aside from Jaakobah. Funny how that works out."

A third hand grew out of Diedre's back. It split open their trench coat and waved them away.

They left the last living myiad alone in the yard.

XX

Magnus

Where a shouting spat between Kiora and April had once shook the hinges of the wood cabin, now an unnerving silence settled in the hallways. With a gulp, Magnus glanced at Gideon, who only shrugged. That was reassuring— it was nice to know Gideon would have his back as they entered a wolf den.

Fallen tomes and notes filled the floor of the entrance hall so that even the walkway that once existed was no longer viable. It seemed to him that a hurricane had come through and taken out the delicate stacks of paper and books. Whether that hurricane was named April or Kiora was anyone's guess. Magnus knelt down to clear the papers, but Gideon's boots landed beside him as the old soldier marched in without a care.

Kiora may have been right in calling the man a brute—the disrespect for the abundance of knowledge and history twisted Magnus' insides. He could only imagine what went through Gideon's mind at the mention of science. The time that the Christian-god-obsessed soldier hailed from wasn't particularly that of scientific enlightenment.

After a moment, Magnus set aside what he had gathered. It would take far too long to organize the mess, and he was far too intrigued by the task at hand. A map to a hidden *something*. Gingerly stepping on the leather-bound tomes so as not to soil any loose paper on the floor, he followed Gideon's lead.

The old soldier kept his eyes high, watching the framework of the walls and ceiling to guide his way. "The map is true."

"Do you recall where we are going?" Magnus whispered. There was a noticeable lack of the two women in the entrance hallway. The only thing more unsettling than hearing them argue was not knowing where they were in the silence.

"This house is a labyrinth." Gideon pressed a hand to a ceiling-high wall of stacked books.

"Why did you stop—"

Gideon's hand pushed through and toppled the stack into an open doorway that had been completely hidden. The room inside was worse than the rest of the house. More than just books and tomes, but trinkets and furniture piled waist high in the room. No trail had been carved out for walking, and considering the doorway had been covered, Magnus was sure it had been long forgotten.

"—Oh. Is this the room, then?"

Gideon looked at him and smirked cheekily. "No. But you thought for a moment, didn't you?" He turned and carried on down the hallway.

"What?" Magnus whispered to himself. Did he just get pranked by a person from the Middle-Ages? That was simultaneously the most embarrassing and fascinating thing that had ever happened to him.

Abruptly, Gideon stopped in the doorway of the piano room where they had first met Osiris.

Magnus nearly walked into the man. Before he could complain, he clocked the discomfort on Gideon's face, as though he had been caught with his hand in the cookie jar.

In the room, Kiora and April shared a seat on the piano bench. Kiora held her face in her hands, while April held Kiora in her arms.

Dread formed in the basin of Magnus' stomach. He and Gideon were invading a moment of tenderness, one that he imagined was rare between the two women. A moment that wasn't his to disturb. Worse yet, the two hadn't seen him. He tilted his head to look at Gideon, who returned an equally uncomfortable glance. Widening his eyes, Magnus nodded an invitation to sneak away before they were noticed. With light feet, they stepped backward into the hallway. Their escape was guaranteed— until Gideon's boot grazed a particularly tall and teetering tower of tomes. A tide of paper and leather rushed to the floor.

In the same instant, Patience flew through the open doorway and pierced the wall where Gideon's head had just been.

"Who's there?" Kiora demanded. Her voice was shallow

and raw.

"Just us!" Magnus whimpered. "Don't throw another dagger! Jesus!"

"Don't speak the lord's name in vain." Gideon smacked his shoulder with a gloved hand.

"You said it in the yard!" Magnus returned in a harsh whisper.

"I have since repented."

"To who? When?"

"The lord above. Just now."

Magnus groaned. "I'm coming out, don't kill me."

He stepped into the room.

The two women stood in opposite corners of the cramped room. Kiora scowled, her knuckles pale with the tight grip on her remaining dagger, Time. April wasn't any more cheery. Magnus suddenly felt a little boy, standing before his parents after they had just had a fight. He cleared his throat and spoke.

"We found—" His voice cracked. "—We found something."

"What?" April asked.

"Well," Magnus said. "We haven't *found* anything yet, but Osiris left a map. Sort of. He drew it on his chest. Anyway, it points to a room in the house. Gideon can find it."

"That I can." Gideon said with a smile. Everyone waited in expectant silence.

"Well?" April asked. Gideon didn't answer, only smiled.

"Gideon," Magnus urged. "What room?"

"Oh," Gideon said. "This one."

"You're serious?" Magnus asked.

"Dead." Gideon answered. He looked at Kiora's puffy face and winced. "Forgive me. A cruel time for such a joke."

Towers of paper hid most of the room's actual walls, and a walking path through ravines had been made to access the two features of the room: the trap door, and the white grand piano. The mark left on the map could have been for the trapdoor, for all Magnus knew. His heart began to sink.

April turned in a circle. "So, something about this room, huh?" She followed the edge of the walkable floor, placed both hands on a wall of stacked books, and threw them down. Ancient wooden walls held more tacked-on scrabble of Osiris' research, alongside hanging frames covered with thick layers of dust. Each had gone so long without a wipe that Magnus couldn't see the pictures underneath. "Guess we'll have to tear through this room and see what we can find."

"Hold on—" Magnus was cut off as Kiora pulled at another stack. They spilled into the thin walking routes of the room, completely covering the floor. Gideon laughed and placed one hand on each side of the doorway. He tore down two high towers of books with a single cross of his arms. Magnus winced and ducked away. "We shouldn't be rash, there's a lot we can learn—"

It was pointless. Forethought lost a battle with present rage, sorrow, and mourning. In Gideon's case, it seemed to be a pure joy in chaos.

Magnus went to inspect the newly uncovered walls and all that hung on them. Perhaps there would be an answer hanging by string and nails. A short climb over mountains of paperwork was all it took to cross to a particularly attractive silver frame. That, and close attention to not be swept by the avalanches that his companions were tossing about. When he came to the wall where it hung, he blew on the dust-caked picture to no avail. How many years had it been hidden away? With his sleeve, he rubbed the silver rose flowers and vines that twisted into the square frame. Even obscured by grime, the detailing in the metalwork was obvious.

A photo hid under the scum. It looked like a school class photo, with teachers standing organized in two lines across, front and back, and students surrounding them in a jumble. The longer Magnus looked, however, the more odd it became. Their clothing was unlike anything he had seen, a variety of wild neon bright colors and patterns, with points and metallic sheens. Even more odd than that, he realized the people weren't all human, as he had thought at first glance. Each figure had a nearly human shape, but possessed attributes of other animals, objects, and aliens. One of the teacher humanoids caught his eye. A large, green serpent's head topped a female human's body. Shai, Seer of the Council. He had only seen her battered and bloodied, but he was sure beyond a doubt. It was the same snake-headed woman in the photo.

Quickly, he scanned over the other figures, until he set his eyes on a tall man at the center of the adults. The bulbous nose struck him. Osiris. Vastly different from the Osiris he had met. A thousand years may do that, Magnus supposed. Beside Osiris, a child with a familiar face smiled at the camera. The features weren't a perfect match, but it was close, and their amethyst eyes gave them away. A young Diedre stood in the photo.

"Hey y'all—" Magnus said.

"—Hey y'all, look at this." April said in unison.

On the far wall from him, once hidden by the walls of books, dusty bricks rose from floor to ceiling in a wide arch.

"A fireplace? In a log cabin?" Magnus asked.

"Hearth." Gideon said.

Magnus stared at him. "What did you just call it?"

"This is a hearth." He squinted at Magnus. "What simple sort would call it a fire place? Fire can be any place with wood or—"

"That's it!" Magnus set down the picture frame and climbed across the room. "Clear a space around the hearth."

Kiora eyed him. "This is what Osiris has left for us to find?"

"The hearth is the heart of the home." Magnus said. "The X was over Osiris' heart. As ingenious as the myiads seem, their riddles have been fairly straightforward thus far."

They all exchanged a glance.

"Good enough for me." April said as she tossed a book across the room. "Get digging."

In a matter of minutes, the four had uncovered the entire hearth. A large, square fireplace that encroached into the wooden floor as well as the wall. The pit was black from char, and held ancient coals that had long since burnt out.

"See anything?" April asked.

Magnus tried to keep his hands from becoming entirely black as he crawled his upper half into the fire place. It was a lost cause. The chimney above was as soot-covered as the fire pit below.

"I don't see anything out of the ordinary." His voice

echoed up the chimney.

"Keep looking, kid." April said.

Something sharp stabbed his hand. He hissed and drew back his blackened palm.

"You alright?"

Wincing, he spotted the charred piece of kindling. An ancient and sharp coal poking up from the pile of ash. A thin bead of blood formed on his hand.

"Fine." He answered. Then, he mumbled to himself. "Just remembered I need to update my tetanus shot."

His blood dripped to the floor and mixed into an inky mix of coal-black mush. The pile of soot formed into a funnel like a filter of coffee grounds, the spilled blood draining underneath. Peculiar. With his other hand, he wiped away the layer of ash and found a thin crack separating two bricks. The murky mixture seeped into the crack and descended into the floor below the hearth. He traced a finger over the brick. As if eagerly waiting for him, the brick reacted to his touch, and depressed into the floor. Unseen mechanisms clicked around him behind the brick walls. They swelled with sound as a panic swelled within him.

"What is that?" April asked.

Magnus didn't want to wait and find out. "Pull me out!"

With a bull's strength, Gideon took hold of Magnus' belt, ripped him from the hearth and threw him into the center of the room. Books caught him, as they always had before.

"How do you fare?" Gideon asked.

"Peachy." Magnus's head spun.

A cacophony of sound grew from the hearth in the form of clicking gears and whirling mechanisms. Magnus ducked under a tower of books. A poor barrier, but, as they had his entire life, the books made him feel secure.

Each wall of the room joined the mechanical chorus. Whirring, ticking, clicking and grinding bounced against wood, rattled the stone hearth, and shook the many papers in the room. April shouted something, her mouth moving without voice. Each followed Magnus' lead and sought cover. They tipped the piano onto its side and hunkered behind it. At some point in the commotion, Gideon found the orange tabby and clutched it close to his chest.

Whirring filled Magnus' ears. Covering them with his hands offered little harbor from the sound. The entire room began to shudder. His eardrums vibrated violently as though sharp stakes were being hammered into his skull. Numbness took over his body like a wave. Muscles lost the will to move. Consciousness faded from him. Just before his vision went entirely black, he saw a tall, dark shape appear in the doorway. Death. He was sure of it. If aliens, time travel and monsters existed, why shouldn't the reaper?

There wasn't room for fear within him, only the mind-numbing sound of grinding metal.

XXI

April

April woke to a harsh slap across her face.

"Wake up!" Diedre whispered, though their voice sounded like an air horn to April's raw ears.

What had happened? The last thing she could remember was the sound of gears clicking. Really loud gears.

The myiad stood over her, hand held high and ready to slap again.

"Do it again and you'll lose it." April warned. "What happened?"

Diedre smirked. "I saved your skin, that's what happened. How are your ears?"

Piece by piece, the puzzle fit together in April's memory.

Magnus in the fireplace. A chorus of sound like they had been trapped inside a broken music box. Grinding metal piercing her ears, driving her senses numb.

"I've been to a few metal concerts," April said. "But whatever that was takes the cake."

April noticed the other three lying motionless in beds of books.

"They're breathing." Diedre whispered. "You triggered a Myiad Sonic Artifice. I've never seen one actually used."

"That was a booby trap?"

"A dangerous one. Stops every known intelligent life form in the universe, except for myiads. Even then, we have to know how to shapeshift the cochlea in our ears to counteract the vibrations emitted into the air. Another minute and your brain would have been scrambled. Get up. We need to talk before the others wake."

"The fireplace—" April began.

"It can wait." Diedre turned on a heel and left the room. Each boot step crunching paper as they marched off.

Before following, April checked Kiora next to her. Raspy, shallow breaths came through. The others shared an equally strained breath. Alive and in need of hearing tests. Could have been worse.

As April stood, her head rolled. The room became fuzzy in her vision. A few intentional blinks helped the walls stop moving.

When she found Diedre, the myiad was leaning against a counter in the kitchen, nervously nibbling on an oatmeal cookie.

Pale green cupboards with dark wooden countertops lined two walls of the kitchen, with more cabinets hanging on the walls above. Scribbled papers covered all but a few spots of the counters— both a basin sink and a metal-coiled gas stove had a foot width between their domain and any stack. A white fridge hummed loudly in the corner, shedding loose leaf papers and brown leaves of a long since dead plant that sat atop it in a water-stained glass jar.

April walked directly to the fridge and opened the freezer door. To her astonishment, paper fell out. Shoveling more frozen paper out and onto the floor, she uncovered the treasure she sought. A bag of frozen peas. As she placed it to her head, a small moan escaped her.

Back against the fridge, she slid down to the floor, and closed her eyes. "What is it, Diedre?"

"Did you hear what Jaakobah said?" Diedre asked.

"He said a lot of things.' April answered.

When no snarky rebuttal came, April opened her eyes to check on Diedre. Bartending had given her a keen eye to tics, but even an untrained eye would notice the myiad's nerves.

Diedre's fingers picked at the nail beds on their left hand. Their heavy boot tapped in quick thuds. Colors shifted as waves of undertones in their skin. In a handful of seconds, they shifted from a sharp crimson hue, to a diminished forest green, then mottled purple. Even the shape of their form started to dance as though the skin couldn't remain contained; it shook and buzzed until most features were blurry. April wiped her eyes to make sure it wasn't her own mind playing tricks.

"What's going on with you—" April began.

Diedre drew a laser pistol from their nylon coat and aimed it at April.

"—the hell do you think you're doing?" April finished.

"There's only one way Jaakobah could have found us here." Diedre's skin flickered crimson.

"Diedre, put the gun down—" April paused. "Wait, you think we have a mole? You think *I'm* a mole?!"

"Prove to me you're not."

"You dumbass!" She shouted. Then, realizing the topic at hand, she whispered. "My saloon was attacked by one of Jaakobah's velexi before I even knew who the hell he was. He's actively trying to recruit me, dammit! Sure, I had no love for the council, but I'm just a goddamn bartender. Coups and xenocide aren't on my menu."

Diedre lowered their pistol.

"Jesus," April's shoulder tensed as if she expected to receive a punch.

"I was 90 percent sure you were clear." The myiad said bitterly. They chewed on their cheek nervously. "Just needed to see your reaction."

"A *mole?*" April whispered. "Shit. A storm of betrayal is coming. Didn't Shai say something like that?"

"Shai wasn't called 'Seer of the Council' for nothing."

April leaned back against the fridge. The cold touch of metal felt good on her hot back. A mole. That was exactly what they needed. Another obstacle on the path. Why couldn't she just return home to the saloon and forget all of this? A whiskey or four sounded excellent. She closed her eyes again and thought.

It could have been any of the others. Even Diedre— April had watched enough true crime documentaries. Simple deception could go a long way; this very conversation could be a ruse.

April glanced at Diedre. The myiad was shaken. April

had known the myiad for years. They would never let their cool slip like that. Not to mention, if they were the mole, there'd be no point in bringing attention to the idea. Could it have been a tactic?

No, it wasn't Diedre. April drew a mental checklist in her mind. With an imaginary pen, she struck Diedre's name.

That left three options.

By the first limitation of traveling, velexi wouldn't be able to travel naturally. Only species with a certain degree of evolutionary intelligence could manifest the traveler genome, and it was well documented that velexi weren't viable. Someone would have had to forcefully travel with the velex that night in her saloon. That drew the suspicion away from Magnus; though he had impeccable timing, he didn't possess the genome. He could have used a pocket watch to forcefully travel. That brought a new question to April's mind: Would Jaakobah have gone so far as to recruit locals?

Gideon was a new traveler, or so he had said when he first arrived at April's saloon and asked for directions to Ireland. It was always a hard conversation to have with a newbie; the explanation that *home* was no longer within the century. The soldier handled the transition smoothly. It was rare to have a traveler from the Middle-Ages adjust so well.

Then, there was Kiora. April's heart tightened at the thought of Kiora betraying her. Their history was a difficult thing to remember, not for loss of memory, but for the pain it stirred. More had been shared than bitter glares and harsh words. Much more. Not more than half an hour had passed since April consoled the woman.

But then, April had seen the sharpness with which

Kiora could become Kekheretnebti, the Egyptian princess. Two entirely different people existed within that body. That was, in part, why their relationship never worked. She loved Kiora, but each day that love was for a different person than the last. Could Kiora have been hiding more personalities?

"What are you thinking?" Diedre asked. They simmered down enough to keep their skin from shuttering, though it still pulsed with a red glow.

"That I need a drink." April stood and dropped the peas on the counter. "Come on, we need to get back."

"That's it?" Diedre's nostrils flared. "We're just going to walk back out there?"

April raised a finger to her lips. "Quiet down. Whatever Osiris booby trapped could be our key to stopping Jaakobah. You think we should just leave that with a potential mole? We'll figure it out. For now, act natural and calm down. Your skin is a dead giveaway."

The myiad's entire body turned blush pink. They closed their eyes and drew a long, raspy breath. The pigmentation in their skin stabilized to its usual soft blue. They nodded for April to lead the way.

Everything had gone to shit and April was pissed. Osiris was dead, along with the entire council, someone in the crew was a rat, and worst of all, the xenocidal maniac that wanted to burn down the saloon wanted her to flip sides. She couldn't help but think it may have been easier to do this alone. That's what she preferred. Just her, the saloon, and countless arms-reach-relationships with travelers who liked to drink. That was the *life*.

Well, it wasn't *the* life. April couldn't convince herself

entirely of that. Being alone meant she had to take both the pros and the cons. Solitude was a pro; loneliness was a con. Either way, it meant she couldn't get betrayed. Lovers couldn't leave her if they were never around to begin with. Family could never die if she didn't keep any.

Thinking about Grandpa Sylas stung her heart like a hornet nest hung in her chest. She'd never felt more alone than when he passed and left her the saloon. Uncle Gainsborough was around, but April often wondered which he cared more about; Sylas' legacy or selling the saloon over to the council.

It was easier to be alone. Just worrying about her and the saloon. No one could take it away. No one could shake up the hornets. She wouldn't let them get close enough. She'd already tried once before.

Kiora stood before the hearth, holding a velvet red box in her hands. It was wide enough to fit in a single palm, and just a little less by height and depth. A soft yellow trim lined the lid. Drawn tight by red ribbon on the top half of the box, a large canine tooth hooked into ribbon loops on the bottom half and held the box closed.

"Was that in the fireplace?" April asked.

As if in a trance, Kiora held her head down. If she had heard the question, she gave no sign.

"Kiora." April stepped uneasily into the room. "Can you hear me? Diedre, is this another trap?"

"Not that I can tell." Diedre said.

Shifting a single hand away from the box, Kiora held it in the air for a moment.

April froze. "Kiora?"

With a quick flick of her wrist, Kiora unhooked the tooth

from the ribbon. The lid rose open on its hinge as though it had been waiting to be unlocked.

A pink glow peered out from it. Rosy warm hues highlighted Kiora's face. A mote of partially translucent pink light floated and hovered above the open box. It stung April's eyes like a miniature, brilliant sun.

"Diedre?" April heard herself say. Despite the blinding brightness, the room grew cold. A shiver traveled down her spine as she noticed her voice press condensation into the air. "What is that?"

"I don't know."

That was not the answer April was hoping to hear.

Abandoning the box to a short plummet to the floor, Kiora rose both hands and cupped the mote of light. A wild smile took over her sharp face. The light began to pulse, each flicker brighter than the last. Shadows danced behind Kiora, framing her shape against the wall in wicked spires. With each pulse, the light pushed air and heat away from it. A soft breeze at first, no more than a ceiling fan. Paper began to flutter away with each gust. Kiora's smile receded. Her face became defiant and rigid. Determined. She tried to touch the source of light. The closer she reached, the more forceful the gusts became. Willfully, defiantly, she tried, but the nova denied her.

"How do we stop this?" April asked.

"We don't even know what it is!" Diedre answered.

The force of each pulse had begun pressing paper, furniture and people alike to the edge of the room. It reminded April of a spinning carnival ride she had ridden at the local rodeo. Gravity pushed out from the light, pinning her to the wall. Diedre hit the wall beside her. The myiad tried extend a shapeshifted arm toward the center of the room. It was no use; with each pulse, the force grew.

Across the room, Gideon's still-unconscious body lay horizontal and pinned to the wall halfway between the floor and ceiling. Kiora had begun to slide away from the mote, fear peering through determination.

Peculiarly, Magnus sat up from a shifting pile of books that had buried him. He blinked sleep from his eyes, rubbed his head and yawned. The mote of light wasn't affecting him at all. There he sat, in the middle of the room, no more than five feet from Kiora, unmoved and unbothered.

"Magnus?" April shouted. The whipping of papers and air filled the room with noise.

He winced and covered his ears. "No need to yell, I'm right here."

Did he not see what was happening?

"Pick up that red box on the ground there!" Her own words were lost to her, but Magnus nodded as though it were a clear command. Now noticing that something was wrong, his demeanor shifted. He stood and carefully approached.

"Quickly!" April urged.

With each breath, her lungs fought to expand. The wall behind didn't budge. If they couldn't stop the pulses, they'd all be crushed beer cans in the recycling bin behind the saloon.

Magnus took up the red box. "What now?"

April read his lips. She couldn't hear him over the tornado of paper.

"Close it on the light!"

Magnus looked around. When he set his eyes on the

mote of light, he tilted his head like a confused puppy. "That?"

She couldn't answer. It felt like an invisible hand was crushing her windpipe. Her ribs creaked near the point of snapping.

Lifting the red box, Magnus stared in wonder at the light. Why wasn't it affecting him as it did her? The light shimmered across his face, dancing over his nose and brow. The whites of his eyes glowed pink. With mouth ajar, he dropped the box and walked toward it in a trance. His hands wandered up and reached for it. April's gasping screams were lost in the whirlwind of paper. As his fingers touched the pink light, it pierced his skin and funneled into his hand.

April fell from the wall and landed in a pile of paper.

"Help!" Magnus squeaked.

He held still as a lighthouse over a bay, his hand the blazing brazier. April thought he looked a bit like E.T., only if the alien's finger had an intensity slider that had been turned up a thousandfold. The pulses of force had stopped, but the light hadn't diminished. It made the skin of Magnus' hand glow so brightly, April could only cast a side glance at it.

"April!" He shouted. The light began to move under his skin. The center of its glow traveled to his wrist, then it slowly wormed up his forearm.

Jumping to her feet, April stumbled over books as she rushed to him. Along the way, she unclasped her belt and whipped it from her pants.

"Blessing upon you!" Kiora called out. She prostrated with open palms held toward Magnus. "Blessing of Osiris!"

"Help—" Magnus shouted. He scratched at the light in his forearm.

"I'm here!" April said. The only thought she had was to stop the light before it traveled all the way through him. What kind of alien parasite or Near-Future tech was trying to take over his body? Why had only Magnus been impervious to its force? "Diedre! Help me out!"

Answering the call with haste, Diedre appeared beside them and held Magnus' spare arm back. He wouldn't stop scratching at the light. Blood trickled from deep fingernail grooves on his arm. Gideon appeared beside April and helped hold the arm still.

"It burns!" He shouted, writhing in Diedre's grip. They shifted their arms and melded them together in a tight vest around him, pinning his other arm down as to stop him from ripping his own skin.

April tightened the belt just below Magnus' elbow, pushed it through the metal clasp, and cinched it as tight as she could. She shoved the end of the belt into Magnus' mouth.

"Bite."

He didn't need the order. Sweat trickled in beads down his face. His teeth sunk into the black leather. Hot breath blew from his open mouth and struck April. She held the best attempt at a calm face she could muster. It wasn't much, but it had to be better than his.

Together they watched the light crawl along Magnus' arm. A bug just under the surface of the soil. It approached the belt and passed through without issue. Magnus spit out the belt and shouted openly once again.

"April!" Diedre shouted. The myiad rose their hand and

mimed scissors.

The light's crawl quickened up his bicep.

"Do it!" April shouted.

"Hold on to him, beefcakes!"

Gideon bear hugged Magnus as Diedre let go. Their hand twisted, flattened, and curved. Skin receded inward, replaced entirely by a flat panel of steel, one edge of which grew jagged and sharp. Diedre's hand became a hacksaw. "Don't worry, my protégé, scars maketh the man!"

April pushed the belt into Magnus' mouth once more as she lifted his arm.

Diedre began sawing. It was quick.

Falling backward onto the ground, April held Magnus' arm in her hands. Blood painted loose paper and stained the floor. The light still crawled toward the open wound.

Magnus weeped in a daze.

"Blessed!" Chanted Kiora. "Blessed!"

"It is done," Gideon whispered into Magnus' ear. "It is done."

Pink light poured over the room once again. It poked through the open wound on the arm like a worm from the earth. Suddenly, the entire arm shook in April's hold. It wormed, rolled, and shot through the air, landing back onto Magnus where it had been sundered. Tendrils of pink light bridged the space between the two wounds and rebound the limb to his shoulder.

"Blessed! Blessed!"

Magnus' eyes rolled up and showed only white. Spittle and froth sprayed from his mouth.

April took him, and with the others' help, guided him to the floor. The light was in his chest, now, crawling toward his heart.

"It's alright." April spoke softly. With one hand she held his, the other she used to comb back his hair. It was hopeless. They had tried and failed. Whatever was happening was beyond her, and certainly beyond the man. He was just a college kid, and she, a bartender. The least she could offer was the comfort of a warm hand and a soft voice. "Easy, easy. It's alright. You're okay."

As the light centered over his heart, Magnus stopped moving.

"Magnus?" April asked. The pink light over his heart grew dull and blinked out. Hesitantly, she tilted her ear to his chest. A heavy, gradual thrum of life beat against her cheek. Rising like waves on a shore, his chest lifted and fell with breath.

"Is he gone?" Diedre asked.

"No." April shook her head. "He's alive."

XXII

Gideon

To Gideon, it was a perfectly clear act of the Lord Almighty.

Though he had never had a hand for writing, the entire journey thus far had set a fire burning within him. Magnus' rebirth was the second coming. Christ himself. What apostle would tell the tale, if not Gideon himself?

God had breathed life into Magnus.

"Jesus." April sighed.

Gideon gave her a stern look and tapped her shoulder.

She rubbed it and spoke. "What the hell was that?"

"The Lord above." Gideon said. "He has placed His grace within our companion. Our mission is a holy one, indeed."

That, Gideon had already accepted. Of the egregious examples of false idolatry that he had seen thus far, Jaakobah was the worst account. Divine justice was necessary. He had surmised that that was why he had been blessed with time magicks, after all. Kings of men hosted great crusades across country and continent for the Lord almighty; Gideon would lead his crusade through time itself. The others would surely come around after seeing the light of retribution seep into the soul of Magnus.

"It was Osiris!" Kiora exclaimed. She still knelt in reverence. It brought a sneer to Gideon's face. "That is the only explanation—

"—It was God's will—" Gideon interrupted.

"—A blessing of Osiris." Kiora said sternly.

He held Kiora's glare. They would see the truth of it in time. He must remain vigilant and trust in the Lord's work.

"Do you think this is what Osiris was researching?" April asked.

"Could be." Diedre nodded. "I've never seen anything like it."

"Nano-tech?" April asked.

Diedre shook their head. "No, nano-tech can't do something like—"

Gideon stopped listening.

Rather, his attention was drawn away by a fuzzy feeling on his leg. The orange tabby brushed up against him. It purred aloud. He bent over and scooped it up. Holding it in front of his face, he looked into its eyes. The furry creature looked back, then rubbed its cheek against his own.

"You don't have an owner now, do you?" Gideon asked. "Can't have that, can we?"

Purring was the only answer it gave, and the only answer he needed. He brought the cat down and held it to his chest. Gideon noticed a tag on the cat's collar he hadn't seen before. A name was etched on the blue metal.

"Alan Rickman?" Gideon asked. "Is that your name?" He scratched the cat's chin. "You can't stay here, alone, Alan. You'll come with me."

Gideon kissed Alan's forehead and returned to listening to Diedre.

"—so no, that's why it can't be nano-tech."

April nodded. "I see. You think it could be how we stop Jaakobah?"

"We'll have to wait and see what actually happened to him."

All eyes fell to Magnus. Instead of the screaming, tormented man he had been a moment prior, he now slept like a newborn baby in a cradle of goose feathers.

"Your guess is as good as mine." Diedre shrugged.

"The Light of the Lord will be an apt weapon against the false one named Jaakobah." Gideon said with a smile. He lifted Alan Rickman onto his broad shoulders, where it happily laid down around his neck. "We should rejoice and drink, for next we meet Jaakobah, the strength of Christ will guide our strikes."

All eyes aligned in a flat stare toward him. Not a single one of them saw the light. What would it take? If not a heavenly vision right before their eyes, what else? The skeptical were a dangerous sort, denying what they had personally observed. Gideon had fought and killed heretics for far less than the hedonistic claims spoken by Kiora and Diedre. The holy-touched one, Magnus, had been open to discussion, though Gideon doubted the future man's faith.

Magnus erupted from sleep. He sat up and sucked in air like a drowning man. The suddenness of it made Gideon tense. Alan Rickman felt it too; he stuck his claws into Gideon's shoulders. Choking quickly led Magnus to vomiting, followed by dry groaning.

"How many times can you puke in a day?" Diedre asked with a mix of curiosity and respect.

"What happened?" Magnus asked.

"Not sure." April said. "How do you feel? Any different?"

"Lighter." Magnus said.

"The holy spirit uplifts," Gideon said.

"Or he just blew enough chunks to make another ring for Saturn."

April squatted by him. "You don't feel anything different?"

"No," Magnus ran his hands down his arm. "You cut off my arm!"

"You still have it!" Diedre said defensively. "We would have reattached it."

April snapped. "Focus! Nothing feels different? What do you remember?"

Magnus cast a distant stare toward the hearth.

"There was something. Floating there. In the air. It kept changing shape. A pen, a cowboy hat, a toy car. When I saw it, I heard a voice. It told me to reach out. To accept it." He looked around the room. Gideon beamed at him with a wide smile.

"The grace of God assumes many forms." Gideon said eagerly. "You have been chosen."

"Alright." April stood up and offered him a hand. "We need to get you checked out. Jaakobah can wait until we figure out what that thing is that went inside of you. I'm willing to bet it's what Shai wanted us to find."

"Inside of me?" Magnus' eyes widened.

"Aye," Gideon smacked him on the back. Magnus grunted heavily. "We are lowly servants deemed unworthy of His grace. But *you!* He has chosen you as his vessel! With His strength, you may move mountains and swim across seas." Gideon capped the sentence off by drawing a cross in the air.

Alan Rickman stretched along his shoulders and meowed.

"Am I dreaming?" Magnus asked.

"No," April said, "But I wish I was. Give me the pocket watch, it's time for us to go."

Fumbling through his coat pocket, he brought out the watch and offered it to her. Gideon squinted at the glowing green light on the pocket watch.

"Aye!" Gideon pointed with a shout.

"What's wrong?" Magnus asked.

April's hand froze above Magnus' outstretched palm. She slowly took the pocket watch and held it in her own. The green light remained.

"Take the watch from my hand." April commanded.

Magnus retook the pocket watch. The green light remained.

"Green means good, right?" He asked.

"A miracle of the lord." Gideon boomed as he laughed. Aside from him, the room was deathly silent.

"Why is he laughing?" Magnus asked.

"An act of God!" Gideon cackled and pointed at the rest of the travelers. "You all doubt the work of the Lord, but can you doubt this? An act only He Above could have carried out?!'

"April." Magnus said urgently. "What does green mean?"

"Portable TDUs like this have sensors that can detect if a user's genetic information has the traveler genome." April said quietly. "Red means a person doesn't possess the genome."

Magnus' eyes widened. "Does that mean—"

"—It means we just witnessed the impossible." April said. "It goes against everything we know about the genome and its limitations, but I think Osiris just gave you his traveler genome."

Gideon's laughter stabbed the walls of the room and shook the support beams on the ceiling. Through faith, nothing was impossible. He had told them, but only the Lord above could open their eyes.

The Lord had an imaginative sense of humor.

XXIII

Diedre

As always, Diedre was right again.

Under the thick umbrella of Gideon's laughter, the myiad smiled wide. Something was special about the kid, that much they knew from the start. Why else would Diedre have made him their protégé? Yeah, Diedre didn't know it was going to be *that* special, but still, it was a testament to their advanced intuition.

Pride swelled in Diedre. The accomplishments of the student were reflected upon the master, after all. Diedre had taken a little, weak, frail, scared local from 2024 and forged him into a traveler-warrior who would lead the charge against Jaakobah. Portum Press would pay three gloags of credits for an interview. They could imagine the headline.

Last living myiad saves the timeline!

A sudden jab of pain stung their heart. The last living myiad. It had been a long time since Diedre cared for the other myiads. They were the progenitors of the *system* in which Diedre wanted to dismantle. Technically, that system was dismantled, but being alone in a universe run by Jaakobah didn't sound fun, either. Osiris was once like a father, and now, he was buried in a shallow grave. Wiped clean. Diedre would never be able to see him in the present, future, or any time in the past. The limitations prohibited it.

Or so everyone thought.

The council had taught everyone, Diedre included, that the limitations were fundamental laws of the universe. Had they intentionally lied to the entire timeline in order to keep the power to themselves? It would make sense; Jaakobah wasn't the only myiad with power fantasies. Shai, Sekhmet, Osiris, every single member of the council had a few screws loose.

Diedre was glad to be the only myiad in all of time to have a head screwed on right.

"My young protégé, we need to get to the Near-Future." Diedre said. "If it is true, we should get your DNA checked. Who knows what happened to that little double helix of yours. Let me borrow your timewire."

"You're thinking mutation?" April asked as they handed them the device.

"I'm no genetics doc," Diedre tapped a quick message on the little black box. "But I know a guy. Setting up a connection now."

Stretching their arm by three extra feet, Diedre took the pocket watch from Magnus' hand. The time wire chimed.

"Great, Rex is ready to receive." Diedre said. Magnus raised his hand into the air. "You don't need to raise your hand. What?"

"If we think— or, if I *do* have the traveler genome, can't we travel naturally instead of using the pocket watch?"

A tear nearly came to Diedre's eye. Their protégé was truly a remarkable student. Curiosity flowed through him like electricity through a carbadium circuit board.

"Traveling so far in one go is tricky. Ninety million years has a lot of time baggage to pull you down and cause variation in where you can land. *I* could probably pull it off on a good day, but if *you* tried? Pieces of you would land in every era from here to the Quaternary. We don't want that now, do we?"

Magnus shook his head.

"Right. Excellent question, though. Keep those up."

Diedre clicked the dial on the pocket watch. Above and below, rings of light formed and pulled at them. They hardly felt it anymore. A slight tug at most. Traveling was natural, even the forced kind. It was simply how they moved to the next destination, like walking, or flying their starship.

A moment later, the familiar glint of titanium alloy surrounded them. Diedre tossed the pocket watch and a proud smirk to April.

The command room of the ship was a wide circular room, with a walkway rounding a sunken area in the room's center. Long strips of neon blue lights curved with the shape of the walkways. Floating above a gravity base, a command table hovered as the room's grand centerpiece. Pale yellow holograms floated above the gravity base of the command table, their warm glow clashing with the cool, metallic tones of the ship.

"Ladies, gentlemen, and those who don't identify within the binary," Diedre twirled on a heel and spread their arms wide to her four companions. "Welcome to the S.S. Paul, my starship."

"Paul?" April blew out air in a single loud laugh. "You named your spaceship *Paul?!*"

Diedre shifted in their coat. What was wrong with the name Paul? There were many gallant Pauls throughout the timeline. Many worthy of a great ship, and many a great ship worthy of the name.

"It's a powerful name." Diedre said defensively. April broke into full laughter. Even Magnus giggled. Their protégé had the gall to laugh. "You two are sleeping in the brig."

Only then did Diedre notice Rex leaning against the door frame of the hallway. His humanoid figure was back lit by blue light, a heavy shadow cast over his inhumanely long head. He remained still, though his tail broke the cool demeanor he garnered. It waved and flicked anxiously.

"Rex." Diedre said.

"Cap'n." Rex's voice was thick and low. A rich undercurrent. Diedre recalled his choice songs during the S.S. Paul's many karaoke nights. Frank Sinatra was a favorite of his; his voice lent itself nicely.

Diedre spread their arms wide and brought him into a tight embrace. "You can't imagine the kind of trip I've been having."

"If I've got any sense, I think I might." With a sweeping gesture, he dragged a small yellow hologram from his tablet into the air, then pushed it forward. Lines of yellow light grew into larger holograms as they hovered and settled above the command table. Some became newspapers, illuminated headlines in a variety of neon blues, green, and purples. Others became hologram screens displaying crystal clear video footage of a burning Portum, velexi in droves rushing down streets of planets across the galaxy, and newscasts with causality numbers rising faster than a Vegas slot machine jackpot.

"Still just doing it for your saloon?" Diedre asked. April's expression hardened.

"Sekhmet." Kiora's hand hovered before the hologram, just shy of touching the light. In crystal clear display, the hologram played video footage over the battlefields of Cydonia, Mars. A news headline on the lower half of the footage read, *The council has lost.* Velexi and traveler corpses alike littered the image. Sekhmet, among the other myiads who had fled Portum, regrouped, and faced Jaakobah in one final stand, hung in the field's center, their corpses staked into the soil.

"Witness accounts say velexi spawn have been found on Mars, Gamma-651, and Leu-Pula." Rex said. "Jaakobah has made a statement to the timeline, promising a peaceful take over, so long as every quadrant roots out any semblance of council rule."

Diedre swiped the holograms from the air. The council were a bunch of bureaucratic, power hungry tyrants who deserved what they got, but these people? Normal, living people who know nothing about Jaakobah, genomes, or why a death horde of velexi appeared on their doorstep? The indiscriminate killing made Diedre sick. Not to mention, hordes of velexi destroying the star system didn't bode well for their piracy business. How could they be Diedre Altair, Space Pirate Extraordinaire, without anything to pirate?

"A black hole. That's what Jaakobah deserves. Stardust, the universe may be ending, but we can at least keep our heads up. Rex, link our comms with Doc Flavo, asap."

"You okay, cap'n?" He asked.

"Peachy. Cowboy back here needs a full GIS."

Rex fidgeted his hands nervously.

"What is it?" Diedre asked.

"Doc Flavo is dead." Rex answered.

Diedre frowned. "Really? Damn. Black market genetics are a real spiral door. I need a geneticist here in under 10 minutes. Double pay."

"Right away, cap'n." Rex saluted and hurried off.

Diedre sighed. Being a beloved captain was exhausting. When they turned, four sets of eyes were glued to them.

"What? Y'all are staring like I'm a blue moon over Neptune." Diedre had seen a blue moon over Neptune. It wasn't half the sight as they were, but it was important to be humble, especially in one's own ship.

"We need to assess the situation." April said.

"Seems like we're heading into the end game, now." Diedre said. Magnus gave them a wry smile. "What?"

"The end game?" Magnus asked. "Did you say that on purpose?"

Diedre had no clue what he was getting on about.

"Jaakobah has an army of velexi, unhindered traveling, a personal forcefield, lightning fast reflexes, secret knowledge of the council, and who knows what else." April rattled off each item with a sinking attitude. "What have we got?"

The five members of the crew glanced around the room at each other.

"Two humans, two religious fanatics, and one dashing space pirate." Diedre answered.

April grunted. "Not much. And we still don't have a way to bypass Jaakobah's defenses."

A double door on the room's edge hissed as it slid open. A cloud of steam formed and fell around it. Rex stood in the door frame caked in sweat and choking on a heavy breath.

"Cap'n," He swallowed. "I tried to stop her— but she wouldn't listen—"

A black-gloved hand wrapped around his shoulder and pushed him aside

Into the room strode a tall, thin woman in black denim overalls. Painted directly onto the fabric in dark reds and browns were cogs, chains, and buttons, which were accented by actual cogs, chains and buttons sewn along the seams. She wore a black, ruffled blouse under the overalls. A long hooked beak of a crow mask protruded out from her nose. Black as the mask she wore on her face, her hair draped down in two long braids behind her.

Diedre whipped out a laser pistol and aimed it across the room.

Mur the Crow, the most dangerous, and most expensive, info broker in the universe. Diedre had dreaded the day Mur would find them. No amount of ignoring comm links, promises of universal governmental loan reimbursements, or prolonged forbearances could have saved them from this moment.

Diedre would have to pay their loans.

"Ah, ah, ah." The crow masked woman said as she

waved a finger in the air. An unnerving smoothness trailed her words, along with the scent of dried roses. The woman's sinister voice bounced inside the beak of her mask. "My crew is rigging microhydrogen explosives to your ship's anti-matter bay. One click, and we'll all take a space walk together."

"Come now, Mur," Diedre said through gritted teeth. "I thought we were friends."

Mur tilted her head. The crow mask pointed glaringly at Diedre's laser pistol.

"A precaution among friends?" Diedre tried. "What are you doing here?"

Casually strolling with a doom device in hand, Mur ventured to the center of the room. She tapped her leather-bound fingers along the command room's center, walking them along the metal table in little strides.

"You owe me a lot of credits, Diedre." Mur walked her fingers up Gideon's arm. "Why, you're just a hunk of muscle, aren't you?"

Alan Rickman, still laying across Gideon's shoulders, held out his nose to sniff the leather glove.

"—and hello, kitty!" Mur's tone took a sharp upward trend in pitch.

"I don't have time—" Diedre began.

"None of us do." Mur twisted her neck to point the long crow beak at Diedre. Her voice returned to a steady slither. "Haven't you heard? The timeline is ending. Time to cash out. There's only one place safe from the hell that's breaking."

"When is that?" April asked.

"April Minnary?" Mur tilted her head like a crow.

"Getting you out of the saloon is like seeing an Optinean flying pig walk. I figured the bar business would be busy at the end of the universe."

"You think there's somewhere you can hide that the Time Council could not?" Kiora hissed viciously.

"Kekheretnebti? Flerovium, Diedre, didn't picture you working with a council dog the likes of her." Mur strutted along the table. As her fingers walked near Kiora, the woman shifted the dagger in her hand. Mur shook her head and tapped the detonator. "I'm taking what I can and heading to the Far-Future. Way I see it, even Jaakobah won't go there. Everything he hates is in the past."

"The Far-Future? *That's* your plan?" Diedre scoffed dramatically. They wished they had thought of it.

"Sure," Mur said. "What, you got somewhere better in mind?"

For a tense moment, the room was silent. Mur inspected each and every person like a crow inspects a bottle cap.

"Goodness and gadgets, Diedre! Don't tell me this little crew is a kill squad. You're going to try it, aren't you? You know he killed every single council member."

Diedre could only imagine the look behind that stupid crow mask Mur wore. A shit-eating grin. That's what it was. Diedre had always wanted to smash that mask to pieces and tell Mur to shove it up her back-stabbing, extorting, self-righteous asshole. Of course, Diedre never said those things. Out loud.

"We'll do more than try." April said.

"Oh." Mur said. "What's a three letter word that rhymes with *try*. Let's think." A cawing laugh echoed from the mask. "I don't usually give advice for free, but this one's on the house. Stick to your lane. I'm an info broker. You're a bartender. We don't fight in galactic wars."

Mur wasn't a fighter, but Diedre knew that she was more dangerous than she let on. The info broker was not the kind of person you wanted to piss off, no matter who was backing you. Somehow, Mur seemed to have a knack for getting information even myiads couldn't, and she had a hand in every corner of the galaxy. That was how it worked. She gave you a little, and you paid her a lot, in credits, or in info.

A light went off in Diedre's mind.

"I don't have the credits—"

"—Then I guess it's *kaboom*—"

"—Do you still take information?" Diedre asked. The room tightened around the question. Kiora shifted so subtly, only Diedre's myiad eyes could have noticed. Gideon was more overt, the tension in his body growing as his muscles did. "I assume the universe' greatest info broker still sees the value in good information. The good stuff. *Confidential stuff.*"

"You assume incorrectly. Whatever you have will be worthless in the Far-Future."

"Even the first known transference of the traveler genome?"

Mur cocked her head sharply. "Bullshit."

"It's true."

"It is impossible."

Diedre nodded to Magnus. "Only way to find out is to test his genetic information."

The room absorbed tension like a black hole, condensing it at the point halfway between Diedre's amethyst eyes and the crow mask covering Mur's. It broke suddenly as Mur rolled her neck toward Magnus.

"There's a thermal cycler in my ship. I take him. I test his genes. If you're lying, I blow up your ship and sell him to the Plutonian slave market."

"You take us both." Diedre said quickly. "They'll stay."

"Deal." Mur said without hesitation. She turned toward the door where Rex stood and walked past the man into the corridor. "Don't dally, you have five minutes before I press this button."

She waved the detonator above her head as the doors behind her slid.

"What the hell?" April shouted. "You're using us as collateral to pay off your debt?"

"Two asteroids, one drill." Diedre said. "I settle with Mur and we figure out if Magnus is really a walking exception to everything we think we know about the universe. Win, win."

April stared with an open mouth. She tried to speak, but nothing came of it.

Another perfect plan hatched and executed. Diedre made a mental note to pat themselves on the back. Not a single person in the universe could match their problem solving skills. Though, none could match their problem *making* skills either. If that's what it took to be the best problem solver, then Diedre would gladly take it in tow.

Now that they thought about it, that was quite the problem itself. One they could probably solve.

"Giddy up, cowboy." Diedre said. "The plague doctor is in."

Magnus fearfully glanced at April.

"Don't look at her, she can't save you." Diedre said.

"April, I'll solve this problem, you've got your own to deal with. Rex, set them up in the guest rooms. The nice ones, not the ones we give to in-laws."

With a tight grip on their protégé's arm, Diedre towed him toward the transfer dock.

April

"Here are the *nice* guest rooms." Rex said sheepishly. "Just as cap'n said."

"What's so nice about them?" Gideon asked.

"Cap'n calls them *nice*."

"How are they different from the others?" April prodded.

"They aren't." Rex said. "Enjoy your stay on the S.S. Paul. The cafeteria is just down the hallway, if you're peckish." With that, he left the three alone.

It was a long, thin room with barracks style beds laid out against each wall. Matching navy blue bedding was tucked neatly into the first bed and each thereafter. A metal locker rested at the foot end of each, and an aluminum dresser sat beside each headboard. April counted eight in total. Dragging a finger along the tucked bedding of the first wiped a thick stripe of dust from it. It had been a long time since anyone had slept there.

April wiped her finger on her pants. "Yeah, to hell with this."

As she turned to leave the room she felt the hair on her neck tingle. Turning slowly, she found Kiora standing so close to her right hip that their noses almost touched.

"Can you give me some space?" April asked.

Kiora shook her head. "I am your blade, and the myiad's ship is no safe haven. We must be ready for whatever comes."

April sighed. She took a step, but the hair on her neck tingled again. By her left hip, Gideon stood so close, the orange tabby standing on his shoulders flicked its tail and smacked her head.

"Seriously?"

"I don't want to get lost." Gideon said sheepishly. He seemed anxious on the ship. April couldn't blame him. She knew all about space travel and it still made her claustrophobic. The open desert was her home, not an aluminum can in outer space.

The tabby reached its front paws down Gideon's back and dove to the floor. It rubbed a cheek on April's leg. Bending over, she smiled and gave it a chin scratch. It began purring immediately.

"His name is Alan Rickman." Gideon said.

April raised a brow. She wondered if Osiris named the cat before or after he went mad. At that rate, she would go mad babysitting the two travelers. If she had to be stone cold sober while listening to another bible quote or some odd nonsense about duty, she would absolutely lose it.

There was also the matter of the mole. In a not-so-inconspicuous way, Diedre had given her an opportunity to investigate.

"Diedre's room should be around here somewhere. If I'm gonna wait around for them, I think it's only fair if I help myself to a drink. Care to join me?"

Gideon raised his eyebrows. "I could drink."

"No," Kiora answered. "I must hold my senses steady."

"Funny," April said. "Whiskey is how I manage that. You go find something for us to eat. I'm starving." She patted Kiora on the shoulder and turned to go.

"I will not leave your side—"

April rolled her eyes and drew out her best managerial voice. "I order you." Talking down to Kiora didn't feel great, but April needed Gideon alone. "Find us something to eat."

A natural comedian, April's stomach let out a growl to cap off the order.

With a freshly adopted death glare, Kiora nodded, turned, and left without a word.

With a sigh, Gideon spoke. "Lover's quarrels."

"*Watch it*. I can send you back to the cretaceous era." April warned. She pulled out her time wire. No message from Diedre. Instead, April started typing.

"Communion with Diedre through the magic box?" Gideon asked.

"No word from them yet. I'm sending a message to my uncle. If it comes down to a fight at the saloon, we should at least be prepared." April shoved the time wire into her pocket. "Done. Let's find those drinks."

It only took about five minutes of wandering the hallways for April to find Diedre's quarters. Short of having a neon fluorescent light hanging from its doorway, it was the most obnoxiously *Diedre* thing in the space ship. Standing in a hallway of sheen metallic and blue light, the wide double door was solid gold, with amethyst encrusted handles and a large platinum plaque with the phrase, *Diedre's Den of Devilry*. Gideon drew a cross in the air.

"You think this is them?' April asked with a smile.

"Yes." Gideon answered flatly.

April shook her head and took hold of the gold door handles. The double doors slid open with ease.

What struck her first was the scent. A thick cloud of blue smoke blinded her as it poured into the hallway. Warm, intense notes of wood and earth seeped into her sinuses. Incense had never been a particular joy for April; she preferred the natural scents that came with a place. The saloon, for example, smelled of whiskey and oak, even chestnut at times, if she had felt experimental with a shipment. In that moment though, the cloud of blue smoke encased her, and against her expectations, it soothed her.

What ease the bizarre incense gave was erased as the cloud settled and April took in the rest of Diedre's den.

Horrific, violet shag carpeting covered the entirety of the large, rectangular room. A semi-circular bed took up an entire quarter of the room, its satin sheets lavender under the warm glow of miniature stage lights above. The rest of the room was dimly lit with a rose tint of ceiling-embedded LEDs. Across from the bed, a brick fireplace flickered with flame. April wasn't sure of the efficacy of a fireplace aboard a starship, but it was Diedre's room after all. Beside two arm chairs, both mahogany and upholstered with red velvet, April found her target. A tall liquor cabinet, also mahogany, with clear glass doors protecting four shelves of bottles.

"Bingo." April said, wasting no time in crossing the room and raiding the stash. She'd made herself familiar with alcohol across the entire timeline, from ancient wines to Near-Future concoctions, but the odd colors of a few drinks made her pause. She took up one in particular; a glowing yellow liquid in a bulb-like bottle with a long neck. Uncapping the bottle with a *plop,* she twirled it, then put her nose to the rim. A jolt ran through her as though she'd dipped her nose in water and touched it to an electrical outlet. Sulfur with a hint of asparagus. Gagging, she hurriedly re-corked the bottle. "I think that is actual piss."

Gideon didn't answer. He stood facing the wall beside the door. Countless framed photos covered the wall floor to ceiling. It looked like the saloon; every inch of available space held some sentimentality.

Alan strode past Gideon, mouth agape as the cat took in the strange scents.

"What are you looking at?" April thumbed over the bottles in the cabinet until she found her mark. A nineteen fifty Macallan vintage single malt. She blew out a low whistle of respect. "I see why Diedre talks down to what I've got at the saloon. This is a thousand dollar bottle."

Taking two glasses down from the shelf, she poured two drinks. Alcohol was the best way to get a secret out of someone, especially one they didn't want to share. If Gideon was her mole, she'd just have to drink him under the table to get the truth out of him. Considering his Irish origin, she wasn't sure it would be that easy.

April joined him by the wall of photos and handed him the glass.

Every photo was of Diedre, of course. Most included their crew as well. One was a selfie Diedre took atop Mount Everest, their star ship floating in the sky behind them with massive icicles clinging to it. Beside that picture, a photo of Diedre in what looked to be a purple swamp. Rex, who April could only assume was Diedre's first mate, or something of the like, had sunk waist deep in the purple ooze. The moment captured Diedre pointing and laughing at him.

"For all of their self obsession," April said. "Seems like Diedre really cares for their crew."

Gideon grunted. He stared at one smaller frame. April leaned over and glanced at it. She recognized the landscape, not from her own experience, but of photos she'd seen before. It was the Cliffs of Moher in Ireland. Diedre, Rex, and an assortment of other wildly shaped alien species, stood together for a group photo on the cliff's edge.

"You recognize it?"

"It is my home." Gideon said. "Feels like many days since I've seen those fields."

"Technically it's been over a thousand years." April said cheekily.

"I suppose it has." Gideon sipped the drink.

April pulled away from the wall and collapsed into one of the red velvet chairs. It felt good to sit down with a drink.

"What do you miss most?" April asked. "When you're traveling."

"My wife." Gideon said. "And my girl."

That news hit April like a truck. Travelers didn't usually keep connections to their local times. She hadn't even thought to ask. "You have a kid?"

Gideon chuckled. "Yes. A little one. Only three." He sat across from her. "And you?"

April stared at him. "And I what?" It took a moment, but the question registered. "Oh, no! No. No kids here. Nope. Nada. Zero children. What's your girl's name?"

"Aoife."

"Pretty name."

"Yes," Gideon rose the glass to his lips and sipped. "You are old for not having children. Are you barren?"

Stunned, April nearly threw the drink at him. She didn't, however. It would have been a waste of good whiskey.

"Things work differently in my time," April said through gritted teeth. Moisture formed in her palms. Was she nervous or just bothered by the comment? The room was unnaturally warm. The conversation had taken a wrong turn. She needed to get it back on track.

"Why'd you decide to come with us when you could have gone home to Aoife?"

The man's body language shifted entirely. April's felt goosebumps race down her arms. A grim look came over the man's face as he cast a long, dour stare into his whiskey glass. Flickering shadows from the flame of the fireplace danced on his face. She shifted, too, just slightly to the right, in case she needed to reach for the revolver on her left hip.

"Why do you ask that?" His voice was low. Nearly a whisper. Holding motionless, his eyes flicked upward and watched her. For a brief moment, as he stared with a lowered chin, April thought he could be cast as a villain in a James Bond movie. He even had a European accent to go along with it.

"I was just wondering—" April tried her best to not stutter. That would show her nerves. Though, Gideon's piercing stare made it difficult to hide the soft twitch of her ring finger on her right hand, or the bead of sweat trailing down her neck. How was she so nervous? She wiped sweat from her brow. Talking over a drink was her greatest strength. Blue smoke trailed from the vents of the room. She sipped carefully. "It's not your fight, is all. If I wasn't dragged into this, I'd have stayed home without a thought, doing inventory in the saloon or something."

Gideon set down his glass. April set down hers. Time felt slow. She watched his movements with as much care as she could. Rigid stone. No fingers twitched on his hand. Not a single bead of sweat. The room warped and bent around him. The purple shag of the carpet rolled and waved. On his face was a grim look, as though he were about to do something he would not enjoy.

What would it be? Had April flown too close to the sun? Was she too blunt? Too forward? Had she let it slip that she knew of a mole, and now he had to blow his cover and kill her? It wouldn't be easy, she'd make sure of that. In her mind, she kicked herself for sitting him down just three feet away from her. Though he was shorter than her, she was far outmatched in size. Not to mention, he was a medieval soldier. April had broken up fights in the saloon plenty of times— some she had straight up ended herself— she had no doubt that Gideon would be a tough match up in close quarters. If it came down to it, she'd rather be across the room with a revolver. Best laid plans, she supposed.

The man brought his hands together in front of him. That was it. He was about to lunge at her neck. There was no reason to draw it out. He wanted to end it quickly. April squeezed her hands into fists.

"I am a sinner!" Gideon burst into tears. With two hands he covered his face and sobbed. "I have abandoned my wife and child. I've deserted the holy fight. My duty was to family and king, but here I sit, fleeing and fled, far from both. The lord punishes the prideful, yet I can not stop. I seek more, in pride and vain. In traveling, I abandon wife, child and king to seek the very domain of the Lord Himself. For it I am branded with sin. But He has graciously made my pathway to penance clear: Serve the lord. Slay the false prophet, Jaakobah."

April closed her mouth, which had grown exponentially agape as the man spoke. She'd had a few catholic-trauma regulars in the bar, but Gideon took the cake. He also brought the ingredients and made the cake.

He sobbed into his hands. Messy sobbing. The kind that April only saw after a customer spent all night at the bar with rum and coke. What could she do? Usually at that point, it was near closing time. Hand them off to an uber and wipe your hands clean. That was her strategy.

Awkwardly, she shifted forward in her seat, leaned across the space, and put a hand on his shoulder.

"It's okay, bud." April said endearingly. She wasn't sure what else to say. So, she told the truth. "I'm not going to pretend like I empathize. I don't have a kid, and I definitely don't get the religious part of it. But, I mean, it ain't like what we're doing isn't for them, too."

Between wet sniffles, Gideon asked. "What do you mean?"

Alan appeared by his side and rubbed his cheek on the soldier's shin. He picked the cat up and placed it on his lap.

"I mean," April sighed. "Aoife will be there when we're done, but she may not be if Jaakobah wins. What we're doing is bigger than us. It's bigger than pride"

She caught herself on her own words. Wasn't she trying to stop Jaakobah for her own selfish reasons? Everything was to keep her saloon. Her grandad's saloon. She had just said admitted a moment before that she would have gladly stayed home. Everyone needed to figure out their own problems. The problem of Jaakobah taking over planets wasn't hers, so long as he avoided planet Earth. Or, at least, Arizona. But he hadn't, and now it was her problem.

Therein lay a question she had only given impartial thought to. She twirled the whiskey in her glass and thought it over.

What if she agreed to Jaakobah's offer?

For whatever reason, he hadn't killed her yet, despite certainly having the capability. He'd conquered Portum with an army of velexi, made a show of executing Osiris, and now, he was laying waste to entire planets. Why did he care so much about her? The better question, could she use that to save her own skin? Either by getting close and putting a dagger in his back, or, if it came down to the wire, cutting a deal.

Yeah, that was a good idea. Cutting a deal with a psychotic, xenocidal, invincible god of time. What could go wrong?

If it came down to it, she wasn't sure there would be

much of a choice. There was one thing she was sure of, though: Gideon was not her mole. He was just a sad, confused catholic. She had met plenty of those in her time managing a bar.

"What we are doing is good in the eyes of your Lord *and* your girl." April smiled gently. "How about we make a deal, you and me."

"What deal?"

"If we survive this whole thing, I'll come visit your time so you can introduce me to Aoife."

Gideon sniffled. "She would like that. That girl is a stargazer, always wandering about and asking questions."

They sat for a moment, in a silence broken only by Gideon's sniffling.

"I'd offer a hug, but it's not really my thing."

The man snorted. "Nor mine."

That made her laugh. The thought of the old, war-grizzled soldier asking for a hug with snot on his face was worthy of Diedre's wall of photos.

"What I can offer is this." April poured him another drink.

"Thank you." Gideon said. It was for more than whiskey. His sniffling stopped. Together, they shared a comfortable silence beside the fireplace. April still wondered about it. Wouldn't it burn the ship's oxygen supply? She shook off the thought.

Enjoy the moment. That was her goal. A noble goal. A rich glass of whiskey, a comfortable chair, and silence. Not to mention she had crossed one name off the list of potential moles. So far, she hadn't had very many successes on this impromptu mission. That deserved a moment to sit back, relax and—

Boom!

A far off explosion shook a distant corner of the ship. The metallic hallways echoed as the blast struck April's head like a drum, leaving a heavy ring in her ears. She jumped to her feet, then wobbled as she fought the trembling ship for balance. Alan hissed, climbed the chair quickly and mounted Gideon's shoulders. With another hiss, the door of the room slid open. April aimed her revolver, Gideon raised his hammer, and Alan drew back his ears in a snarl.

Blue smoke unfurled into the hallway and was made purple by crimson alarm lights flashing above.

April held her breath for a bated moment as a shadow emerged. Her finger touched the trigger of her revolver.

"He has found us." Kiora hissed. She stepped out of the cloud with daggers drawn and dripping. "Velexi have boarded the ship."

XXV

Diedre

The many chains and buckles that Mur wore clinked together as she led Diedre and Magnus through the black hallways. Scarlet tubes of light overhead filled the onyx-toned walls with a sinister sheen, reflecting rays off of the Crow's many brass accessories.

Diedre found it infuriating. What kind of criminal would want their enemies to hear their brass ass clanging so loud it could cut through the void of space? Not to mention how difficult it was to see anything in the ship. The lighting was dim and drab. Sure, the steampunk aesthetic looked cool, but what about *practicality?* They glanced over at Magnus and pointed.

"She sounds like maracas." Diedre mouthed silently.

Magnus squinted and shook his head. They mouthed again. *"Maracas."* He still didn't get it. Diedre shifted their lips into a long tube. Long enough to reach the three feet between them and Magnus. He cringed at the sight, but kept quiet. Their lips lingered in the air right beside his left ear and whispered quietly.

"Maracas."

Diedre sucked back the tube of their lips and smacked them against their teeth.

"Here we are." Mur said.

A puff of steam blew out from a stretch of smooth wall and revealed the seams of a hidden doorway. The wall depressed, and slid open.

"Now we're talking!" Diedre's shouted.

Large dark pipes, cogs and valves covered each wall of the wide room in a spaghetti pattern, which Diedre wasn't a fan of. Too mid-18th-century-warehouse chic for their taste. What really titillated the myiad was the plethora of Near-Future tech. Tables full of gadgets, gizmos, apparatuses, dingalings, doodads, and each other word that came to their mind.

"An atomic proton displacer!" Diedre marveled at the tall cylindrical machine before their eyes latched onto another long, flat bed. "Is that a Morpheus somnology table? Those are worth more than an outer ring planet." They placed their hands on the cushion. A wave of exhaustion overcame them, as if every atom in their body was being pulled down and lulled to sleep. When they tore their hand from the cushion, they felt utterly weightless.

"What is this?" Magnus asked. Diedre turned to see him inspecting a wall-mounted helmet connected to a terminal.

"That's just a Manchester 2440 Craniofacial Reconstructor." Diedre tossed the name aside bitterly.

"It isn't *just* anything." Mur added. "That's the best facial reconstruction module credits can buy. Some say it cleans up features better than a myiad. I suppose there's no competition now." She cocked her crow beak at Diedre. "Sorry, too soon?"

Diedre grit their teeth down to dust, reformed them, then grit them down again.

"Why don't we get on with it." Diedre said through clenched, fresh teeth.

"Great idea." Said Mur. "I'm eager to see your face when I press this button and your ship gets blown to JADES-GS-z13-0. The sight will almost be worth what you owe me."

She slammed a fist against the wall beside Magnus. He flinched as a section of the wall began to fold out and land as a waist-high counter.

Once again, Diedre marveled, though, they did their best to hide it from Mur. It was a difficult task when there was a Vostok cryogenesis rifle *and* a Hadron micro particle accelerator in the same room. Diedre had to give it to the Crow; she had a fine taste for Near-Future tech.

In a far less exciting fashion, Mur ignored the fun stuff and took a standard issue thermal cycler from the wall and set it on the table. The clear casing looked to be made of cheap plastic, and the small touch screen resembled an Ipod touch from two thousand and seven.

It was a tragedy. Diedre felt their fingers grow longer and reach toward the wall of fun gadgets as though they had a mind of their own. They held down their roaming fingers. It wasn't time for fun. Even the kind of fun that could come from pointing a Vostok cryogenesis rifle and a Hadron hand-held micro particle accelerator at each other. But, oh, the sweet vapor layers they could drum up. A firework show of particle decay.

No. Diedre took a deep breath. They were already breathing heavily. More was on the line than a few missed explosions. If they made it through this whole ordeal alive, they could simply borrow the gadgets from Mur and have fun with them, then. Blow up an asteroid or two. Maybe drag Magnus along and work on that anti-violence quirk of his.

"OW!" Magnus yelped.

Mur plucked a hair from his blond bun and placed it into a small compartment on the thermal cycler. The plastic cover lowered, the cycler beeped twice, and began whirring.

"How long is this going too-"

The machine beeped again.

"Done." Mur tapped a quick sequence in the table. Pale, white light resonated with the touches of her fingertips and sent ripples across the table's surface. Once she finished tapping, more instruments unfolded from the flat wall. Diedre eyed the wall respectfully. It was certainly an economic usage of floorspace.

A live-feed electron microscope with eye pieces shaped to fit Mur's crow mask descended on a robotic arm to the table. Beside it, another arm laid down an array of test tubes in holders, and a stack of flat microscope slides. Mur removed her leather gloves to reveal pale, human hands. She quickly turned a few knobs on the machine, then squeezed a drop of the cycler's solution onto a slide and placed it under the microscope.

Diedre held their breath. It was the moment of truth. Had their protégé broken all known conventions of traveler law? It wasn't impossible. All facts were only facts until proven otherwise. Diedre couldn't count the amount of times in history that a single advancement broke every preceding rule that had been generally agreed upon.

If it were the case, Magnus deserved a better title than protégé. Maybe even a spot in Diedre's crew. *Ship boy*, or something or another. He would still have to work his way up from the ground. Just because he was their protégé, didn't mean they cared for crew members taking shortcuts.

"Janus, Juliet and Jupiter." Mur whispered.

"How long has he got, doc?" Diedre joked and playfully shouldered Magnus. He stared at them with a grim face.

"Look for yourself." Mur said. She stepped back from the microscope.

Diedre stepped forward and leaned over the microscope. Their human face didn't quite fit into the mold, that is, until they shifted their nose into a long crow's beak to match the shape of Mur's mask.

A single strand of Magnus' DNA sat center stage of the microscope flat. What Diedre sought was the one physical piece of evidence that science had found in those with the traveler genome; a molecular inconsistency in how the two bases of DNA helices formed. It was a simple thing to see if one knew what they sought. What Diedre found, however, sapped the breath from their lungs.

The DNA wasn't a double helix. Where individual bonds between nucleotides should have connected the two glucose bases of a helix, there was a solid band. Rather than two strings twisting with threads between, Magnus' DNA looked to be a thick strip of twisted ribbon. It was no longer human. As far as Diedre knew, only one known species in the entire timeline had a solid band genetic sequence.

Magnus' genetic information matched that of a myiad.

Diedre's face trembled as it reformed into a human shape.

"What?" Magnus asked. "I don't like that look. What's wrong? Oh god, what is it?"

"You really want to know?" Diedre asked. They held her voice low and raspy.

"Jesus, it's that bad? Tell me." Magnus covered his face with his hands. "No, don't tell me. Okay. Say it. What do I have? Is it some sort of space tuberculosis? Am I a goner?"

"You're no longer my protégé," Diedre said with a sudden burst of cheeriness. "You're my brother!"

"What?"

"Welcome to the family!" Diedre took his head in both hands and kissed his forehead. "Wild how things turn out, huh? Yesterday you were human, today you're a myiad. Can't say I've ever heard of that before, but you're full of surprises."

Magnus breathed heavily. "What are you talking about? I'm a myiad? How is that possible?"

"Shouldn't be." Mur said.

Diedre shrugged. "Wish I could tell ya. My best guess? Osiris figured out a way to meld two sets of genetic code, one with the genome and one without."

"Combining two sets of genetic information into one organism could circumvent the known issues with genome transference." Mur added.

"Whatever it may be, genetics don't lie." Diedre said.

"You're as much a myiad as I am. That is some information for the millenia! More than enough to square my debt away, right Mur?"

Mur nodded slowly.

"Maybe." Mur said. "Leave the gene samples and we're even."

Diedre wagged a finger in the air and made a game show buzzer sound with their mouth. It was time for some real negotiating. Diedre had leverage, and no good Space Pirate Extraordinaire would settle for less than twice a good trade is worth.

"Not the deal." Diedre smiled a wide, toothy smile. "I traded *info* for my debt. The samples will cost you extra."

Their eyes wandered to the wall of gadgets. Mur followed the glance.

"What do you want?" Mur sighed.

"The Hadron. And the Vostok. Hot and cold, baby!"

"I'll give you the Hadron for the samples. If you want the Vostok, I get one of his limbs."

Diedre tilted their head back and forth, considering the trade. They glanced back at Magnus.

"You're not cutting off my arm, again." Magnus said. Sweat rolled down his face.

"It'll grow back! You're a myiad, now!"

That was it. His eyes rolled back, his knees buckled, and he dropped to the floor like a sack of potatoes. Shock had taken him. Diedre only eyed him long enough to make sure he was still breathing.

"Okay, I hear you." Diedre dragged the words then turned to Mur. "What a drama queen, right? You know he can't stomach the smallest bit of violence? Even killing a mosquito!"

Mur whistled. "Lucky life he's lived getting on like that."

"That's what I said!" Diedre said. "We'll take the Hadron for the samples."

Diedre spit in their hand and offered it forward.

"Deal." Mur lifted her mask just enough to show a pale human chin. She spit in her own hand, then smacked it against Diedre's. "Always a pleasure, Diedre. For what it's worth, I hope you can pull this suicide-mission off."

Their hands shook; it was the closest thing to an honorable deal a space pirate could get in the twenty fourth century. Sure, Mur and Diedre had their disputes, quarrels, various sharp objects in each other's backs on countless planets, but when they shook, Diedre knew Mur was always good for it. At least, for that deal and that deal alone. The next one? Well, that would be another deal for another day.

Diedre reached over, took the Hadron micro particle accelerator off of the wall, and slung the strap over their shoulder like a laser rifle. It wasn't much larger than a common laser rifle, save for the extra-long chrome barrel of the accelerator. The base was a slightly wider cylinder, decked out with a graphic interface and a double poriddium-leather grip. It was lighter than they expected, but it felt good in their hands.

"Alrighty then," Diedre said, wandering toward the door. They gingerly stroked the barrel of the Hadron. "Be seeing you, Mur."

"Forgetting something?"

Diedre inspected the Hadron. Check. Their hands wandered to the hidden explosives flap of their coat. Check.

They didn't think they had forgotten anything. The deal was made, DNA samples for the rifle. What else was there?

Mur cleared her throat and kicked Magnus' leg.

"Ah, right."

XXVI

Diedre

Diedre dropped Magnus on the floor just inside the loading dock of the S.S. Paul. They fiddled with the switchboard and detached the two ships. Mur's ship split from the connection and floated away gently through the cosmos. Diedre looked down at the sleeping myiad next to them.

Myiad. That was a strange thing to call Magnus. Somehow it felt like a weight had been lifted off their chest. Diedre wasn't the only myiad left. Technically, they were even related.

The myiad genetic code was unique among the many living, sentient beings of the universe in that it was a sequence that assimilated every other sequence of genetic information it came into contact with. That flexibility of myiad genetics was how a myiad could shift their body to their will. Magnus' new genetic information, just as Diedre's, possessed a part of every life form in the universe, across the entirety of time.

Osiris had given him a gift, all right. The mad fool. Diedre tried to imagine what the poor geezer did to his own body to extract his genome. Hell, they didn't have to imagine much, now that they considered what all had happened. The scars on Osiris' chest, the utter lack of sanity, the self-imposed solitary confinement; it all fell in line together like puzzle pieces. Whatever Osiris did to separate his genome from his body had twisted his mind and warped his body.

What side effects would it have on Magnus?

The list of questions burned a hole into Diedre's mind. The new, the old, and the ugly.

How could they use this to stop Jaakobah? If it came down to a fight, could Magnus actually do it? How could being a myiad help fight Jaakobah if he had already killed the entire council?

Did the mole of their group just receive the only weapon they had in fighting Jaakobah?

Diedre clicked their tongue.

"Unlikely." They said to themselves.

Diedre had a good knack for reading people. It came with space piracy. One needed to know who they could trust, and who they couldn't. It didn't always work— some people were too good at playing a part. But this kid? This dorky, history-manic college-aged human? He wore his entire history on his sleeve. Diedre was almost certain he was clear, but that exact moment gave them a chance to be sure beyond a shred of doubt.

It was time for Diedre's ultimate, secret move: the *Truth-Teller's Handshake*. They were quite pleased with the name, too. It added a flair of drama, and, more importantly, mystery.

The *Truth-Teller's Handshake* was Diedre's personal take on an ancient myiad trick. When they were a myiadling, Shai had told them an old story about the myiads before the genome awoke within their species, long before they involved themselves with intergalactic politics and xeno-wars. Diedre's myiad ancestors had devoted their long lives to mastering the myiad art of shapeshifting. The greatest of the ancients could shift their matter by single molecules. As far as Diedre knew, no myiad of the council had ever come close to that level of perfection. Diedre hadn't either, but they *had* developed a trick or two of their own.

They took Magnus' limp hand in a handshake hold and concentrated on the space between their palms. The air held tightly in the sealed vacuum of their flesh. Shared space. Shared energy. The warmth of blood flowing just under the skin. Electric currents through nervous systems.

The center most point of Diedre's palm unraveled into microscopic tendrils. Their tiny points met the pores of Magnus' palm and entered into his hand without breaking skin.

Diedre exhaled. This was the hard part.

Slowly, Diedre shifted the inserted tendrils into axons capable of connecting to a human nervous system. One by one, they fused each end of their own axons to each nerve ending in Magnus' hand.

Diedre was connected directly to Magnus' central nervous system. They could feel each neuron firing through nerves all the way up to the electrical signals within the hemispheres of his brain. Therein lay the trick to the *Truth-Teller's Handshake*: penetrating a person's mind and finding the truth at its root.

Still, it wasn't a perfect method.

Though Diedre was connected to his meaty, human brain, feeling signals and understanding them was entirely different. Sensing how another being's nervous system worked was akin to hearing a language that only that person knew. The words were a jumbled mess of sound that held no meaning to a foreign ear. The electricity coursing through Magnus' brain held no meaning. But, just like a stranger speaking a foreign language, there was more to communication than words and their meaning.

Hints of nervousness rattled his neurological network, sending pulses like pistons firing into every corner of his body. Quick, sharp, sporadic. Excited trills topped the nervousness like a harmonica in a Billy Joel song. Diedre liked Billy Joel, especially some of his slower tunes, like *Vienna*. A steady underbeat thrummed gently through Magnus, carrying a steadiness like a raft in stormy seas.

It was hardly what Diedre would expect from a double agent hiding his identity, and Diedre had rooted out a few liars their day. The electricity that drove him was warm and inviting. A sign of a good-willed person. An anxious wreck, maybe, but good all the same.

Diedre was convinced. Magnus wasn't the mole. They nearly thanked Gideon's God for that.

"Beef jerky!" Magnus woke with a jolt. Diedre dropped

his hand, which he promptly raised to his forehead. "Oh god, what happened?"

"You passed out from shock. Hit your head on the way down." Diedre didn't tell him that they had actually knocked his head on a doorway while carrying him back to the ship. They snapped two fingers in front of his eyes. "What year is it?"

"I don't know."

Diedre considered the answer. Did he know what year they were in to begin with? Probably not.

"Eh, you're fine."

Again, Diedre reached out a hand. This time, he took it consciously.

"I had the most peculiar dream that I was a horse. I galloped across an open plane, but when I looked down, my hooves were chicken feet. And I had six of them!"

"Ah, shapeshifting nightmares." Diedre reminisced. "I had them when I was myiadling. They'll pass once you start shifting regularly."

Magnus' face hardened. "Oh."

"What's wrong?"

"I was hoping that was part of the dream too."

"Not a chance. You're a myiad, now, bold and beautiful." Diedre slapped him on the back. "And, you helped me settle a debt. I call this a total, complete, and infallible success—"

A heavy *boom* rattled the hallways and echoed into the wide, two story loading dock. The ship shuttered and rippled. Crimson light overtook the blue-white fluorescent tubes of the ceiling, faded to black then flashed again. Across the dock, titanium security doors leading to each hallway slid closed and clicked as they locked.

"What's happening?" Magnus asked.

"Could be one of two things." Diedre said. "Either it's someone's birthday, or we're under attack."

"How do we know which it is?"

The intercom system spit static and turned on. A nasally voice spoke through a tinny microphone.

"Attention crew of the S.S. Paul, today is Gweneviere's birthday!"

Diedre let go of the breath they had been holding.

"We will not be celebrating it, however, because we are under attack! Multiple velexi have been found on the ship. Please make your way to the—"

The nasally voice was cut short by a squeal in the pitch of a high C, followed by gurgling in a low B, then a click as the intercom turned off. A blaring, long winded siren followed in a D flat. Diedre pulled out their laser pistol. They were glad to see Magnus draw the peashooter April had given him. Progress.

Jaakobah's mole worked quickly this time. Their ship should have been off the grid entirely. Only someone from within would have known in which sector of the universe they hovered. They ran quickly to the nearest titanium door.

By a space pirate's fortune, Diedre counted their stars at the sight of the functional dock terminal. It wouldn't have full access to the ship's main controls, but they could get an understanding of what was happening.

Diedre placed their eye to the retinal scanner.

"Hello, captain." Serene and disjunctive, the voice of a New Zealand man sounded from the terminal.

"Paul, show me a layout of the ship. Add on alpha

layers of an oxygen map, structural integrity, and a heat map. Offset each by one micron."

"On it."

The terminal blinked dark. Four tiny dots of light appeared and expanded outward into a multi colored highlighted map of square rooms, long hallways, curved viewing decks, a mess hall, living quarters, various internal circuitry access points, and at the very center, four orange-red points where life forms stood in Diedre's own private quarters.

"Son of a bitch!"

"What?" Magnus asked.

"They're drinking my booze!" Diedre shouted.

"The velexi?" Magnus pinched his face in confusion.

"April!" Diedre squinted. "Jokes on them, I have my radmercybin ventilators on full time."

"What is radmercybin?"

"For myiads, part-muscle relaxer, part-aphrodisiac." Diedre said. "For humans, it just piques out a person's existing anxieties."

They scanned the hologram map. The entirety of the O2 synthesizing chamber had disappeared from the blue lines of the structural map, and the green highlights of the oxygen map were fading outward from the missing rooms.

"We're draining oxygen."

Another explosion rattled the ship. Diedre was swept off their feet that time. When the rattling stopped, their feet didn't return to the floor. That wasn't a good sign.

"Diedre!" Magnus yelled. "Help!"

He floated through the air toward the walkway's ledge. Behind him, cargo crates hovered freely through the loading dock. Diedre twisted their hand and extended it to the terminal, anchoring them to the wall. Another section of the hologram map had gone dark: the ship's gravitation well.

Diedre stretched out their free arm and shot it toward Magnus like a harpoon toward a tuna. They clasped their fingers over the tuna's jacket, reeled him in, and made sure he had a good hold on the rail before letting go.

They turned to the terminal and tapped the hologram keyboard at lightning speed. It wasn't fast enough. The command center had been targeted, likely to disrupt the internal mainframe of the ship. Diedre had to patch together each loose end of the S.S. Paul's systems from the tiny loading bay terminal. As their hands moved, they sprouted five more fingers from each. They figured that would double their typing speed.

"Paul, prep every escape pod for emergency evacuation and upload yourself into each. Also, reroute six percent of the Paul's energy to the auxiliary gravity well."

"Verbal confirmation needed—" Paul began.

"Captain Diedre Altair gives confirmation." Diedre said. Softly, their toes touched to the floor as gravity increased to a near-normal effect. "Well, it ain't perfect, but it's something. Link me through to the intercom, Paul."

The terminal chimed and the intercom hissed with static. Diedre cleared their throat.

"This is your captain, Diedre Altair. Get to the escape pods, your lives are more important than a lost ship. April, I see you in my quarters, you whiskey-depraved *plutarch*! Meet us in the armory."

A surge and hiss took over the intercom. Another portion of the blue map faded to a dark screen. The communications deck was gone. Diedre snarled. Velexi were a royal pain in the ass. They'd be lucky if half the crew made it to the escape pods at this rate. There wasn't anything more they could do for them.

"Paul, release all security doors not linked to structural damages and engage internal defense systems. Target genetic makeup of the velexi, excluding myiad crossover."

"Yes, Captain."

Each titanium security in the loading dock hissed as they slid open.

Magnus pulled himself closer to the terminal. "What do you mean, *excluding myiad crossover?*"

Another great question from their protégé in yet another terrible moment. Now that they thought about it, with Magnus being a myiad and all, their whole teaching syllabus would need to be reworked.

"A safety precaution."

"I'm part velex?"

"You and me both, baby! Myiad genetics are like a sponge; they soak up everything we've ever come into contact with. That's how we can shapeshift." Diedre shifted their hands back to normal sets of five fingers. They drew their two laser pistols, kissed each barrel, and turned off the safety catches. "Now come on. We've got some humans to find."

XXVII

Magnus

Something in Magnus' stomach turned worse than the night in college when he had eaten bad sushi right before a Sun Devils game. Paired with a growing throbbing in his head, he could hardly make out Diedre's words. Something about finding April and the others? Obscurity plagued his thoughts like a derailed train. His legs felt equally derailed as Diedre all but dragged him by the wrist through chrome hallways. The myiad's grasp felt like a leash of flame had been tied to his arm. He was amazed when he looked down to find his skin unburnt.

Thurump. Thurump. Thurump.

He became distinctly aware of his heartbeat. It pounded against his chest rapidly. The more attention he gave it, the faster it seemed to move. It made his breath turn shallow. Attention spread to his mouth, where his tongue felt deplorably dry. He needed to distract himself.

"Can I ask you something?" He asked.

"Shoot." Diedre had reverted completely to their myiad form; a blue skinned alien humanoid with long eye stalks. Their left eye stalk curved back to watch him as they walked.

"How do your clothes change with your shape?" Magnus asked in an attempt to pull his mind away from his own body. "Your trench coat reappears when you shapeshift."

"An old myiad trick. One of the first ones we're taught as myiadlings. I suppose it's a good place to start."

Magnus' heart skipped a *thurump*. He swallowed through a dry mouth.

Diedre's left elbow crunched as it bent inversely to reach backward toward Magnus. They lifted a hand and pointed an index finger to the ceiling.

"We can pretty much shapeshift into anything, as long as you can imagine it."

The skin of their index finger peeled away in strips and folded into their palm seamlessly. Muscle receded into the palm. Jointed bone morphed like clay into small, interlocked ovals. It's color changed to match the chrome of the starship's hallways. Diedre's finger had become a rigid, 3-link metal chain.

"Even non-living things. But there are limits, like anything."

In an instant, the chain-finger shifted into a thin green stalk of a dandelion. Frosty white seedlings formed a sphere at the top. The seeds fell away, floating a few feet before they blinked out of existence.

"Pieces separated from our bodies won't last long unless we keep them close to our core."

Magnus looked down at his own hand, innately aware of each pore, nerve ending, muscle fibre and vein.

"So your trench coat—" He said slowly. "Is a part of you."

"Bingo." Diedre said. "It's easier this way. If we wore normal clothes, they'd tear to bits each time we changed shape."

We.

That word seeped into Magnus' brain like a poison. Could he truly be something other than human? Would that mean he was even himself? Was he still Magnus Duvall?

Of course he was. That was ridiculous. Time travel, gods and genomes. It was getting to his head, digging its way into his brain and burrowing itself a little den of insanity. He needed to hold himself together, especially now that he had a body built to unravel.

But there was the matter of the veins in his fingers. Bulging, they pulsed in thick rhythm with his heart. Magnus stared at them. Each thin vein vibrated under the flesh like strings of a guitar. If the throbbing in his skull wasn't so damned loud, he was sure he'd be able to hear them strumming a song.

"Stop." Magnus said to his veins.

"What? Did you hear something?" Diedre asked.

Lifting his forearm to his ear, Magnus listened to the song. Muted under layers of skin, his veins *did* strum with sound. A G note. Then a C.

"Stop it!"

The guitar strum of his veins grew silent.

Thurump. Thurump.

His heart continued beating, but no blood traveled the veins of his arm. He had told the veins to stop, and they had. That cut through Magnus' brain fog enough to warrant a scream.

"Keep your voice down!" Diedre hushed him. "What's wrong with you?"

"Oh god," Magnus said to his veins. Diedre's words came as muffled sound. He watched their mouth move silently under the drum beat. *Thurump thurump.* It bounced against the inside of his skull. His stomach lurched as he looked at his hand. Without blood flow, his fingers felt cold. They adopted a blue tint. Choking down bile, he forced out a shout. "Flow!"

The veins of his forearm began pumping in tune with his heart. *Thurump.* They poured more and more blood forward until the veins outpaced his heart. *Thurump.* The tips of his fingers grew dark red as the flesh pooled with an overbearing amount of blood. *Thurump.* Suddenly, they burst, and blood shot forward onto Diedre in five tiny lines, one from each of his finger tips.

Through hazy thoughts, Magnus clung to a desperate wish that the holes would close. Muscle fiber and bone erupted from the tips of his fingers, and new joints formed. Each of the five fingers on his right hand extended out an inch from his nail bed with an additional joint, fingertip, and fingernail.

"What is happening?" He clutched at Diedre with extra long fingers. "Help me!"

Diedre held his face still and looked into his eyes. The myiad's mouth moved silently.

"I can't hear you!" Magnus shouted. He couldn't hear himself. Diedre kept repeating something, but he couldn't make out the words. Reading lips had never been a strength of his. "What are you saying?"

Like dynamite had been set off right behind his head, Diedre's voice poured into his mind. The throbbing pain in his head dispersed in an instant. In its place, an odd tickling sensation, like a feather in his ear.

"Open your ears." Diedre whispered repeatedly.

"I can hear you!" Magnus whispered. "I can hear."

"Listen to me carefully. You're shapeshifting for the first time. Your body will do strange things, but you are in total control. You had a headache and closed your ears to isolate the pain. Focus on your ears. Visualize them. Imagine the holes that should be open. Open them."

"Aren't they open now?" Magnus asked. "I can hear you again."

Diedre gave a toothy grin. "Not exactly. Let's just say I had to break a window and sneak in."

Again, there was a strange tickle in his skull. Only then did he realize that his ears were completely covered by Diedre's palms. His eyes widened with horror. The myiad had shaped tiny tentacles from their palms and forced their way into his head. Diedre was literally inside of his skull, petting his brain.

"Relax," Diedre said. "I'm qualified in pretty much every surgery you can imagine. The sooner you open your ears, the sooner I can pull out."

Diedre winked.

Magnus closed his eyes and tried to imagine anything but Diedre's tentacles combing over his brain. He'd seen a diagram of the inner ear once in anatomy 101. The outer ear led to the eardrum, then the ear snail was behind that. No part of the ear was *actually* called the ear snail, but in every diagram, it looked like a snail, and that had helped him remember it for exams.

He felt an awareness in his ear drum that he had never felt before. He'd never thought he could be aware of an ear drum. As acutely as he could isolate the feeling of one finger or toe, he could feel his ear canal. He could *move* it. No. Not *move*, exactly. It wasn't quite movement like a finger or toe, but it was a function. Something that had never been there before. Something that his myiad genes allowed.

As Diedre had told him, the ear canal was entirely blocked. A wall of cartilage had filled the tube like a dam, save for the worming probe of Diedre's shapeshifted hand. Magnus engaged this new function as he would flex a muscle. The wall of cartilage quivered and tensed in response. It grew thicker. It tried to squeeze out the invading tentacles from Diedre's palm.

"Visualize what you want your form to become." The myiad said. "You are in complete control."

Magnus tensed his brow and imagined a tunnel. A long, stony tunnel through a mountain. His mother was driving. He would be in the passenger seat, breathing in a deep, heavy breath right up to the tunnel's entrance. Just as they entered, he would stop and hold his breath the whole tunnel through. It grew dark for a few moments. The tunnel curved, the far off opening poured light through the windshield.

Fresh air and sound filled the open passageway of his ear. The tickling stopped.

"That'll do." Diedre patted a hand on his head.

Before he could answer, the skittering of a thousand tiny claws on metal struck Magnus' fresh ears.

Between flashing crimson light and blaring alarms, a velex crept from a branching hallway and tackled Diedre to the floor. Each talon glistened with liquid made dark under the red light. A dozen tiny claws jabbed into Diedre's coat, shredding fabric and skin alike.

"Shit, my coat!" Diedre grunted. Each of their arms splintered into a dozen smaller limbs to fend off the velex' own. "Run!"

Magnus froze. Air became thick within him, like honey flowed through into lungs with each breath. On his hip, the pistol he wore burned a hole in his mind. He drew it quickly, and aimed it at the velex. The round body of the monster chattered with countless mouths of snapping teeth as it nipped greedily at Diedre's arms.

Again, Magnus' stomach rolled. Bile and more raised all the way to his mouth, ruining his taste with a foulness near that of the velex' putrid scent. His hands shook violently. He fought for control over his nerves.

Pull the trigger. He wished to pull the trigger. Urged his finger to obey. It had always been that way. Even as a child, play fighting with his siblings had made him sick. Age had only made it worse.

He wanted to scream at himself.

Pull the trigger.

Diedre was dying for god's sake. Either Diedre died, or the velex died. He wanted the velex to die. He wanted to kill it.

The gun fell from his hands.

Magnus imagined a club. A *gada*. An old Persian mace he had seen once in a history textbook. A long shaft with a metal sphere at one end. A capable instrument for bashing an alien. An image of it crystallized in his mind and took over his arm. Swelling to the size of a pumpkin, his palm smoothed out, absorbed his fingers, and hardened into a dull metal sphere. His skin had become bronze. *Literal* bronze. Diedre had shown him how myiads can shape into non-organic matter, yet it still shocked him. But there wasn't time for shock or curiosity. He rose his gada-arm into the air, preparing to strike the velex.

"Hit it!" Diedre shouted. Indigo blood dripped in tiny streams down their many defending arms.

At the height of its rise, Magnus' arm trembled uncontrollably. He remembered the saloon basement, watching the velex threaten to bore into April. The blood, the screaming, the axe in his hands. He couldn't do it then, could he now? The flesh and bone of his forearm wavered and unraveled into indistinct, sagging shreds of flesh. The metal club-head drooped limply. Even after forming his body into a weapon, he couldn't strike. His mind was still that of Magnus Duvall. That hadn't changed. At least, it hadn't yet. He couldn't force himself to enact violence. He had always called it his curse. Unable to raise a finger to fight, he'd watch Diedre die, and then, the others soon after.

No. That wouldn't happen. He didn't need to kill the velex, he just needed to save Diedre.

A thousand images flashed in his head like a hyper-speed power point presentation. What could help? A net? He could shapeshift into anything in the universe, and a net was his first thought. He envisioned a fished net made of finely twined line.

On his still-human hand, his nails shot out and morphed into black lines. They laced over each other and weaved a velex-sized net in an instant. He cast it over the velex like he had seen a fisherman do in a documentary once. At his fingertips, he reeled in the outer two threads in an attempt to cinch the line around the velex.

The dozens of free hands on the velex' back cut through the net like warm butter.

"Are you serious?" Diedre shouted. "Saw it in half! do anything!"

Magnus envisioned a buzz saw. His drooping club-arm morphed into a half-hearted spinning fan of half-metal-half-bone flaps. It wouldn't work, but it gave him another idea. He focused on the flaps, forcing them to stretch out farther, spin faster, and shift into steel rectangular plates. Six flat, steel rectangles clung to his wrist, each at least four feet long. They began to slid around his wrist, spinning in a whirlwind of metal. He'd made an industrial-sized fan at the end of his arm.

He aimed it at the velex. Flexing that new control over his own matter, he spun the rotating mechanism of his forearm. The fan blades sped up, drafting a current down the chrome hallway. He tensed every muscle in his body, pushing his new ability as far as he could. The fan blades sucked in the air behind him and pushed it forward. The velex' spare arms braced against the wind tunnel, its talons scraping against the chrome walls like nails on a chalkboard. It was working. Magnus pushed further. The velex drew back its arms from attacking Diedre, stabbed a dozen claws into the floor, and crawled against the wind toward his fan. The alien didn't seem pleased that its feast was interrupted by the universe's largest hand-held fan.

Magnus' arm felt like jell-o. Shapeshifting felt like working a new muscle, and just as overusing a muscle, his fan arm started to lose its pace. The velex crawled further toward him through the weakening wind. That was all he could do; spend his energy and life to delay the inevitable. He couldn't fight. He certainly couldn't kill the velex. All he hoped was that Diedre had time to get up and run away while he put up a distraction.

A looming storm in the dying wind, Diedre's body rose without standing. They shapeshifted upward, building a thick, black, armless silhouette that towered over the velex and Magnus both. Magnus watched in horror as the myiad grew a single limb; an immense double-axe head. It was the size of Magnus' entire torso. Diedre had grown to at least ten feet tall, their body a thin shadow without features. Color had abandoned their flesh, leaving behind a void, rough skin. The myiad looks dangerously similar to their sibling, Jaakobah.

"This is for my coat!" Diedre's voice was as shadowy as the form they had taken. A hissing whisper that dripped with rage. Their axe carved through the air like a bat on a moonless night.

For a single breath, the velex hadn't realized it had been cut. It took one more scuttling step toward Magnus before it fell apart in two, cleanly sliced pieces. Violet oozed from the two halves and pooled underneath.

Magnus hadn't realized he'd been holding his breath.

"You looked like Jaakobah." Magnus said after catching his breath. Diedre's color returned to its blue hue, their form shrinking down to a humanoid shape.

"Don't compare me to him." Diedre said dismissively. The outer layer of their flesh peeled off and took the shape of their trench coat. They adjusted the collar and spat. "Jaakobah wishes he had my eye for fashion."

Magnus almost let out a laugh, but the sound of chattering turned him on his heels. A second velex had skittered close under the cover of whirring fans and roaring myiads. It raised eight arms toward him, each adorned with talons already painted red by the blood of some other unfortunate soul. He raised his own arms to cover his face.

That was it. He had saved Diedre without violence. That was all he could offer in this campaign against Jaakobah and the velexi. As he closed his eyes and waited for the velex' talons to stab his chest, rip apart his insides and feast on his organs, Magnus found that his thoughts were depressingly absent. Death was coming, and he had no visions of his childhood, old lovers, his family or friends, or even his recent escapades through time. His mind was blank of thought, save for the acknowledgment that, in a moment, he would be dead. He should have known this time travel business would kill him. At least he had seen a few cool things before the inevitable came to pass.

It would come to pass in a second's time. Or this one. Or maybe another.

Magnus opened his eyes.

Only a foot away from burrowing into his chest, the velex hovered, frozen in the air. Its back side wriggled to get free, but the arms nearest Magnus were completely still, as if the air around them had solidified. Peering past the eight sets of talons directed at his face, chest, stomach and various other parts, Magnus could see the alien's tiny mouth's chattering in slow motion.

A whirring sound came from behind him. Yellow light sparked under the velex' skin. It grew in intensity until the velex' body bulged, as if the light were rooted in its body and pushing outward. Hundreds of velex mouths squealed as its body struggled to hold itself together. It failed. The velex' black body erupted, sending violet innards floating every direction.

Diedre laughed, their face wild with rage, their hands gripping tightly to the steaming Hadron micro particle accelerator.

"That's what happens when you mess with us! Internal particle acceleration!"

Like the velex they had belonged to, the violet guts hovered frozen in the air a foot from Magnus as though an invisible bubble surrounded him.

"Who's looking like Jaakobah now, huh?" Diedre leaned the Hadron against their shoulder. "How are you doing that, anyway?" They raised an eye stalk at him. "You think you could get through Jaakobah's forcefield like that?"

"I don't know."

Magnus found that, now that death wasn't of immediate concern, his mind had too many thoughts. It reeled with all the things he had expected; flashback memories to his childhood, the scent of his mother, the feeling of reading a good book. They all faded as his eyes landed on his right hand. What had been steel fan blades now looked like limp pasta noodles. They were an unnerving site. Human skin and steel melded into each other as if his body had tried shapeshifting back and stopped for a smoke break.

Magnus shook his hand gently, though he wasn't surprised when nothing changed. He visualized his hand as best he could. A pale and pink thing, with wrinkled knuckles and a scar by his thumb where he had burnt himself against a hot stove top as a kid. The fan blades rescinded into his palm like worms into dirt, leaving five spindly fingers roughly the size that they had been before. He wasn't sure exactly how long his fingers had been— he could honestly say he'd never thought to measure them. In an almost animated-fashion, five little fingernails emerged from under the skin with a *pop*.

"You're a quick learner." Diedre chimed. "Can't say I'm surprised. You've got yourself a great teacher."

A grin stretched unnaturally wide across Diedre's face. Magnus wiggled his fingers. He couldn't help but smile.

Absurdity. That's what it was. All of it. Everything that had happened since he stepped into that saloon. Absurdity had seeped into his mind and taken root in the growing cracks of his reality. Weeds in cement. He had tried to pull at them along the ride, but as he pulled, the cracks grew further. Now, at least, flowers seemed to bud. Dandelions growing between the shattered remnants of life as he once knew it. The universe as he once knew it. So he smiled at Diedre, because for the first time, he understood how the myiad's mind operated.

A cracked sidewalk full of dandelions.

To his amazement, a round cloud of white seedlings grew from his fingertips. Dandelions sprouted and blossomed from his hands. He blew at them gently. Countless seeds took to the air and floated away from his fingertips. They hovered a few feet from him, then evaporated.

"I'm not really human anymore, am I?"

Despite the unavoidable truth he faced, Magnus had hoped this was all somehow a dream. In Diedre's sympathetic stare, he accepted the answer.

"You'll help me, right?" He asked.

"Yes." Diedre said tenderly. It was a rare form for them. "I'll give you the crash course of a millennium as soon as we're clear of this titanium deathtrap."

As though on cue, the clatter of velexi claws echoed through the halls.

"Deal." Magnus said. "Let's get out—"

A distant shout bounced along the hallway ahead. Deathly quiet, both Magnus and Diedre peered down the long corridor. It carried on forty yards before meeting a wall and splitting off to the right and left. The nearest corridor to Magnus, where the velex had pounced from, was only a few feet away. Together Magnus and Diedre caught each other's look, then began to creep toward a side corridor on their tiptoes.

"— DIEDRE!"

Another shout reverberated from the distant hallway's end.

Skidding around the corner, April led Gideon, Rex, and half a dozen crew members of various species in a dead sprint. Kiora trailed the pack. After the Egyptian princess had cleared the turn by five long strides, a torrent of black legs and chattering teeth spilled into the hallway. Four velexi clawed over each other in a roaring tide down the hallway, tearing flesh and scraping metal all the way to the ceiling.

"Run!" Diedre said.

Turning, Magnus and Diedre only made it three steps before two more velex turned a corner at the opposite end of the corridor.

"Shit." Diedre fiddled with the Hadron. "This thing needs a recharge, and I don't think I can axe all of them!"

Magnus looked down at his hands. He had stopped one velex without violence, could he stop six? Would his body even be able to shapeshift after he pushed it so hard? His arm was mostly numb. He wasn't sure he could conjure up another dandelion, let alone an industrial fan for six velexi. His fingers twitched. An anxious pinch in his chest turned his stomach. The flat of his palm turned a sickly green color to match how he felt.

"The pocket watch." Magnus said. Then, he shouted. "The pocket watch!"

April understood the prompt. She ripped the watch from her pocket and twisted the dial. A green light glowed sharply against the flashing crimson of the hallway.

"Diedre, can you reach them?" Magnus asked.

"Bet your ass, I can."

The myiad's hand shot out like a harpoon. April and the others were thirty feet away at least, but the myiad's shot was true. Silhouetted by green and crimson light against a backdrop of black arms and yellow teeth, Diedre's hand found April's.

Magnus immediately felt the warm glow of golden rings. His eyes stretched beyond the traveling horizon a moment before the velexi hoard descended upon them.

XXVIII

April

April breathed in short, raspy breaths. Diedre's ship was a labyrinth, and she had practically run a marathon through it. Velexi swarmed each twisting hallway so that she and the others had to double back, run in circles, duck, dip, dive and dodge every which way to avoid them. Her lungs burned like the sun and her stomach felt as heavy as the moon. She needed to lay off whiskey-n-wing Wednesdays and hit the gym.

"Where are we?" Diedre asked.

Opening a single eye, April discovered a familiar looking ceiling, laces with dark wood scaffolding and a few rec league jerseys hanging by fishing ling. April opened her other eye. While running for her life, she hadn't thought much about when to set the pocket watch. *Take me away from this shithole!* That was the only thought she had considered, and in that endeavor, her goal was achieved.

Gideon knelt next to her, breathing heavily as well. Alan sat beside him, rubbing his cheek on the soldier's calf and purring. The cat seemed the only one of the group content with the outcome of their escape. Kiora stood near Diedre and Magnus, hardly winded, yet stiff with alertness. Rex sat among four blue-suited members of Diedre's crew, already drafting a report on a tablet attached to his wrist.

"The saloon." April said in a hoarse voice.

The familiar photos on the wall brought an ease of comfort. Family portraits of April, Grandpa Sylas, Gainsborough, and the older generations of saloon owners. A few jerseys and local sports paraphernalia hung framed in a corner beside a wall mounted TV. Circular tables scattered the open room and wore their share of stacked stools. Behind the bar, a dozen long rows of bottles glistened in the warm light. A cold breeze slithered into the saloon's front door and passed by McQuade, the taxidermy duck.

"*When* are we?" Diedre clarified.

Judging by the cool air, empty saloon and lack of light, April supposed it must have been early morning. Without the TDU operating, the saloon wouldn't host travelers after two AM. Then it dawned on her what Diedre was truly asking.

"Uncle G!" April tried to shout. It came out as a half-wheeze.

"Uncle G!" Diedre echoed with a bolstered volume that was surely the effect of shapeshifted lungs. The shout rattled the framed walls, the delicately stacked stools, and even the floor boards themselves. Magnus covered his ears.

"Could have given me a warning." He said.

"Your ears are fine. Myiads don't have to worry about things like hearing loss." Diedre said.

"Still hurt." Magnus said.

The kitchen door swung open and clattered against the wall behind the bar.

"April?" Gainsborough's voice crossed the room and picked April's head up.

"Uncle G, what day is it?" April said.

"Saturday." He said in a flat, rusty voice. He wore a matching set of red and black plaid pajamas.

"The date, man." Diedre hissed.

Gainsborough paused for a moment, then spoke. "August thirty first, two thousand and twenty four. Morning of. About three AM."

April's stomach sank. It didn't give her time to react before it bounced back up. She rolled over and puked Diedre's thousand dollar whiskey all over the floor.

"I'll get the mop." Gainsborough sighed as he left.

"How did the velexi find your ship?" Kiora asked.

"Good question." Diedre spat. They threw back their coat and drew two laser pistols. One they trained on Gideon, the other, Kiora.

Gideon froze, still kneeling on the floor. Kiora spared no time in reaching for her blades.

"Nuh-uh, princess, I'll shoot before you can draw them."

"What's going on?" Magnus asked.

Groaning, April wiped her face with a sleeve and climbed to her feet.

"We've got a mole." Diedre said. Their skin adopted a sharp red hue.

"You call me a traitor?" Kiora's glare was as sharp as her daggers.

"I lost my ship. Most of my crew is dead. I don't know which of you it is, but I'll drop you both before I let one of you get away with it."

April lifted her hands shakily. "Diedre, calm down. I spoke to Gideon, it's not him, and—"

Both laser pistols swung to aim at Kiora.

"Should have guessed," Diedre said. "Couldn't stand being kept under the myiad thumb, so you teamed up with Jaakobah to take them all down, huh?"

A snarl curled Kiora's lips. "Watch your tongue, else I will rip it from your skull. I am the proud blade of Sekhmet."

Diedre laughed emphatically. "Where were you when Sekhmet was killed by Jaakobah? Feeding him our location you traitorous, power hungry, walking identity crisis of an Egyptian princess—"

Kiora drew Time and Patience. Diedre shot both laser pistols. Kiora lunged.

Time stabbed into Diedre's right arm and pressed it up, sending one photon laser beam into the ceiling above the bar. Patience pierced Diedre's chest directly over the heart. From the second pistol, a white-hot laser struck Kiora's thigh, spilling the smell of smoking leather and flesh into the saloon.

"I have yearned for this moment, myiad." Kiora smiled as she twisted the blade in Diedre's chest.

A third hand erupted from Diedre's chest, bursting through the front right flap of their trench coat, and sucker punching Kiora square in the jaw. The Egyptian princess stumbled back in a daze.

"Took the words out of my mouth, princess." Diedre said, plucking Patience from their chest like a rose thorn. The wound sealed over instantly. "Forget something?"

A lion's roar of a battle cry sprang forth from Kiora's mouth. Diedre responded by shaping their face into a lion's snout and letting loose an actual roar. The two charged toward each other.

"Stop it!" Magnus shouted. His two arms shot forward and splintered into a dozen fleshy tentacles. Like fish in a net, he scooped up the two and held them apart.

Stunned silence beset the saloon.

April was sure she was hallucinating. She must have slipped and fallen on the ship, banged her head, bled out and lived her final moments in an imaginary timeline of her mind where Magnus could shapeshift like a myiad.

Gideon's bellowing laughter cut the silence. There was no dream that could sleep through the man's laugh.

"The lord works in mysterious ways!"

"What is this?" Kiora squirmed to break free from Magnus' hold.

Magnus audibly gulped. "I'm uh— a myiad. Now. I wasn't before."

April wanted to lie down again. She had a mild headache, her lungs still burned from running, and now she was losing her mind.

"How is this possible?" Kiora asked.

"Yeah, you don't know everything, do you?" Diedre stuck out their tongue at Kiora. It slithered out to a sharp point and wiggled like a serpent. "Too late to report back to your boss! We found our weapon!"

"That's not exactly what—" Magnus began.

"—I do not serve Jaakobah, you mindless sandworm!" Kiora spat. She turned her gaze so sharply at Magnus that the man flinched. "How have you gone from human to myiad? Such a thing is impossible."

"Osiris." April pieced the puzzle together. "He couldn't extract his genome, so he infused his genetic code with yours. He didn't break the limitations, he found a workaround—"

A slow clap at the saloon door set her nerves on edge. A chill trickled down April's spine as she turned. Standing in the doorway, black robes stood against a twilit night sky. Jaakobah's hood was raised, its shadow covering his face as though light was barred from passing its veil. Long, charred fingers on black palms came together in slow rhythm.

"Well done." His voice sent a second chill down her spine. "Isn't it fitting? They exiled me for the truths I had uncovered, then experimented with it themselves. The limitations are no more than—"

Time soared across the room. The bronze blade froze in the air before the shadowed hood.

"Seriously?" An amused tone overcame Jaakobah's harsh voice. Somehow, April found it undercut the threat of him. His scary, killer-voice was more forced than he let on, like an action movie villain.

"You speak too much." Kiora said.

Diedre nodded. "Got that right."

"As do you." Kiora hissed.

"Two for two, traitor." Diedre's stuck out their serpentine tongue again.

"Traitor?" Jaakobah cackled like thunder on a black night. "You think I swayed the blade of Sekhmet to feed me your timestamps? Dear cousin, Diedre, you are dumber than I thought."

Kiora clicked her tongue in agreement.

The mole. April had been too focused on escaping velex claws that she had nearly forgotten. Kiora wasn't the traitor. For that, April was able to take in a slight breath of relief. Diedre and Gideon were crossed off her mental checklist, too. She eyed Magnus-turned-myiad. Painted on his face was fear, worry, and a smidge of queasiness. The man looked like the mere thought of lying would give him a stomach ache.

April didn't think any of her companions were traitors, and yet, Jaakobah had known where they were at every step of the journey. He'd followed them to Osiris' cabin, he found them on Diedre's starship, and he knew the exact moment they had arrived at the saloon.

"Who?" The thought spilled from her mind to her mouth. Before she could ask it with intention, the kitchen door swung open and slammed the bar back.

"I've got the mop, but you're gonna have to clean your own—" Gainsborough's voice trailed off.

Like a brick to the face, the answer struck April. Like a second brick to the face, Jaakobah laughed another harsh, gravelly chortle.

"No," April turned slowly. "Uncle G?"

Gainsborough's gaze wandered to the floor. He rung his knuckles on the mop stick.

"Jaakobah has shown me that the limitations aren't set in stone. They can be bent. Imagine, April? I could hold my sweet Lara in my arms, again. And you could visit Sylas, or meet your parents." His voice trembled. "He promised he would spare us if I gave him your time stamps—"

"—He's lying!" April shouted. The words were hollow in her mouth. Was he? Jaakobah was a xenocidal maniac, but had he ever lied to her? Magnus was living proof that at least the first limitation was false. Jaakobah had been telling the truth.

Gainsborough crossed the room slowly. He drew a wide berth around Kiora and flinched as a hiss escaped her mouth.

"Do not listen to them, April." Kiora said rigidly. "The laws of the universe exist with purpose. It tainted Osiris' mind and body. What toll has it taken from you, Deceiver?"

A snort came from Jaakobah's hood. Ten charred fingers drew back the veil from his face. Patches of charred black skin wrapped his oblong head. Large lumps pressed out like bones had grown against the hold of his skin. An echo of a human head was present, but far removed. Green and yellow sludge dripped down from the seams between patches, spilling into hollow pits that once held eyes, and a lipless, yellow-fanged mouth. Three more tiny mouths adorned his face, one set beside his left ear, another above his left brow, and the final, over his right cheek bone. They chattered excitedly, but it was only from the larger mouth that he spoke.

April wanted to gag. She choked it down. The sight was unholy, but the smell was deathly. It pierced her raw sinuses with the scents of rotten meat and sulfur.

"There is a price to pay for freedom. Osiris understood. The human will, soon enough." The patches of skin on

Jaakobah's face stretched at their seams as his jaw moved.

She cast an inspecting look toward Magnus. He looked like the same lanky guy that had walked into her saloon before, save for his blond bun being a bit messier. There was something else. Something in his stare. A distance, or absence, as though he wasn't entirely present. April's focus turned back toward Jaakobah.

Jaakobah raised a single hand to her, his long, black fingers reaching forward, scorched palm open. "Join me, or die with the others."

Gainsborough watched her with sunken, urging eyes. The old man looked fragile. He shivered anxiously under the shadow of his new master. Softly, he spoke.

"That wasn't the deal. I gave you their timestamps. You said you'd spare April."

A blackened hand swept through the air and landed firmly on Gainsborough's nape.

"I agreed to offer mercy. It is hers to accept or refuse."

Electric silence filled the saloon. It pulsed in twitching fingers over daggers, a hammer, and laser pistols. All eyes were cast upon April; all hands waited for her answer.

April's mind raced. Gainsborough, her only living family, had betrayed her. April had been the traitor. She had inadvertently given Jaakobah their whereabouts, led him to Osiris, and brought the velexi to Diedre's ship. How had she gotten into this? How did it all come down to her? She was a bartender. All she wanted was to pour a drink for herself and call it a day.

"And the saloon?" She asked.

"April—" Diedre hissed.

"—The saloon will burn either way." Jaakobah

answered. "It is a relic of the old system. A system that harbored unnecessary despair. My timeline will have no need for it."

"You can't honestly be considering this, right April?" Diedre scowled. "You would take a deal with that monster?"

"I—"

What chance would they have at stopping Jaakobah? Diedre had said something about Magnus being a weapon, but the kid looked as worn out as a used doggy bag. Not only that, she wasn't sure Magnus was entirely himself at the moment. Kiora had a hole in her leg from Diedre's pistol, and that was the *first* time April had ever seen Diedre actually hit a mark they aimed at. That left Gideon, a medieval soldier with a long hammer. Their odds weren't great.

She could save herself. If Jaakobah could bend all three limitations, she might even be able to bring her grandfather back. It shouldn't have been possible, but what ground did impossibility have to stand on? Was anything she had known real, or was it all a fabrication of some powerful alien tampering with time, unhindered and all powerful? Could her grandfather have been saved?

In that single moment, April felt hopeless.

"You can really do it?" April asked.

A wicked smile returned to the patchwork face. "Take my hand. By sunrise, you will be laughing by your grandfather's side."

Her hand twitched. An unconscious reaction. It wanted to reach forward. Each molecule of her body desired to know the truth. To save the saloon. To save herself. Grandpa Sylas would never have struck a deal with the devil. She wasn't her grandfather.

April felt her mind crumbling apart.

"I— I can't— I don't—" April stuttered.

The others stood behind her. She could feel their tension. Their bated breaths. What tie did she have to them? Two strangers, an ex lover, and *Diedre*. What would happen to them if she accepted? Jaakobah had made it a point to offer mercy to April alone.

Gainsborough pleaded with sullen eyes, urging her to give in.

The decision twisted her gut and set it aflame. Air burned like gasoline in her chest. Her nerves were a thousand lit flames. The flame rose, not from her mouth, but her eyes, melting down her cheeks.

"Time— I need time—" April managed to say as she wiped her tears. The room grew dark in her vision, and she felt her body drift. Natural traveling came easy. It was an old friend after a series of forced traveling. Much kinder to the body than forced traveling. All it took was a push. There weren't any rings of light, nor any stretching of the body. A single thought, a slight urge, and she could whisk herself away from all the worries of any given present.

April traveled through time. Not to anywhere or when, only away from that moment.

XXIX

April

A curtain of fog rolled over the dark asphalt of main street. Hidden under that curtain, a barefoot, rag-covered little girl wept for all to hear.

There were none to hear, though. On a Wednesday night in spring, Tombstone was a desolate place. Where tourists roamed and raved of historical shootouts by day, a haunting solitude possessed the night. Some believed spirits of miners and cowboys remained in such crowds as to outnumber the permanent residents. Strange things happened at night in Tombstone.

The little girl knew nothing of spirits or ghosts. The little girl knew nothing of anything in particular. She wasn't sure how she had arrived in Tombstone, or where it was. A vague thought of her mother tickled her head like wispy fog tickled the rooftops. Music tickled the rooftops, too, swirling the fog like an oil painting. Rings and twangs and chimes foreign to her little ears. She paused her pouting just long enough to decide on which road the melody drifted. Then, once she had settled on one, she returned to crying as she toddled on forward.

A dirt parking lot sat at the far end of the road. Bright light shone through tall windows of a building. It was the first light the little girl had seen since becoming lost. Wearily, she sniffled. Her little heart not able to weep for a second longer, she set on toward the front door. Her little bare feet stung with each step.

A woman stumbled out of the double saloon doors. The little girl watched as the woman gathered her bearings, took a step, smacked a pack of cigarettes til one came out, and leaned against the building's wall as she lit it. The tip of the cigarette glowed brightly as the woman breathed in, and the little girl noticed her eyes glow as well. In the dim light that floated from the windows and into the night, the woman's eyes glowed a soft amethyst color.

"Flerovium!" The woman jumped. They hadn't seen the little girl standing only a few feet away. Harshly blinking, they weren't quite sure the little girl existed. "You're real, right?"

The little girl nodded.

"Well that ain't gonna cut it. Little girl ghosts silently gesture all the time in scary movies. You gotta speak if you want me to believe you're real." The woman slurred their words. "I don't trust ghosts, but I trust whiskey less." Their two eyes blinked out of sync. "You real?"

"Yes." The little girl whimpered.

After a long drag of their cigarette, the woman spoke again.

"Give me your hand." Holding the cigarette in their mouth, the woman held out a long fingered hand. The little girl offered her own. Pulling a small, circular device from their coat pocket, the woman touched it to the little girl's hand. A tiny bulb illuminated with a dull green glow.

The amethyst-eyed woman sighed deeply. "Okay kid, wait here a minute."

After snuffing out the second half of their cigarette, they combed their hands through thick, black hair, blinked away drunkenness, and stumbled back into the saloon. The little girl found that she was just tall enough to peer through the window.

Life bustled in the place. Strange life. Odd colored people the little girl hadn't seen. Red and green and blue. Some of them had many heads, or lines of ears down their arms and bodies. Others were see-through, like they were made of water, or glass. A strange half-spider woman played cards with a creature that looked like a man with a German shepherd's head and another man who sat inside of a standing mirror. When he needed to move chips, he reached out of the mirror, a glassy arm sparkling like a monastery mosaic. At the bar, there sat three green things, each the size of the little girl's feet, with ears longer than their bodies. Beside them, a golden sphere hovered above a stool. A glass defied gravity and rose up to its center, pouring liquid directly into the sphere, though no hole or seam could be seen.

The amethyst eyed woman stood behind the bar,

speaking to an older man with white fluffy hair and light, sun-touched skin. He turned, his soft brown eyes settling on her. She quickly ducked and turned away from the window as though she hadn't been caught.

A moment later, the woman walked steadily through the doorway and placed themselves in the same spot on the wall they had leaned on before. They drew another cigarette from their pack. The fluffy-headed old man stepped out from the melodious building. He blew air out in a whistle and wrapped his arms around himself.

"Phew, it's a cold one." The deep voice rocked like an oscillating fan; persistent and slow, with a steady breeze in each word. It swept the little girl's worry away, and laid it down to rest in a gentle cushion of vibration. He squatted down with a belabored sigh and looked into her eyes. "Are you cold?"

The little girl nodded. He took off his black leather jacket and wrapped it around her. She swam in the tall man's coat; it was a full length dress to the little girl, and even still, it bunched up at her feet.

"Better?"

"Yes." The little girl wiped her eyes.

"Told you, Sylas." The amethyst eyed woman said. "My drinking ghosts don't speak. Figured that one out in Alpha Centauri at a hole-in-the-planet pub called Kenta—"

"Diedre." Sylas said, his breezy voice a momentary harsh wind.

"Right." Diedre said. "I'll shut up. You're the professional at this kind of thing."

Sylas smiled gently.

"What's your name?"

The little girl did not answer. She didn't know what her name was. She wasn't sure she had a name.

Sylas' gentle smile held strong.

"How about your parents? Mom? Dad? Moms or dads? Do you know where they are?"

The little girl shook her head.

"What do you remember? Are there buildings like this where you are from?"

The little girl's face creased into a frown. She couldn't remember anything before that night.

"Hey, that's alright. No need to get upset. We'll find your home, alright?" Sylas reached out and pulled a lollipop from the leather jacket's pocket. "Here. Oh, root beer flavored. Not my favorite, but it's all I've got right now. Wait here, alright? We'll get you some warm food and clothes, in a minute."

Sylas stood and turned away. The little girl stared at the root beer lollipop in her hand. Her stomach grumbled, though she didn't find the root beer lollipop appealing.

"What's the protocol, Sylas?" Diedre whispered. "You get kids like this?"

"Doesn't happen much anymore." Sylas said. "Since the council started sending their hounds out, time orphans are a rare sight. They find most genomes when the hosts are still newborns. Ain't like when I was younger."

"Three hundred years ago?" Diedre smirked.

"Try thirty." Sylas eyed the little girl. The lollipop's wrapper lay on the dirt next to her, though she only sniffed at it. "We can't let her wander about. She's lucky to have landed here."

"What do you want to do?"

Sylas sighed. "All lost traveler children go straight to Portum."

"Doesn't sound like you to give the council what they want." Diedre smiled. The little girl stared in amazement. Diedre's grin grew from ear to ear, and had far too many teeth. They noticed the little girl watching them, and blinked their eyes sideways. The little girl's jaw dropped.

"She'll stay here." Sylas said. "These time orphans who accidentally travel too young, they're exactly what the council wants to find. No past. No memories. Easy to raise into their dirty work. At least here, we can help her try to remember. See if she has a family."

Diedre nodded and took a long drag from their cigarette. Sylas knelt in front of the little girl again.

"Would you like to stay here till we can find your parents?" Sylas asked.

After the break from crying, the little girl's reservoir of tears had been refilled. The dam broke, and hot streams ran down her cheeks.

"Oh, no need to cry, dear. I won't bite." Sylas leaned in and smiled. "Diedre there might, but only if you get on their bad side." He turned, and together they watched as Diedre thoughtlessly picked at their many teeth with a long nailed finger. "But I'll tell you what; you cry as much as you need to, alright? You ever hear that saying about April showers?"

The little girl shook her head.

"April showers bring May flowers." Sylas reached out and plucked a marigold from the planter under the saloon's window. He combed back the little girl's thick hair and tucked the flower onto her ear. "So you cry all you need to, just like April, and when we find your parents, you'll have a whole bouquet of flowers for them."

Sylas took her little hands in his own. They were calloused and confident.

"I bet you're starving. There's some stew left over from the dinner shift. You can just call me Grandpa Sylas, alright?"

Diedre laughed. "Grandpa Sylas? That's a riot." They peered down at the little girl. "What are we gonna call her?"

April's face burned with hot, thick tears. She cradled herself, squeezed her eyes shut and tried to dam the flow. Her fingers rubbed against her back, grasping at the familiar comfort of the leather jacket.

Another hand touched her gently. Her skin shivered. She threw herself forward, twisted, and aimed with a finger on the trigger.

"Don't shoot!" Magnus said. He raised his hands up. To his own surprise, they continued to grow upward from the elbow, until his forearms were three feet longer than they should have been. April supposed what *should have been* was relative after seeing him shapeshift at the saloon. Only when April lowered the gun did his arms shrink to a relatively-regular proportion. "I haven't quite figured this *'you're a myiad, now'* thing."

April watched wordlessly. Her face was numb.

"I also haven't figured out traveling, but I grabbed you right before you left." Magnus scratched the back of his head. "Guess I don't need the pocket watch anymore."

The revolver fell limply from April's hand. It landed in tilled dirt. They had traveled to a wheat field near dusk. The time period remained a mystery. Brisk air drew steam from wet hot cheeks.

Nearby, a time local stood no more than twenty feet away. A man of medium height, maybe an inch or two shorter than her. He wore a heavy blue coat over a color stained shirt, and a hat atop a cushion of red hair that wrapped around his chin and mouth in a thick beard. His left ear was marred and misshapen. In his hand, he wielded a paintbrush thick with yellow paint, but his attention had been drawn away from the standing easel and onto the two strangers who appeared out of thin air.

"You got a problem?" April shouted harshly.

The man slowly shook his head, then returned to his easel.

Magnus watched her with a face twisting in thought. *Literally* twisting; his nose wandered to the left side of his face, then, as he changed what he intended to say, it returned, and his left eye sagged to his cheekbone. "So, what's the plan?"

The wind swept the wheat fields and whistled into oncoming dusk. A murder of crows cawed ravenously in the distance.

"There is no plan." April said.

"Why did we come here, then?"

"So I didn't do something I'd regret." She kept her face hidden. Magnus shifted uncomfortably.

"What's that?" Magnus asked. "You were going to take the deal?"

Hearing it spoken felt like a thousand needles pinned her heart.

Magnus grunted. "I didn't think—"

"—you thought wrong." April said sharply.

"You've seen what he is." Magnus said. "What he does to people. He's a murderer, April. You would work with him to save a building?"

"The saloon is my home. My only home. Grandpa Sylas built it for people like me. It's more than just a building. It's a home for travelers who knew nothing, came from nothing. Older folks who wandered helplessly. Kids who lost their parents and didn't know why. He gave that place to me—"

"—April—"

"—How could you understand it? You can't even raise a hand when lives depend on it. You don't know what this life is. All of time at your fingertips, and still there isn't enough to spend with the ones who matter. It's a cosmic joke. Yes, I'm afraid that I will take Jaakobah's offer. If there's even a chance that I can save my home, a *fraction* of a chance that I can see my grandpa again, there will always be a part of me that craves it. And that *building*? That saloon is everything Grandpa made with his life. He handed it down to me. It is my grandfather, and mine, and all I have left of him. I can't lose it. I don't want to make a deal with that *monster*, but I could. I know I could. I'd hate myself for it, but at least the saloon would still be standing."

The one eared painter sneezed. April turned and glared at him again. He hurriedly took up his easel and paints, and left.

"There's no plan." April continued. "I got out of there because we can't beat him, and I sure as hell can't let myself join him. If I sit in the past, at least I can die knowing the saloon was never lost in my life."

The words hung in the air a moment before a breeze carried them away.

"You're right," Magnus said. "I don't know what it means to be a traveler. It's new to me." His facial features twisted in a slight spiral as he raised a finger and tapped his temple. "My mind doesn't feel like my own anymore. Neither does my body. Not quite me, but not quite someone else. It's strange. I shouldn't be here, or in Ancient Egypt or the future, but I was. I am? I don't know, time is tricky. All I know is, at some point in time, you stuck your neck out to save mine. You had no motive or compensation. It was compassion. Whoever your grandpa was, he didn't give you a dusty old building, he gave you *that*. Compassion. That's yours now. That's what you carry. And that *monster*, Jaakobah? He's evil, April. A fairy-tale kind of evil. Pure. Like the devil, or the CEO of a bank. Temptation doesn't make a person that way, but giving in might."

The look in his eyes pierced April like a bronze dagger.

"How about you, huh? Easy to call out other people for being afraid, but you're no better." April's anger held for one final jab at the man. "What will you do against Jaakobah? Watch him kill the rest of us while you sit back. Can you even throw a single punch?"

"It doesn't matter." His lips thinned into a pained smile. "That kind of evil? I couldn't live with myself if I didn't try. Can you?"

In defiance of a quivering lip, he forced a smug smile, as though he knew the answer before asking the question. Then, he was gone. The seamless act of natural traveling. No stretching of the body, nor of the mind, no wormhole of golden light. There one moment, and the next, gone.

"Of course it matters." April crumbled once more. Lifting her knees to her chest, she wrapped her elbows around them and tucked her face. She could have laughed at herself. A little girl alone in an unknown time and a strange place.

Hidden behind her knees, April's frown sharpened into a violent scowl. Red dripped from her nails squeezing into her palms. Anger rolled through her like a tempest.

Magnus was right. That pissed her off.

She had run away. That also pissed her off.

What pissed her off the most of all was Jaakobah. The manipulating myiad threatening what she loved. *Who* she loved. What kind of person would she be to turn her back on the entire timeline for a selfish reason like saving a building? Seeing her grandpa? How much blood would be on her hands if she had accepted Jaakobah's offer. All for what? A chance that Jaakobah could be telling the truth. That he may be able to bring back her Grandfather?

"It doesn't matter." April found the words in her own mouth. Magnus was right. If she didn't try to stop Jaakobah, then why had she ever run the saloon in the first place? Why had she helped Magnus, or anyone, for that matter? Why did she hold onto what her grandfather had taught her in life? "I've got to try. Even if Jaakobah has found a way to break the limitations, or at least the one—"

Her voice tapered off to the sound of cawing crows. An idea came to April. A plan. She wasn't sure it would work, but that didn't matter. She would try.

"I'm sorry Grandpa. I got a little lost there for a minute." April wiped her face with a leather sleeve. "It's time I should be getting back to the saloon. There's a bar fight I need to wrap up."

XXX

April

Experienced travelers could arrive within ten seconds of their target moment in time, and within a foot of their target location. April had tested her own skill and found that, at most, she was only ever six seconds late, and three inches off. So when April materialized in the bar just about where she had been, no more than six seconds had passed.

In those six seconds, things had gone to hell.

Every table in the bar lay on its side and shared the floor with the broken glass of countless shattered picture frames. Dozens of shattered bottles littered the room, mostly in the far corners where they sat as the basis for rising pyres of flame. April assumed Diedre had the bright idea of Molotov cocktails. A mix of smoke and every kind of alcohol stung April's nose. Where weaker booze didn't light, a collegiate jungle juice seeped into the floorboards. Against her own senses, she spared a millisecond of thought to how difficult it would be to clean out of the wood.

"Ah," Jaakobah growled. Gainsborough was nowhere to be seen, but the velex beside him still twitched eagerly. "Welcome back. I presume you have decided—"

April raised her revolver and shot three times. She knew it wouldn't do much, but she couldn't handle another monologue. Three bullets struck the air and slowed to a crawl. He grinned, plucked a bullet from the air and flicked it to the floor.

"April!" Diedre shouted.

The myiad rose from the bar and aimed the Hadron micro particle accelerator. April dove over the counter just as a yellow glow formed at the tip of Diedre's rifle. With a sleeved arm, Jaakobah picked up the large velex and held it as a shield against the rifle's line of sight. A yellow light formed in the velex' black body. It clawed at its own body before suddenly erupting from the inside out. Slime and innards splattered to each corner of the room, velex mucous sizzling as it half-doused the rising lines of fire. The smoke had a nauseating stench of burning grease. A thick sheet of velex innards hovered in the air before Jaakobah before cascading to the floor in thick, chunky ribbons.

"Howdy." Diedre said as April landed on the rubber mat next to them. "Thought you lost your cool."

"I did." A thick sweat had already formed on her neck. The flame was spreading quickly up the walls of the room. "What happened?"

"My crew went out the back, your piece of shit uncle out

the front."

"Where is the boy?" Kiora asked. She crouched against the bar counter, the dagger, Patience, in her right hand. Gideon crouched behind her, peeking over the counter.

"Magnus isn't here?" April asked.

She could have punched herself. Of course he wouldn't be on time. He was brand new to traveling. He might be hours late, if he could find the right moment at all. Without a guide, he could be lost for weeks before getting the hang of traveling. Even then, it wouldn't be precise to the exact minute.

"Cover!" Gideon shouted.

A table flew over the counter and crashed into the glass bottle display. The vodka section shattered and spilled onto the floor. April sighed in relief. A second table flew over the bar and crashed into the row of whiskey bottles.

"I'll kill you for that, Jaakobah!" April shouted.

"You have decided your fate, April." Jaakobah said. "Face me and wipe away the ways of the old timeline. You have no place in mine."

Diedre opened up the flap of their coat and unclipped an oblong metal canister. "Eat shit, asshole!" They pulled a pin and tossed it over the bar counter.

BOOM.

The saloon rattled with the grenade's detonation. An eye-watering note of sulfur joined the brewing mixture of smells. Velex guts, sulfur, booze and smoke mingled together into a nose-numbing concoction.

"Jesus, Diedre," Gideon said. "What was that?"

"*Garadrin* feces grenade" Diedre grinned. "Top quality black market —"

Two heavy thuds turned their heads to the end of the back bar. Jaakobah stood behind the bar, his two hooved feet sinking into the thick rubber mat.

"Lord," Gideon whispered. "The Devil walks among us."

As with his patched face, a twisted, stitched together amalgamation of different species' formed Jaakobah's body. A goat hoof carried his left side; an ill formed horse hoof, his right. Tree trunk thick legs coated with patches of fur, skin and scales held up a hulking humanoid torso. Four arms of different lengths sprouted from him, two on either side. Where hands should have been, each arm carried strange appendages, each more unnatural than the last. On his left two arms, a falcon's talons and a lion's paw; the right two, an amorphous, gel-like globule clung to one, and a massive chrome hammerhead made the other. Black fabric stretched across his chest and waist in torn shreds. Underneath, where his scarred flesh could be seen, it constantly shifted, his flesh folding in on itself and twisting back out in a grotesque, everlasting phase of myiad shapeshifting.

Jaakobah roared. It pierced April's skull. She covered her ears, as did the rest. What was left of the bottle display erupted one by one, raining glass and booze over them

When his roar ended, Jaakobah raised his chrome hammer-hand and dropped it into the bar. The wood folded like playdoh.

"Agonize while you can, April!" The voice that came from his largest mouth was gargled and heavy. "I will create a universe without despair, without hunger or pain, and you have chosen to deny it!"

"Create this, asshole!"

Diedre pointed the Hadron micro particle accelerator at

him. It whirred for only a moment before Jaakobah's talon-tipped hand shot forward, tore the rifle from Diedre's hands, and snapped it in half like it the titanium frame was a twig.

"Aw, I just got that."

Gideon stood up. Compared to Jaakobah's hulking frame, the soldier looked to be a child before a grown man.

"*Allow me to wear your whole armor, God, that I may be able to stand against the wiles of the devil.*" Gideon stamped the butt of his lucerne hammer into the rubber mat. Shifting his feet into a battle stance, he took the hammer in both hands, and stood resolute. It may have been a trick of fire light or reflected glass, but April thought, for a moment, that a warm glow surrounded Gideon as he spoke.

Jaakobah laughed a thick, oily laugh. It seeped into April's ears and skin, each peak rattling her bones.

"No god can save you." Jaakobah swept his arm forward in a blur of charred flesh. Gideon braced for impact with the shaft of his hammer. Another blur, bright orange and furry, traced a line like lightning through the air.

Alan Rickman yowled as it anchored its claws into Jaakobah's shoulder. Hissing nastily, it unhinged its mouth unlike any cat April had seen. The sound of sinew stretching and bones cracking rang from the jaw as it opened a foot wide. Three rows of sharp teeth spun in its mouth like drills. Alan bit into Jaakobah's chrome-hammer arm, its spinning teeth tearing the limb from the body. With a heavy *thump*, the sundered arm fell to the ground in a puddle of green puss and black ooze.

"Remind me to pick up some cat gogurt for Alan." April whispered.

"What is gogurt?" Kiora asked.

"God's blessing is named Alan Rickman!" Gideon pointed and laughed at Jaakobah's dismembered arm.

Jaakobah snatched Alan's nape with a hand of falcon talons. Alan hissed to the tune of whirring drills. Jaakobah returned a wet hiss of his own as he threw the cat across the saloon. Alan collided with the far wall just beside a still-hanging photo of the saloon's previous cat, Java Chip. Both Alan and the photo of Java fell to the floor in a lump pile of fur and broken glass.

Gideon stopped laughing. "Devil!" He shouted as he swung his hammer. It collided with the air a foot from Jaakobah's chest.

"How will your god stop this?" Jaakobah raised his lion's paw. The thick padded paw was the size of Gideon's chest, with five claws that extended out the length of Gideon's face. He swiped toward the old soldier's neck.

"No—" April screamed. Just before the strike landed, another blur of color formed in the air. She squinted as her eyes tried to decipher the moment. "Magnus?"

Above Jaakobah, a man who wasn't quite a human anymore, appeared. Though it was far too quick for April's eye to discern as it happened, Magnus' feet phased into existence first, and they settled directly on top of Jaakobah's striking arm. His body followed and weighed down the arm so the only torn flesh was not that of Gideon's gullet, but the rubber mat on the floor. Jaakobah's claws sunk into the mat. Magnus balanced on the arm like a surfer riding an angry wave.

"Thank God!" Magnus exclaimed.

Gideon nodded furiously. "He protects!"

"I traveled to two different saloons and a handful of

other times before I got the hang of it." Magnus said, not bothered by the hulking form of Jaakobah directly behind him.

Jaakobah's face shuddered in maroon and violet hues. Rage painted his twisting face, but small strokes of something else peeked through his eyes as he watched Magnus. The first April had seen of it. Concern. Magnus was *touching* Jaakobah. Now that April had a moment to think about it, she realized Alan Rickman had done it just a moment before. The expressive singularity defense didn't affect them. Why was that? April's mind reeled for an answer.

"Seek out Osiris. He holds an answer to defeating the Defiler."

Shai's words fell into place. Osiris had not only given Magnus his genome, but he had changed Magnus' genetic code. If the forcefield wasn't a result of an ESD as they had all assumed, but rather a product of a mutation in the myiad genome, they might have a fighting chance.

That was, if Magnus could fight.

"Get off of me!" Still struggling to pull his arm out from under Magnus' feet, Jaakobah threw a side hook with the glob hand. Gideon leaned away, but Magnus kept to his balancing act.

As Jaakobah's glob fist neared Magnus, his stomach stretched back like taffy and bent around the punch. The strike flew past the man and slammed into a sink. Jaakobah's liquid flesh dripped from the glob hand and melted the steel sink basin like water over cotton candy.

"Nice one!" Diedre stretched out their arm and offered Magnus a high five. He smacked it high and stepped off of Jaakobah's arm. "Look out!"

Jaakobah slugged a hook at Magnus' head. Without looking, Magnus shrunk his head to the size of a tennis ball. Razor sharp talons trimmed a single lock of his blond hair as they floated overhead.

"Take this!" Kiora threw Patience.

In one fluid motion, Magnus caught the dagger, twirled it's point forward and thrust it at Jaakobah's heart. It was an easy strike; the target was large, off balance and over extended. The tip of Patience slipped through the air well past the forcefield.

Magnus' hand paused just before sinking the blade into Jaakobah's chest. The features of his face twisted in pain.

"Kill him!" Kiora shouted.

It was too late. Jaakobah stepped back and launched himself away from the bar. His heavy feet splintered the wooden floor as he landed in the center of the burning saloon.

"Osiris, you really have outdone yourself. A shame that your parting gift is wasted on this human. At least the dumb one has conviction." Jaakobah nodded at Gideon.

"The Lord gives wisdom. Through His mouth comes knowledge—"

"Silence." Jaakobah pointed a long finger at Magnus. "I misspoke. It appears the council still lives. Tell me, human, what is your name?"

"Magnus," His gaze carried far beyond the walls of Time's Tap. "But my body shares the history of Osiris. The truth lies somewhere between. I am both, but something other than each." He cast the gaze down to his feet, where April and the rest sunk behind the cover of the bar.

An icy shiver scratched at her spine when she caught

sight of his irises. Peering down from Magnus' face were a set of foreign eyes of shifting colors between the soft blue she had come to know, and foreign shades of teal, cyan and emerald.

"I'm not entirely Magnus, and I am not entirely Osiris,.I am both and both are I. I can hear myself in each of my cells. I scream at the thought of hurting another. I cry out for the children I have lost. I have a fury that demands his death. I have will can not be wrenched into aggression. Even against one as wretched as him, I desire his end. I can not cause it."

That was lovely, April thought. An ultimate weapon granted by an Egyptian god-alien, and the only man that could wield it was a pacifist with a radically skewed sense of identity.

Just her luck.

"Thanks," April said, trying not to let her appreciation drown in annoyance. "I've got a plan, but I need a minute. Can you buy us time?"

He nodded, planted a hand on the bar and jumped over. As he approached Jaakobah, a third arm grew from his left side. It split open his shirt and pushed open his tweed coat, flexing an excessively large bicep. He was still smaller than Jaakobah, but now, they had the same number of limbs.

"Osiris!" Jaakobah boomed. "You have fathered despair for too long! I will cleanse the timeline of your genome and your hypocrisy!"

A downpour of strikes fell upon Magnus. April could hardly follow the speed of Jaakobah's three remaining fists. She had hosted plenty of MMA watch-parties in the saloon, but no fighter had ever come close to the quickness of Jaakobah's strikes. To her amazement, Magnus seemed more than capable. With his three arms, he blocked, dodged and diverted each strike without a single counter. His myiad arms shifted shape to greet Jaakobah's every move.

"What's your plan?" Diedre asked.

April snapped back to her own body. If she were being honest with herself, an alternate timeline where Magnus overcame his aversion to killing was preferable, but it didn't seem the man would be coming out of his identity crisis any time soon. How could he rationalize having a fist fight, but not *ending* the fist fight? She didn't know, nor did she think she could ever know how that man's mind worked. One thing was clear: he could never be a saloon manager if he couldn't throw a few punches once in a while. She shook off the thought.

The plan. April considered it. An insane gamble that may just work.

April took the pocket watch from her jacket. The light flicked green in her hand. Three sets of eyes analyzed her movements. It almost made her more nervous to say the plan than to actually try it. She closed her eyes and twisted the dial as far forward as it could turn. Year 2467.

Diedre spoke first. "Flerovium, April. You're insane—"

"—I know—"

"—but it might just work—"

"—what might work?" Gideon asked earnestly.

"The Far-Future." Diedre and April said in unison. April continued. "The second limitation. No traveler has ever returned from beyond 2467. I just need to touch him and I can force—"

"I do not accept this." Kiora cut in. "You can not push someone through time. At best, you must drag him. You will not do this. It is certain death. I can not allow it."

April eyed her. It sounded as if a sob threatened to break through Kiora's defense and spill out.

"I need to." April said. "This is my saloon."

"Jaakobah is our enemy, not yours alone." Kiora challenged. "I am your blade, allow me—"

"No!" April said. She surprised herself with the sharpness of it. She clasped her fingers tightly around the pocket watch and cradled it defensively. A stab of pain lingered at the thought of Kiora traveling to a place April could never reach. She glared, but the shame of it struck her immediately. Her own fears were reflected in Kiora's eyes.

"I need to do this. I caved, Kiora. If it wasn't for Magnus, I'd still be god knows where, throwing a pity party for myself. This isn't about the saloon, this is about me. Who I am. The person grandpa and this saloon helped me to become. He can burn down my saloon, kill me and half the universe, but I won't let him take that from me."

Kiora reached out to her. April tightened her grip on the pocket watch, but the princess only took her hand and squeezed it. The touch left April with the lingering thought of what could have been if they had time to mend what had been.

"Sorry to ruin this touching moment," Diedre whispered. "But there's a hole in your plan. If he's broken the limitations, he can just travel back."

April turned to Diedre. "Maybe he figured out how to transfer the genome, and maybe Osiris copied his work, but I don't think he can bypass the other two limitations. He still needed us to find Osiris for him."

"What does that have to do with it?" Gideon asked.

"If he could bypass the third limitation, then he wouldn't have to worry about paradoxes. He could have found Osiris in any time that he had been before, but he didn't. He needed us to find Osiris in a new time where he hadn't, in order to avoid the paradox limitation. I thought his force-field might have been Far-Future tech, but Magnus just proved it's a mutation of myiads, or genome transference, I'm not sure which. Either way, I don't think he's broken all the limitations. This can work."

"A one way ticket to the Far-Future, no return service?" Diedre grinned a toothy grin. "No point in hopping off this roller coaster now. We'll find out Jaakobah's limitations soon enough."

"I do not know what a roller coaster is." Gideon added. "But I am a servant of God and I believe this is His will. He has granted you insight, April. Your plan will lead us to a righteous outcome."

"Right." April watched Kiora. Her expression returned to tempered steel.

"I am your blade." She nodded. "Whatever you need, I will give you."

"Alright. Here's the plan."

April

A moment later, April stood on the bar counter.

Despite a newfound agility in his myiad body, Magnus was slowing down. Blood trickled from grazes drawn across his arms. Thick gashes made by lion claw and falcon talon. Sweat beaded on his face from the constant shifting of his body. Diedre had told April once how difficult it was to shapeshift in quick sequences. Now, the lesson truly sunk in. Magnus acted so coolly, but it was clear that he was approaching his limit.

The hulking tower of charred flesh that opposed him, however, wasn't even winded.

"Hey, stitches!" She yelled.

Magnus blocked a gut punch with two hands. The force

of it sent his feet skidding across the bar floor like a beer mug on a counter. He slowed to a picturesque stop beside April. A pair of lips formed on the back of his neck and whispered.

"What do you need from me?"

The back-of-neck lips breathed heavily.

April raised her hand to cover her mouth. "Can you get me through his forcefield?"

A miniature hand sprouted from his neck. It gave April a miniature thumbs up.

Clearly bothered by the disruption, Jaakobah roared in a mix of lion, falcon, and grinding metal. It carried on for at least ten seconds. April waited patiently for him to finish.

"I bet your friends love you in a karaoke bar." April said. "Do velexi prefer ABBA, or are they a Dolly Parton crowd?"

Scooping up a chair in his lion paw, Jaakobah lifted and heaved it at her. Magnus's arm split into a three foot wide catcher's mitt of woven sinew and muscle. He caught the chair and twisted it down to its feet, placing it gently beside the bar.

A few more seconds. That was all Diedre needed to get into position.

"I personally think you could belt out Nine to Five like no other. You know, if you give up trying to destroy my saloon, we host karaoke every Sunday night—"

"Bargaining will not save you." Jaakobah hissed.

"You sure?" April held her eyes on him. "I'll give you a year of half-off drinks. I make a great old fashioned—"

"Enough—"

The floorboards underneath him erupted. The trap was

sprung.

Diedre, who had taken the form of an ant and crawled through the cracks of the floor board, expanded like an airbag. They swelled instantaneously to the size of a small hippopotamus.

The first gamble had paid off. April wasn't sure it would work, but from what she could tell about the ESD forcefield, Jaakobah could decide what passed through and what didn't. She figured that out by the fact that he didn't hover over the floor— he allowed his feet to touch. Instead of trying to break through the forcefield, they manipulated what was already crossing the boundary: the floorboards.

Oak plank and Jaakobah alike soared ten feet upward toward the high ceiling of the saloon. April silently thanked her grandfather for renovating the building years ago. The high ceilings were a nice touch.

 As quickly as they expanded, Diedre shifted to their natural blue-skin humanoid shape, save for their two arms, which had taken the form of titanium swords.

Gideon and Kiora met their cue perfectly in sync. They curled toward Jaakobah in parallel, low sprints. April wasn't sure who was faster. Kiora was the quickest person she had ever met, and yet, Gideon streaked like silver lightning, his hammer a dull blur. They planted themselves in a tight formation with Diedre, and prepared to catch their prey in descent.

Jaakobah plummeted down toward a pitfall trap of bronze, steel and titanium. He never met them. A foot above the reach of Gideon's lucerne, Jaakobah froze. He floated effortlessly in the air. The ESD force field pressed down on Gideon and his weapon until the shaft of the lucerne snapped where it was planted on the floor. Growling through a twisted grin, Jaakobah flexed his palms downward and forced the ESD forcefield onto all three of them. Diedre's knees buckled under the weight. Gideon and Kiora fell to their knees in suit, all struggling to hold the Atlassian weight.

The second step of the plan had gone off without a hitch. Just as April had thought, Jaakobah was all too eager at the opportunity to crush the three. He hovered in the air, untethered, the bubble of his forcefield pressing downward on Kiora, Diedre and Gideon below.

"Magnus!" April leaped from the counter. Magnus' hands stretched out to catch her feet. One by one, he placed his hands under her stride, catching each step and walking them through the air like stones in a creek.

"Yes, April! Let us end this!" Jaakobah shouted, pointing two of his inhuman hands toward her.

With one final leap, she lifted off Magnus' hands toward Jaakobah. Like diving into honey, April struck the invisible force field. Her arms pumped through the air like hot glue. The air seemed to solidify and encase her, a fly in a jar, completely frozen in the air.

"Now!"

Shooting out like tendrils, Magnus stretched his hands and brought them together in a tight clasp in front of her. They blended and morphed into a thin panel of flesh, like a shield guarding April's face. A hole formed in the shield's center and spread until it was a single, thin ring of Magnus' flesh, wide enough for April to fit her entire body through. He reeled his arms back and passed the ESD force field around her.

The world moved again. April lurched forward. From her jacket, she brought out her revolver and shot Jaakobah twice in the chest. The two bullets struck his sooty flesh and spun to a stop without piercing the surface.

Falcon talons wrapped April's throat; the massive lion's paw wrapped her arm and squeezed until bone shattered. The revolver clattered on the floor. She sucked thin wisps of air through a clenched throat. Her broken arm hung limply at her side. With her other hand, she clasped onto Jaakobah's wrist and held tight.

"This was your plan?" Jaakobah said amusedly. "A human gun? You humans are so resistant to forethought. Bashing your heads against the same wall, hoping each strike will shatter the stone and not your skulls."

Sweat beaded down April's forehead. It seeped into her eyes and blurred her vision.

"It is over." Jaakobah said. "Unless, you have something more to offer this fight?" He raised a brow at Magnus.

The man-turned-myiad watched with a pale, stiff face. The three below fell to their stomachs, crushed between the earth and the weight of Jaakobah's force.

"That's humanity for you." Jaakobah laughed. "A species of irony. Strength to fight, no courage to use it."

April tried to speak out a choked word.

"Begging for your life?" Jaakobah asked. The talons around her neck eased just enough for her to inhale a whistled breath. "Amuse me."

"No speaking," April said weakly. "No moving. Relax your body."

"What?"

April lifted a single finger where she held Jaakobah's

thick wrist. Soft green light peered through.

"What do you think you can do with that? There is no moment in time where you can stop—"

Terror crinkled the puss-covered creases of his face. The expression was clear under the illumination of golden light forming above and below.

"I have shed the limitations" Jaakobah shouted. "This will not stop me. I will return. I will raze this saloon to the ground! I have surpassed time itself!"

April closed her eyes and clung with all of her might. What could the Far-Future hold? Maybe it was the end of time all together. Maybe she and Jaakobah would be the only two things left in existence. That would be a severe disappointment. She let her mind wander and hope. Maybe time was cyclical, as plenty of crystal-toting locals believed. It would wrap around again, and she could travel forward to a future where the saloon was built, and Grandpa Sylas had never gotten sick to begin with.

Maybe heaven was at the end of time. She hoped Gideon had punched her on the shoulder enough to cleanse her of the many sins she had tallied.

"Stop this!" Jaakobah shouted as the rings of light pulled at him. His forehead stretched into the wormhole above, his toes spiraled into the one below. "I will return! Not even the Far-Future—"

"I'd be quiet if I were you." April said with a smirk.

Jaakobah's mouth crossed over the boundary, ending his speeches. His body thrashed and twisted. Floating in the air, he was out of reach of any anchor.

Golden light touched the top of April's head. Only a few feet below, her friends were bathed in the glow of it. She looked down at Kiora and smiled. The princess had tears rolling down her cheeks.

"Don't —" April began to speak.

Countless tentacles erupted from Jaakobah's chest, each pencil thick. They shot outward in all directions, jabbing the ceiling, walls and floors of the saloon. A dozen shot downward toward the three on the floor below. April screamed as she held Kiora's teary gaze.

A disk of milky-white flesh sprouted over them and blocked the tentacles. Magnus knelt beside them, heaving and sweating, raising his shapeshifted arms as a wide, flat shield.

April took in a breath of relief, but pain swathed over her body. Four black tentacles pierced clean through her stomach, thigh, the bicep of her broken arm, and the shoulder of her healthy one.

"April —"

She heard someone speak her name. It was distant and foggy. Her head bounced up as she fought for consciousness. Pain surrendered to numbness. The green glow of the pocket watch slid from her grasp and fell in front of her. She commanded her broken arm to move. Her left hand needed to catch it. The limp limb didn't answer.

Then she fell.

"Magnus, the pocket watch —"

" —On it —"

" —Will not be stopped."

Through the misty film of pain, April heard Jaakobah's voice rejoin reality.

Diedre's blue arms caught her before she hit the floor. The jolt of it cleared her mind just enough to see what was happening, though she could hardly make sense of it.

Through his tweed coat, Magnus forced tentacles out from his own body. Pale white cords of flesh sought out each of Jaakobah's violent whips. Where they met in the air, the light wrapped the dark in twisting binds. They sought out others and came together in larger braids. Magnus poured the entirety of his matter into the effort. His legs and arms split apart, his head unraveled, his torso nothing more than a joint that held the many cords together. The two bodies lost all shape as they became a unified, twisted mass of braided pale and black tentacles. It hovered in the air, swirling like a galaxy. At its center, April caught glimpses of green light.

She tried to lift herself. She wanted to crawl out and take the pocket watch. Save Magnus from this cursed existence that he had wandered into. Traveling wasn't his life. The saloon, aliens, Jaakobah. It was hers, and Diedre's, and Kiora's. She promised him that she would keep him safe.

"Stay still," Diedre chided. "You've lost too much blood. I'm pumping more in just to keep you alive while I stitch you up."

A wave of nausea struck her as she realized Diedre's fingers had wandered into the open wound of her stomach. Warmth of freshly shapeshifted blood flowed from the myiad's hand into her cold chest.

"Magnus," April's voice was shrill and airy. Her mouth tasted of blood. "I can't let him—"

"It's already done." Diedre said.

They watched as two golden rings encompassed the massive ball of flesh. Where black tendrils of Jaakobah tried to escape, white tendrils of Magnus constricted and braided them back into the main body.

The golden rings closed in toward the center of the mass. It was a silent event. Jaakobah's voice did not speak of despair, nor did Magnus comment on the ridiculous nature of time travel. Diedre, Kiora, Gideon and April simply watched as the golden rings met, and the twisting mass of two shapeshifters was gone.

April held her breath for a long moment. Part of her believed it couldn't be finished, that Jaakobah would travel back to that exact moment and laugh at her one final time before killing the rest of them. Lying cradled in Diedre's arms, she realized the myiad was holding their breath as well. She would have bet Gideon and Kiora were doing the same.

After a long moment, nothing happened. Jaakobah did not return. Magnus didn't either.

April allowed herself breath. It hurt. Her entire body ached, from her bruised neck to the hole in her leg. But she was warm. She hadn't noticed how cold she had become until Diedre took her into their arms.

"Kiora, Gideon, Help me carry her." Diedre said.

"I must get Alan!" Gideon answered.

The saloon was an utter mess. The walls were fully aflame, their decorations scattered and broken in charred piles across the floor. Well, what floor was left, at least. Not a single table had survived the fight. Each had been rendered to scrap firewood. The bar back roared with the burnt smell of alcohol. The counter had begun to catch as well. Igor above the door had lost his fur. It crisped and fell in sprinkling ash over McQuade the taxidermy duck, who somehow managed to avoid the encroaching flames.

April felt the distant touch of Kiora's hands on her back. She was lifted from the floor, though Diedre's fingers in her stomach still worked as they moved.

"McQuade." April whispered.

"What?" Kiora asked.

"The duck."

Kiora scowled. As they passed through the saloon door, she kicked the taxidermy duck up with one foot and caught it under her arm.

They laid April down in the dirt lot a good distance from the saloon. Fire swelled and engulfed the building. It flickered and danced in the black night, the cracks and crackles of the falling lumber drifting down the street in a haunting melody.

Kiora held April's head in her lap, wiping sweat and blood from her face. Diedre worked, stitching together veins and organs with string made of their own matter. Gideon landed beside April in the dirt, cradling Alan in his arms. The cat licked at matted blood caked onto its shoulder.

The saloon burned. That was it. They'd stopped Jaakobah, and in the process, lost both Magnus and the saloon.

April let out a weak snort. It became a laugh, which made her wince, then laugh again twofold.

Kiora stopped combing her hair. The princess' expression turned sharp.

April barked with laughter. Then wheezed in pain. Then barked again. It infected Gideon, who kissed his cross and whispered a prayer between bouts of laughter. Diedre broke into a smile and started giggling, though they remained focused on their operation.

"Why do you laugh?" Kiora asked in a rigid tone.

"Because," April winced. "The bastard did it. Magnus actually did it."

"You laugh at his sacrifice?"

"Of course not." April said. "I'm laughing because he didn't throw a single punch."

Kiora's face was blank. A small smile crept over her mouth.

"That's my protégé for you." Diedre said proudly. "You know, I really nurtured his inner pacifism. Glad my lessons stuck."

AFTER

Gainsborough Minnary

Whether it was for shame or for fear of what punishment April may conjure up, after the fateful night in August, Gainsborough Minnary never returned to the saloon.

The One Eared Painter

Inspired by April and Magnus's conversation, the one-eared painter went on to be a somewhat well known figure in the Post-Impressionism movement in France at the end of the 19th century.

Struck by the wandering features of Magnus' face during the conversation, the One Eared Painter painted a portrait by memory of the human/myiad traveler from 2024. Contemporary critics at the time found the portrait unsightly, uncouth, and undeserving of love.

In a fit of self-doubt, the One Eared Painter destroyed the experimental portrait of Magnus Duvall in a fire.

Rex

The monononymous Rex, right hand extra-terrestrial-lieutenant to Diedre Altair, led the surviving crew of the S.S. Paul through the back door of Time's Tap just before things got dicey. He, of course, wanted to stand and fight, but on Diedre's order, he made a tactical retreat to Tombstone's local Motel 6— a wonderfully hospitable place Diedre had told him about.

There, they waited patiently for word from Diedre. Using a holographic disguise beacon, Rex was able to book the best that Motel 6 had to offer. They drank free lobby hot cocoa and watched old reruns of The Simpsons in their combined suite.

Come morning, they enjoyed a free continental breakfast, a quick dip in the pool, and, after no word had been received from Diedre, accepted their fates as extra-terrestrial strandees on earth.

Diedre had simply forgotten which Motel 6 they had told Rex to go to.

Two days after the fight with Jaakobah, Rex warily led the troop back to the saloon, with the hope of burying their fallen captain. They found Diedre alive and well with the others, picking up rubble and laying plans for a new saloon.

Mur

In the vacuum of power left by the council's demise, Mur's influence grew unchecked. It reached out from the underworld and swallowed Portum. In turn, Mur the Crow found herself as the leading political figure in time traveler society.

Mur despised it.

She quickly learned of the difficulty in remaining a faceless operator when the entirety of time looked to her for leadership. Each waking moment of her existence became eaten up by the trillion woes of societies from every planet, and every era. In a desperate attempt to offload the weight of ruling time traveler society and return to her old life, she sought out Diedre Altair, the last living myiad. The Space Pirate Extraordinaire laughed in her crow face when she offered the high seat of Portum. With a little finessing, however, Mur convinced Diedre to say yes.

Mur's life returned to normal. That is, her personal flavor of normal; Mur the Crow, broker of information in the underbelly of time traveler society. Her first act after returning to her favored post: experimenting with Magnus' genetic information in an attempt to gather what she could about the phenomenon of genome transference. Her work has proved fruitless thus far, but she continues on, hiring the best black-market geneticists she can reach— and as far as the universe may extend, Mur has quite the reach.

Diedre Altair

After the battle in Time's Tap, Diedre held an honorary space-pirate funeral for their protégé. This included putting a blond wig on a mannequin, lighting it on fire, and shooting it into space. Then, in Magnus' honor, Diedre drank heavily, consumes copious amounts of space narcotics, and hosted multiple extra-terrestrial orgies. All things Diedre was sure Magnus would have enjoyed.

After the wake, Diedre busied themselves with anything they could find. April needed all the help she could get with renovating Time's Tap, so Diedre helped there. The S.S. Paul needed to be rebuilt entirely, so they rebuilt it. A new crew would be needed to replace the lost crewmates, so Diedre went to every scummy bar filled with villainous types they knew of in order to find recruits. Once that was done, Diedre even offered to help Kiora manage ancient Egypt, a request to which the princess sturdily declined.

When the busy work settled, all that was left for Diedre to face was the one truth they had avoided facing.

They were the last living myiad.

At first, when they believed the council had all been killed by Jaakobah, Diedre thought it was worthy of celebration. Only when Magnus became a myiad did they realize how much the title bothered them. They didn't want to be the last living anything. Diedre Altair, Space Pirate Extraordinaire, was supposed to go out in a blaze of glory, a space-shoot-out of epic proportions, or something else of grand nature. But no. They had outlived every one of their boring, council-based, rule-setting, power-tripping family members. How lame was that? It was a harsh blow to Diedre's self confidence.

So when Mur came to them and asked if they wanted to take over Portum and lead time traveler society, Diedre offered the obligatory laugh that would be expected, then eagerly said yes. If their family members in the council were going to take their spot and die in an emphatically dramatic way, Diedre would take their livelihoods and do it better than they ever did.

Thus, Diedre Altair, Space Pirate Extraordinaire, became Diedre Altair, Timeline Emperor. Their first edict was to change the pronunciation of "emperor" to "emper-air" so that it would fit the rhyming scheme.

To everyone's surprise, including Diedre's own, though they would never admit it out loud, the timeline blossomed under the last myiad's leadership.

After their first edict, Diedre enacted a slew of directives and mandates to dismantle the council's more autocratic systems.

The Magnus Mandate was the first Diedre placed into time travel law. It stated that locals who were known to have discovered time travel, no matter the means, would be protected without exception. Memory removal was still necessary in *most* cases, though Diedre was known to grant amnesty to the occasional local.

The Sylas Mandate followed soon thereafter. It dismantled the former limitations on localized gathering places. Using April's saloon as a guideline, Diedre helped to establish multiple permanent TDUs around the universe.

With each action Diedre took as the sole leader of Portum, and in turn, all of time travel society, they chipped away at the blueprint of oligarchy their family had left behind. Localized governing bodies sprouted across the timeline, and in time, Diedre relinquished universal control in favor of a network of self-governing sectors. Diedre still acts as the high seat of Portum, but as a peace-keeping entity within the universe, rather than an all-powerful tyrant.

Through it all, when Diedre had a rare moment to themselves, they would travel to Time's Tap and have a drink of cheap whiskey with their second favorite human, April Minnary. And sometimes their third, Gideon Oengus. And even occasionally, their six hundred and eighty fifth, Kiora Kekheretnebti.

Alan Rickman

Aside from a limp in his front right leg, Alan Rickman walked away from his spat with Jaakobah alive and well.

Taking a particular liking to the calloused-yet-gentle chin scratches of Gideon, Alan stayed close to the old soldier in the aftermath of the fight in Time's Tap. When time came for Gideon to return home, Alan returned with him.

Living most of his life with Osiris in the Cretaceous period, Alan Rickman was a simple cat of simple needs. 11th century Ireland was more than enough. He received plenty of pets from Gideon, and found a great snuggling partner in Gideon's young daughter, Aoife.

Everyone who had seen Alan attack Jaakobah shared in wondering what exactly the *cat* was, but none had cared to seek out an answer. They were thankful that Alan seemed to like them enough to not saw off their limbs with his drill-like teeth. That was enough.

Gideon Oengus

With his history of carpentry, and April's permission, Gideon took the lead in renovating Time's Tap. Of his two professions, Gideon much preferred the work of building homes than slaying enemies on a battlefield. Jesus was a carpenter, after all.

Of course, Gideon returned home to live in his local time. He retired from the military and took to a peaceful life with his wife Aghna, and their daughter, Aoife. He worked wood by day, spent time with his family by evening, and by night, he would visit April and her saloon.

His search for God in the expanded universe continued. For each new traveler he met, he sought out Godliness, and in its absence, planted the seed of it. April kicked him out more than once for disturbing a new traveler, but she made sure he knew there would always be a seat for him at her saloon.

One evening, as Gideon came home from a day's labor felling trees and treating them for a new lodge, he heard Aghna's wail across the village. When he arrived at his home's open door, heaving with labored breath, he found Aghna weeping on the floor, clutching Aoife's blanket.

"Where is she?" Gideon asked.

Aoife Oengus

A little girl with carrot colored hair and pale white skin walked alone through a strange street. She'd never seen houses like the dark frames on either side of the road. She'd never seen a road made up of one long, black stone. It was a strange sight. Her da built houses and roads, so she would know.

A quiver of fear twitched in her stomach. She pouted and thought about her da. He would never be afraid, even now. Even if he had gone to bed at home and woken up in a strange place like she had. Da would pray to the Lord and find a way home to her and Ma.

So the little girl mumbled a prayer and set out to find a way home.

There wasn't any particular direction that looked promising, so she followed her ears.

The bouncing music was unlike anything the little girl had ever heard. It tickled her ears with high pitched squeals and rumbled in her chest with heavy *thrums*. She found herself walking in tune with the heavier sounds, stepping over the black stone, then onto neatly packed dirt. Before she had realized it, she stood in front of a wooden house that she recognized. It looked like da's work.

Yellow light shined through and spilled over the dirt lot. Marigolds lined planter boxes on either side of a big double door. The little girl loved marigolds. They were her favorite.

The twitch of fear returned to her stomach. She shook her head, took a deep breath like da always told her to, then marched toward the door with confidence.

A whistle to her left made her nearly jump out of her dress. She swiveled on a heel and put up her fists to fight.

"Woah, we've got a fighter here. Look at that form, the Plutonian fighting champ wouldn't stand a chance if you signed up."

From a shadowy stretch of the wall, a woman stepped toward the little girl. Her little fists fell to her side as she marveled at the stranger. The woman was pretty. Almost prettier than ma. No one could be prettier than ma. That's what da said. The woman had dark hair over a silky face, bright green lips, and eyes that glowed like two purple jewels. She recognized the woman from da's stories.

"Dee-druh?" The little girl sounded out.

The woman froze.

"How did you—" Diedre said. "April!"

The doors swung open and another woman stepped out. The little girl didn't think her eyes could widen any more, but she was stunned. The second woman had hair curlier than even her red mop, and she had the curliest hair in her village. Not only that, but the second woman had dark brown skin, and a shiny black coat.

"What is it—" The second woman asked. "Oh. Hello little one."

"Ay-prul" The little girl moved her mouth deliberately to shape the sound correctly.

April froze. Then, a smile grew across her face.

"I think I recognize those red curls." April's spoke warmly. "Let me guess. You're Aoife, aren't you?"

The little girl nodded happily.

"I've heard a lot about you." April said. She squatted down to the little girl's level and fished a lollipop out of her pocket. "Root beer. Here." She put the lollipop into Aoife's hand. "Why don't you come on in. It's a cold one. I'll have your daddy come pick you up, alright? He must be worried sick."

Cleopatra

Cleopatra's reign lasted for 21 years. It has been well documented by historians and historical fiction authors alike. One seeking accurate information should invest their time reading the former rather than the latter.

One seeking inaccurate information would be pleased to know that Cleopatra's suicide was actually a historical inaccuracy. As Egypt was invaded by Octavian, a passing party-star-barge, en-route for Jupiter and in need of an Egyptian wine restock, accidentally caught Cleopatra in its tractor beam. Octavian, eager to usurp Cleopatra, claimed that her absence was due to her death, a suicide that he had "witnessed."

After a speedy recovery from culture shock, Cleopatra joined the cross-universe bound party-star-barge and is said to still be partying somewhere in the cosmos to this very day.

Kekheretnebti

Kekheretnebti, princess in the Fifth Dynasty of Ancient Egypt, lived a short life, and passed away unexpectedly.

Her daughter, Tisethor, outlived her. To her closest advisers, Tisethor spoke of a visage of her mother visiting her in the darkest hours of the night. The visage offered leadership advice, warning of ill omens to come, and reassurance of a mother's love.

Kiora

Despite the success of their quest against Jaakobah, Kiora sunk into unruly depths of despair. Only after the fight of Time's Tap did the weight of the council's death bear down on her. Rebuilding one's entire sense of purpose is no easy thing.

The rebuilding began with death, or rather, a fabrication of death. Kekheretnebti's disappearance unburdened Kiora from the responsibilities of leading a civilization. While attending her own funeral, she found that she could breathe deeply for the first time in years. She was free to live a single life as the traveler Kiora, though, she often visited her local time to see her one and only child, Tisethor.

For a time, she drifted through the cosmos, working odd jobs that befit her skill set. A bouncer gig on Qwering here, a body guard job on Jop there. A simple life where the title, "Blades of Sekhmet" could rest in the passing of time, just as the council would.

After assisting with the saloon's renovations, Kiora stopped visiting. She avoided it like the plague. Her greatest failures were eternally marked by the place. She had failed the council as their defender. She had been powerless to save Magnus. She had failed April long before any mention of Jaakobah. Kiora could not return to Time's Tap. Failure was her crime, separation was her punishment.

"Look who it is." A familiar face made Kiora's ear perk up. She was working as a bouncer at a club on Cerivl-9. Two amethyst eyes on long, blue talks caught her own. "Kiora, blades of—"

Kiora hissed. "I do not use such a title any more. What do you want?"

"Woah now, I'm a VIP client here, you should treat me with respect." Diedre winked. Their nylon blue trench was covered collar to fringe in sequins. "I just wanted to say hello to an old friend. We are friends, aren't we?"

Kiora glared at them.

"Harsh." Diedre grinned. "You haven't gone to see her since we fixed up the saloon, have you?"

In her best attempt to ignore the myiad, Kiora pressed her stare down the bustling street.

"We all make mistakes," Diedre said. "But we can change. Look at me. I was a pirate, now the whole universe loves me. You know how many baby's heads I've signed just this week alone?" Diedre's hand slithered through the air in a serpentine gesture. They slipped a card into Kiora's hand. "I'm sure you've heard, but I'm running Portum now. Trying to clean up the mess. You want to atone or whatever, help me make things better."

A week later, Kiora rolled out of bed, wiped the sweat of a week-long binge off of her forehead, and traveled to Portum.

"Thought you'd come around." Diedre said with a smirk.

"I am here to ensure you do not destroy the entire

timeline." Kiora answered.

April Minnary

The first thing April did after the dust settled was run to the local liquor store and pick up a cheap bottle of whiskey. She poured shots in the best semblance of glasses she could find in Time's Tap— most were shattered to bits and black with soot— and handed them out to Gideon, Kiora, and Diedre. She made sure to pour a splash over the last spot where Magnus had stood.

Renovations came thereafter. Gideon led the rebuilding process, and despite his medieval origin, he learned to use modern machinery quite well. With the benefits of a shapeshifter, a crew of extraterrestrials, and Near-Future tech, Time's Tap looked better than it ever had in just a few short weeks. April cleaned up what she could find of the old photos, sports gear and knick knacks and made sure to hang them all again, along with a few additions that included photos of the crew, a mount for Gideon's broken lucerne hammer, and a memorial plaque for Magnus.

Once Time's Tap reopened, it was back to daily life.

During the day, April would pour drinks and serve curly fries to the locals of 2024. In the night, travelers would pack the saloon, filling it with extra-terrestrial music and merriment.

Gideon often visited, though April had to keep him away from newbie travelers. At times, he was worse than an LDS missionary in a third world country. Against the incredible odds of the genome lottery, his little girl Aoife turned out to be a traveler herself. Eventually, she began to visit the saloon with Gideon, and April came to be known as "Aintin April." The name stuck, and all who visited the saloon came to know her as Aintin April, daughter of Grandpa Sylas. April had never wanted kids of her own, but she had to admit, that damned little red-head was a cutie.

On more rare occasions, Diedre visited when they could break free from managing Portum. It surprised April a bit, seeing her friend take a position in time traveler politics, but then again, Diedre always had an opinion on the matter. They turned out to be pretty good at it, too. April would read every message through the time wire about a new directive or program Diedre had started.

Late on the coldest of winter nights, April would sip old-fashioneds alone at the bar, listening to the everlasting magic of Fleetwood Mac through the jukebox. For the first time in a long time, she could remember Sylas without weeping. Then, naturally, her eyes would turn bleary at the thought of Magnus.

"The stupid fool." She said on one such night. "It should have been me."

"Do not speak ill of the dead."

April spun around so quickly on her stool whiskey shot from the glass in her hand and sprayed Kiora in the face.

"You can't sneak up on a person like that." April offered Kiora a floppy bar napkin.

She wiped her face. "I did not intend to alarm you."

"Intent don't mean much if it happens anyway."

They watched each other in silence for a lingering moment.

"So, you want a drink?" April asked as she reached over the counter and lifted a glass from the drying rack.

"Aye." Kiora nodded. She sat beside April and sipped.

Thurump. Thurump. April's heart beat heavily.

"Haven't seen you in a while." April tried to say coolly. "I heard the news about Kekheretnebti. Sorry for your loss."

"Not a loss." Kiora's face was unreadable.

A flutter tickled April's gut. She knew how much Kiora struggled with the upkeep of the two egos. She had seen the stress first hand, how it ate away at Kiora's heart and sapped her confidence. The news had made her glad for an old friend.

"Well, here's to Kekheretnebti." April threw back what was left. Kiora smiled and followed suit.

April poured another round for each of them.

"Do you think of him?" Kiora asked.

She didn't need to say who.

"Every day." April answered. "Diedre says they've got a team researching the Far-Future. Maybe they can find a way to bring Magnus back. But if that's possible—"

Her voice trailed off. Kiora grunted. They sat with the silent repercussion of such an outcome. If Magnus could return, Jaakobah could, too.

"Do you think of us?" Kiora asked.

Heat flashed in April's face. What the hell was she supposed to say to that?

"I—"

"—Forgive me—" Kiora added quickly. "—an unfair question. I do not have the right—"

"—It was hard, you know." April gave her the honest answer. "I never knew who I'd be talking to from one day to the next. Kiora. Kekheretnebti. I tried my best, but I couldn't handle it. I knew it hurt you, I could feel that, too. But trying to love both of you was like being laid out bare in the desert. I'd burn in the sun and freeze under the stars. You shifted like a myiad changes shape. I could never tell. Dammit I wish I could have. It was impossible to love both Kiora *and* Kekheretnebti."

April's old fashioned was ruined by a few drops of tears.

"Sorry," April said. "I've had a bit to drink tonight—"

"—I know too well the impossibility in loving both."

They caught each other's watery gazes. Kiora and April sat in a single moment of time, a moment behind, a moment ahead.

"Hello, I'm Kiora. Only Kiora. I believe this is the first time we have met."

"Hi Kiora," April spoke through blurry eyes. "I'm April. A pleasure to meet you and only you."

Jaakobah

Once Jaakobah was forced into the Far-Future by Magnus Duvall, his legions of semi-intelligent velexi reverted to their expected, primal natures. What lasting groups had been deposited on various planets across the universe tore themselves apart, or were hunted down by local militias. None were sure how Jaakobah was able to tame the species, but researchers of Diedre's Portum suspected it was a specific mutation he had forced within his myiad genetic code that allowed a hive-mind-like system of communication.

Soon after the universe had cleansed itself of the velexi threat, Jaakobah fell into anonymity. None but April, Diedre, Gideon, Kiora and Diedre's crew knew that Jaakobah had been the actual mastermind behind the council's downfall— all else who had come face to face with the Deceiver had lost their life. This, of course, spilled a slew of theories into the mind share of the general populace as to what actually happened to the council. Some believed it was an underworld takeover by Mur the Crow. Others believed it was a successful coup by Diedre, the Outcast.

Most agreed that it didn't matter much one way or another. The oppressive rule of the council was gone. Each traveler across the timeline breathed easier under Diedre's rule, and in turn, the new social systems Diedre set into place.

Jaakobah's name would be forgotten in the passing of time. As for his intent to erase despair, one might wonder if he succeeded, for a time. Soon after Diedre's ascension to the high seat of Portum, traveler historians dubbed the intra-temporal era as the "Golden Era of Traveling." For all intents and purposes, despair was at an all-time low.

Diedre wondered on occasion. Was it Jaakobah's actions that truly led to the "Golden Era," or was it an inevitability for the council's rule to be disrupted and replaced by the traveler's they ruled over?

In the end, it was beyond Diedre's interest and energy to find the answer. Jaakobah's name would be forgotten, and the Golden Era would live on as far as Diedre could carry it.

May Duvall

On the morning of August 31st, 2025, May Duvall nearly tripped over a bouquet of strange flowers lying on her doorstep. The fluorescent green petals gleamed in the morning Arizonian sun like emeralds. They weren't a plant she'd ever seen before. In fact, they looked more like flowers from one of those space-movies her son used to enjoy as a kid. She lifted them and discovered a folded note underneath with her name written on it.

Mother,

> *I'm sorry I left without saying goodbye.*
> *I won't be returning*
> *I can't explain why.*
> *I love you.*

Magnus

> *P.S.*
> *If you find yourself in Tombstone*
> *and want a good old-fashioned,*
> *stop by Time's Tap.*

The next day, May Duvall slammed the note down on the bar counter of Time's Tap and demanded to know where her son was.

"Well ma'am, I'll need to know who your son is before I can figure if I know where he is." A bartender with a black leather jacket said.

"Magnus Duvall." May said. The bartender went flush. She knew something about Magnus. May would be damned if anyone kept her away from her boy.

"Miss Duvall, how would you like an old fashioned?" April asked. "I think I'll make one for myself, too."

"I would like you to tell me what you know about my son's whereabouts. You clearly know something. I'll call the police right—"

April offered a warm, professional smile. The kind a bartender would train for years to perfect. A welcoming grin with a sharp edge to warn people from doing anything stupid in her saloon.

"Lady, you've got unrestricted clearance direct from Diedre Altair, Timeline Emperor. I'll give you every answer you want to hear, honest truth" April leaned over the bar counter. "But trust me, you're going to want a drink for this."

GLOSSARY

Annihilation

Diedre Altair's favorite word.

Cantanea

A bipedal species known for its dog-like appearance.

Carbadium

A Near-Future metal alloy.

Celestial calendar

The generally agreed upon calendar for time traveling society.

Deshret

A red crown of pharaonic ancient Egypt.

Duat

The underworld in ancient Egyptian mythology.

ESD (Expressive Singularity Defense)

Near future tech utilizing the inverse-gravity-well effects of quantum white holes. Usually deployed on star ships as a force field capable of catching even light-based projectiles.

Far-Future

Any time beyond 00:00, January 1st, 2467, per the celestial calendar.

Flerovium

A synthetic chemical element with the atomic number 114. In Near-Future societies, used as a curse akin to any other curse word starting with the letter F.

Garadrin

A quadrupedal species known for the distinct scent of its feces.

Gloag

A million.

Gomo

A species known for its 'ooze' like form.

Hadron Microparticle Accelerator

A Near-Future hand-held particle accelerator.

Hedjet

A white crown of pharaonic ancient Egypt.

Kemet

A name given to the land by the ancient peoples of what is now Egypt.

Lorouxias

A large, quadrupedal species of the planet Kaa-ah-a. Known for the unique scent and hangover-healing qualities of its pheromones.

Lovinians

A species known for its tentacle-based form.

Lumenglass

Crystallized light. A Near-Future evolution of glass. Crystal clear and as durable as titanium.

Manchester 2440 Craniofacial Reconstructor

A near-Future device that can completely reconstruct the head of any known species, given they have a head.

Marsdvark

An endangered creature native to the planet of Mars.

Mnemosyne machine

A Near-Future machine that can erase a being's memories.

Morpheus Somnology Table

A Near-Future tool that can monitor the sleep patterns and dreams of the user.

Myiad

A species of shapeshifting alien.

Myiadling

An adolescent myiad.

Near-Future

Any time between the years 2200 and the beginning of 2467, per the celestial calendar.

PEA (Psilocybin Enveloped Astronomorph)

A species known for its natural ability to produce a thick layer of psilocybin-based mucus. Originally a defense mechanism on their home world, PEAs have come to be favorites at parties around the cosmos, and often get into events without paying a cover charge.

Pocket watch

A handheld TDU.

Pschent

A double crown worn by rulers in ancient Egypt.

TDU (Time Dispersal Unit)

Near future tech allowing one to direct the flow of time travel. Can be used as a receptor to gather travelers to a specific point in time, or as a tool to move one or more species across the time line. A being does not need the genome to operate a TDU.

Time Council

A select group of the eldest living myaids. The Time Council directly oversees the coordination of time traveler society.

Timewire

A communication device that can send and receive messages across time. Don't ask how it works.

Traveler

A sentient being with the traveler genome. A time traveler.

Traveler genome

A specific mutation in the genetic information of certain beings in the known universe.

Uul

A species that isn't really known for anything.

Velex

An aggressive alien species. Known for their unique bodies, velexi have are round, black masses of flesh with more than a hundred tiny mouths, and dozens of spindly arms. It's talons are sharp enough to tear through steel, and it has been observed to consume any and all organic matter within its reach.

Vostok Cryogenesis Rifle

A ear-future weaponized cryogenesis ray. (It makes things cold. Really cold.)

Wicntibfos

A species known for having skin so soft to the touch it can pass through air without disturbing any resting molecules.

Zoombaatis

A species of bio-mechanical humanoids. Due to their biological ancestry, they can develop the traveler genome.